THE MEN ON THE FARM

A JOE COURT NOVEL

BY
CHRIS CULVER
ST. LOUIS, MO

This is a work of fiction. Names, characters, places, and incidents either are the product of the author's imagination or are used fictitiously. Any resemblance to actual persons, living or dead, events, or locales is entirely coincidental.

Copyright © 2020 by Chris Culver

All rights reserved. No part of this book may be reproduced or used in any manner without written permission of the copyright owner except for the use of quotations in a book review. For more information, address: chris@indiecrime.com

First paperback edition June 2020.

www.indiecrime.com
Facebook.com/ChrisCulverBooks

Contents

1. 1 — 1
2. 2 — 8
3. 3 — 19
4. 4 — 26
5. 5 — 35
6. 6 — 43
7. 7 — 49
8. 8 — 58
9. 9 — 74
10. 10 — 81
11. 11 — 90
12. 12 — 98
13. 13 — 107
14. 14 — 114

15.	15	123
16.	16	133
17.	17	146
18.	18	159
19.	19	167
20.	20	176
21.	21	183
22.	22	191
23.	23	199
24.	24	208
25.	25	217
26.	26	227
27.	27	237
28.	28	246
29.	29	256
30.	30	266
31.	31	276
32.	32	284
33.	33	294
34.	34	301

35. 35	309
36. 36	319
37. 37	331
38. 38	339
39. 39	348
40. 40	355
41. 41	363
42. 42	372
FREE JOE COURT NOVELLA	387
Stay in touch with Chris	388
About the Author	389

Chapter 1

Nadine exhaled through her nose to avoid fogging her rifle's scope. The morning chill pierced the thin insulation of the sedan's trunk but did nothing to deter the dozens of men, women, and children ambling through the mall's parking lot. Blinding sunlight reflected on the mirrored glass of the nearby Dillard's department store. Nadine could use that.

The car smelled like automotive grease and old milk. An empty baby's bottle rolled around on the floorboard beneath the driver's seat. Nadine and her colleagues had stolen the vehicle that morning and cut a hole in the trunk through which she could aim her rifle. They had gotten the idea for the setup from the DC sniper in the early 2000s. Unless the sedan's owner happened to need something from his vehicle in the middle of his shift at Mercy Hospital, he wouldn't realize it had been stolen for hours more. By then, they would have completed their job and abandoned the vehicle in the middle of nowhere.

Without taking her eye from the rifle's scope, Nadine reached down to her phone and held it to her lips.

"You guys still in the food court?" she asked.

This would be the eleventh armored car she and her colleagues had robbed, which meant they had one more to go after this. Once they finished the twelfth job—a capstone that would double their earnings and for which they had been planning for months—she and her husband would leave the country. Nadine looked forward to it. She needed to get on with her life.

"Yep. We're still there, and we're eating a Cinnabon. It's delicious."

The voice belonged to either Wendy or Robin, but Nadine couldn't tell which. They were sisters, and Nadine had met them years ago when they were still young women with all the idealism of youth. Now they were older and a little wiser and much more cynical. Nadine had met Wendy first. They had been in a mess hall outside Baghdad at the time, and they had commiserated over the sorry state of their love lives. She had met the other ladies later.

"Am I on speaker?" Nadine asked.

"Yep," said Ursa, their unofficial leader. All four ladies had spent time in the military, but Ursa had been the only officer. "You holding up okay, hon?"

"I'm good," said Nadine. "Just waiting for Mr. Right to come along."

"Hold tight, and I'm sure he'll be along shortly," said Ursa. It was as close an order to shut up as Ursa was likely to give on an open channel. Nadine drew in a breath and listened to the soft murmur of the building on the other end of the line.

"I hope you're right," she said. "See you soon."

She set the phone down but didn't hang up. Robin, Wendy, and Ursa continued chatting. Though they didn't know the precise tactical situation they'd face when the armored car arrived, they knew it would have at least two armed guards but no more than six. Each guard would carry at least one pistol, and each would have significant firearms training. Some would be former or off-duty cops, while others would be former soldiers. Few would hesitate to shoot if they perceived a threat.

The car itself presented a unique tactical challenge as well. Its armored windows and exterior plating could withstand anything they could throw at it, which meant they had to wait for the guards to open their doors.

Those simple facts dictated the tactics Nadine and her partners utilized. They were patient and restrained when necessary, but absolutely brutal and efficient. Their work had no margin for error. Any hesitation would mean Nadine or one of her partners would die.

"Hey, Nadine, how's the car smell?" asked Wendy, her voice light. "Just curious."

Nadine rolled her eyes but couldn't help but smile as she picked up the phone.

"I'll make sure you get a whiff before this is all done," she said. "I think Mr. Clean spilled about a gallon of milk on his backseat and decided he didn't need to clean it up. You ladies got the better end of this deal."

"You can't blame Mr. Clean for the state of his car," said Robin. "He's got a toddler, and toddlers are horrible people. Six months ago, Summer shoved two hard-boiled eggs under the couch and didn't tell us. Three weeks later, the dog ate them and had diarrhea for two days straight. He killed three azaleas in the yard and a patch of grass the size of a kiddie pool. Kids are the worst. Trust me. If his car smells like rotten milk, it means he's a good dad."

Nadine smiled but said nothing. Her friends' voices sounded light. Some of their gaiety was an act but not all of it. After months of work, they were nearing the end, and they all knew it. Their homes and families and friends were thirty miles away in Illinois. If the risks weren't so high, they could have driven over after finishing this job and seen their families. They wouldn't do that just yet, but the thought still made Nadine smile. It was like sitting in a classroom in May and knowing summer was just around the corner.

Two more jobs. This one wouldn't be bad. Their next one would be the hardest they'd ever done, but once they finished it, they'd have more money than any of them could ever earn in a lifetime behind a desk.

"Let's button it up, ladies," said Ursa, her voice softer. "We're drawing attention. You've not seen any sign of Mr. Right?"

Nadine lowered her phone and put her eye to her scope again. As she panned it toward the mall's entrance, she shook her head.

"Not yet. He's late."

"I'm going to take a walk," said Ursa. "Wendy, come with me. Robin, finish the Cinnabon."

"Yes, ma'am," said Wendy and Robin in unison.

Nadine focused on her rifle again. Their armored-car target came twice a week to fill a specialized ATM inside the mall that catered to Bitcoin traders. Neither Nadine nor anyone else on the crew knew much about Bitcoin or cybercurrency, but it didn't matter. The machine dispensed hundred-dollar bills, which meant someone needed to fill it with hundred-dollar bills on a regular schedule. That made it perfect for their needs.

Had life been fair, Nadine would have been a stay-at-home mom. Life, though, was a motherfucker. When she was twenty-three years old, she married the love of her life—another soldier—and had planned to live the American dream with him. They'd get a little house together once they both finished their military contracts, and then she'd get pregnant. She'd raise their kids while Charlie became a policeman. They'd be happy.

God, or the universe, or somebody, though, decided she didn't deserve to see her dreams come true. On August 3, 2007, forces from the Islamic State of Iraq ambushed Charlie's Humvee. Two of the soldiers with him died. He survived, but he sustained a traumatic brain injury. His fellow soldiers kept him alive, but not even the best surgeons in the world could repair the damage to the prefrontal cortex of his brain.

After the Army discharged him, Charlie became a full-time mechanic. He was great with his hands and could fix anything—at least when he could focus. Prior to his injury, Charlie had been her rock. Afterwards, though, he changed. Doctors said that was common with his type of injury. He couldn't stick to a schedule, he skipped work, and he had difficulty focusing. Nadine's calm, stable, dependable husband became a flake. Within six months, he had lost three jobs.

Eventually, Charlie's world shrank. He was still the sweet, compassionate man she'd married, but their dreams changed. They stopped focusing on the future and began focusing on survival. He couldn't keep a job, so he worked around the house. He grew vegetables and flowers in their backyard and built end tables and kitchen cabinets in their garage. He stopped talking about children because he was afraid he'd be a lousy father. It broke Nadine's heart to see her gentle warrior hurting.

Every woman on the crew had similar stories. Robin was a single mom who had joined their group so she could better provide for her kids and a brother with Down syndrome. Wendy didn't have children, but she had joined to support her sister and their brother. Ursa had joined because her friends needed her.

When he turned eighteen, Charlie had put his life on hold to join the Army. He had wanted to protect those who couldn't protect themselves, and, because of that, he had lost everything that mattered to him. His old dreams of being a father, of watching his kids grow up beside his wife, would never come true. Nadine had joined their group so she and Charlie could afford to dream again. They wouldn't have kids, but they could have a wonderful life together. She'd make that happen no matter what.

Nadine heard the truck's diesel engine before she saw the boxy off-white vehicle stop in front of the curb near the food court's entrance. It was a hateful thing she and her colleagues did, but they acted out of love. One day, she hoped God would understand even if the world didn't.

She reached for her phone.

"I've got eyes on Mr. Right."

Nadine dropped the phone and looked through her scope. The armored vehicle's rear door remained closed, but she positioned the reticle to the right spot to make her shot.

"We're in position," said Ursa. "Nadine, you've got point. Robin, be prepared to move. Good hunting, ladies."

Chapter 2

I parked in the visitor spot beside the St. Augustine County Sheriff's Department headquarters building and drew in a breath through my nose. The building, a former Masonic temple, was just as pretty as it had ever been, but it had changed since I last saw it. The Doric columns in front seemed cleaner and crisper, the carvings on the oak front door seemed sharper, and the steps looked steeper somehow. When I had left St. Augustine a little under a year ago, I hadn't expected to return, but then this place had pulled me back. I still wasn't sure how I felt about that.

Before getting out of my car, I grabbed my briefcase and took a couple of deep breaths to calm my churning stomach. Then I looked at my phone and the text messages I had already received that morning. *You can do it,* read one. That came from my dad, Doug Green. *Kick some ass.* That one came from Audrey, my sister. *I love you.* That one came from Julia Green, my mom. I had read those messages a dozen times already and smiled every time. Those messages reminded me I wasn't alone, and every message meant more to me than its sender probably realized.

THE MEN ON THE FARM

This was the second time I had interviewed for a job with the St. Augustine County Sheriff's Department. My first interview seven years ago must have gone well because Sheriff Travis Kosen had offered me a job immediately afterward, and for six years, I had been proud to put on my badge every morning and go into work. I had helped people and made the world a better place.

Then, life got complicated. I exposed things about the county that some powerful people would have preferred that I had kept hidden, and I had stepped on a few toes. A year ago, I turned in a letter of resignation to the former sheriff to avoid being fired. After that, I traveled for a while and did a few other things, but now I was back, and I was ready for the next ride on my roller-coaster career.

I climbed the limestone steps, pulled open the heavy oak door, and looked over the lobby. Since I had left, the county had finished a top-to-bottom renovation and turned the old building into a modern, functioning police department. The lobby had a slate tile floor, white walls, and a white and gray granite information desk, behind which sat Trisha Marshall, the station's dispatcher. When she saw me, she stood and smiled and walked around the desk with her arms outstretched. I didn't usually like hugs, but I had missed her.

"I'm glad to see you again," she whispered.

"Me, too," I said, squeezing her tight before taking a step back and looking around. "This place is fancy."

"And you've only seen the lobby," she said. "I'll give you the full tour when you finish up with the sheriff and get your badge back."

I smiled and looked down.

"Let's hold off on that badge talk until I get the job."

"Okay," she said, squeezing my elbow and smiling again. "The sheriff's upstairs in George's old office. You can either take the elevator or the stairs."

"They put in an elevator?" I asked.

"An elevator, a gym, and a full kitchen. This place is nicer than my house."

"Mine, too," I said. "I'll see you soon."

"Good luck."

I thanked her and took the marble steps to the second floor. It was quiet up there. Prior to the renovation, the second-floor hallway had been long, dark, and narrow, but the contractors had ripped out the old drywall and plaster walls and replaced them with metal beams and sheets of floor-to-ceiling glass, giving the space a much more airy and open feel. The private offices had blinds, but the overhead lights cast an even, bright white on the floor in the hallway. It was the nicest police station I had ever stepped foot inside.

I walked to Sheriff Dean Kalil's office and knocked on the open glass door. The sheriff looked up from his desk. He was about fifty and had light brown skin, black hair, and brown eyes. When he saw me, he smiled and stood.

"Come on in, Ms. Court," he called. I thanked him and walked inside. The station had changed, but it looked like Sheriff Kalil planned to use the same heavy oak desk as his predecessor. I appreciated the continuity.

"Thanks for considering my application," I said, crossing the room to shake his hand. "I know I didn't leave under the best circumstances."

He smiled and nodded toward a chair across from his desk. I sat down, and so did he.

"You have a knack for understatement," he said. "My predecessor accused you of murdering a suspect in custody."

Butterflies fluttered in my stomach. I swallowed and sat straighter.

"Your predecessor was an asshole," I said. "The accusation was personal and had little to do with the evidence."

The sheriff considered me and then tilted his head to the side before smiling.

"They told me you weren't afraid to speak your mind."

"I'm not," I said. "And I'm a dedicated detective. If you hire me, I'll work hard for you, and I'll close cases. I may not always agree with you, but I'm a good cop."

"That's why you're here," said the sheriff, leaning back. "That's why my predecessor, George Delgado, is in the building, too. I understand you don't like him, and you've got ample reason for that. Can you work with him, though?"

I cleared my throat and shifted.

"I'm a professional."

The corners of the sheriff's mouth turned upward, and he lowered his chin.

"That's not an answer, Ms. Court."

I swallowed.

"Yes. I can work with him."

"Good," said the sheriff, pushing back from his desk. "You've been away from St. Augustine for almost a year. What have you been up to?"

He already knew what I had done because I had written about it in my cover letter, which was on the desk in front of him. I crossed my arms.

"I did some police work in North Carolina, so I've kept my skills up. You've read my cover letter, and you've also talked to people in North Carolina. Unless you've got specific questions, I'm not sure what you need me to say."

He smiled a little.

"I was just trying to make conversation. If I hire you, we'll see each other every day. Letters of recommendation and resumes only tell me so much. I'd like to get a sense of your personality."

It made sense, so I nodded.

"What do you want to know?"

He considered me.

"You like Ethiopian food?"

I closed my eyes and drew in a breath, surprised.

"I don't know that I've ever had it."

He looked as if he had expected that answer.

"You mind working twenty-four hours in a row if a case requires it?"

"No," I said, shaking my head. "That's the job. If I wanted to work nine to five, I'd go back to school and become a lawyer."

"You thinking about that?" asked the sheriff, lowering his chin.

"No. I don't like lawyers. No offense if you are one."

He smiled again.

"I'm not."

Neither of us spoke for a few moments. Then I raised my eyebrows.

"Do you have any other questions for me?" I asked.

Once again, he smiled, but it didn't reach much past his lips.

"What's your biggest concern about the job?"

I shifted on my seat and looked down.

"The world's a messy place, St. Augustine included. That makes the job hard."

The sheriff said nothing. Silently, I hoped he wouldn't ask me to elaborate.

"That's an interesting answer," he said, pushing back from his desk and opening the center drawer. He pulled out a detective's badge—my old badge, by the looks of it—and laid it on the desk. "The job's yours if you want it. I'll be reinstating you at your former salary and rank. Officer Trisha Marshall has some forms for you to fill out, so stop by the front desk sometime in the next couple of days. In the meantime, I need you to go by St. John's Hospital. There's a young lady there you need to see. I was going to send Trisha, but now that I have a female detective on staff, you're up. Assuming you want the job."

I picked up my badge and studied the embossed Missouri shield stamped into the metal. For a very long time, this badge had represented everything I admired most about the world. I had grown up in the foster care system and bounced around from house to house every few months. Some houses were good, and some weren't. One of my foster fathers hurt me when I was a teenager, and I never thought I'd recover. If not for a brave and compassionate woman who carried a badge very much like the one in my hand, I probably wouldn't have.

I ran my thumb over the word DETECTIVE and swallowed a lump in my throat. My eyes felt wet, so I blinked. I hadn't realized how much it had meant to me until I held it in my hand again.

"I didn't know that I'd ever see this badge again," I said, my voice soft.

"It's yours if you want it," said Kalil. "That one's a little tarnished, so I can get you a new one if you want."

"I'm proud of that tarnish," I said, allowing a tight smile to form on my lips. "I'd like the job."

"Good," he said. "You were the only qualified applicant willing to work for the salary the County Council allowed me to offer."

I laughed and stood. That sounded about right.

"Who's the girl in the hospital?"

He pushed back from his desk and then reached into a drawer for a manila file.

"Makayla Simpson," he said. "She's sixteen, and she was found yesterday at the foot of some steps in her high school. She has a pretty serious head injury, so I need you to talk to her and make sure she wasn't pushed down those stairs. You'll be working this case with George Delgado."

The moment he said Delgado's name, muscles all over my body tightened. I forced a smile to my lips and hoped I could keep my voice even.

"Detective Delgado is a gifted officer, but I can interview a young woman on my own. If you're worried about our findings holding up in court, I can record it."

The sheriff's lips curled into a tight, humorless smile of his own.

"I'm not worried about your interview skills," he said. "This is a simple case. That's why I'm giving it to you both. I want to make sure you can work together. Detective Delgado's in his office, and he's expecting you."

"Who's the lead detective?" I asked.

The sheriff blinked and then pushed back.

"That's something you two are going to have to figure out," he said, standing. "I'd advise you to choose the detective best suited for the specifics of the case."

"So me," I said.

Kalil considered me and then smiled. This time, it seemed genuine.

"Somehow, I thought you'd say that," he said, holding out his hand. "I'm sure you two will figure it out. Good luck, Detective Court. Welcome home."

I thanked him, shook his hand, took the file he handed me, and grabbed my briefcase before stepping out of the office. My fingers trembled, and a bubbly, light feeling swelled inside me. My legs wanted to run, and my heart raced. I didn't want to look too giddy in case I ran into somebody I knew in the hallway, so I held my breath and forced myself to walk at a regular pace to the second-floor restroom. Once I got inside, I locked the door and squeezed my fists tight and let myself smile.

Home.

The word felt almost foreign to hear, but the sheriff was right. I was home again, and this time, I wouldn't let anyone force me out—even an asshole like George Delgado. I stayed in the bathroom and took deep breaths until the initial surprise—and delight—at being hired faded. Then I looked at the file he had given me and read it as I walked down the hall to George Delgado's office. The documentation was thin so far. The school's principal had called 911 after a student found Makayla unconscious at the bottom of some steps. It looked as if she had fallen, but then he noticed red marks on her biceps that could have been handprints. He snapped pictures in case they disappeared.

Paramedics took her to the ER at St. John's Hospital, where the physicians examined her. Beyond that, I knew nothing, which meant we had work ahead of us. It was entirely likely that she had fallen, but I was glad the sheriff had assigned it to George and me. This was an opportunity for the two of us to put things right.

Delgado had a corner office at the end of the hall, and unlike most of the offices around him, his had its window blinds drawn shut. There was a handwritten note on his door.

To whom it may concern: I'm at St. John's Hospital working a case.

To Detective Court: you're late. Meet me at the hospital.

At least his personality hadn't changed in the year I was gone. He was still a dick. I took the stairs to the lobby and smiled at Trisha.

"So," she said, "you're Detective Court again, aren't you?"

"I am," I said. "And I've got an assignment. George Delgado and I are working a case involving a young woman at St. John's Hospital. She may have had an accidental fall, or she may have been pushed. We don't know yet."

Trisha furrowed her brow.

"Sheriff didn't waste any time," she said. "Good luck."

"Thank you. I need all the luck I can get," I said. I started toward the door but then paused and looked back at her. "You want to get a drink after work some time? And bring your husband, too."

The smile left Trisha's face, and she tilted her head to the side. My skin started tingling, and my stomach tightened just a little.

"Did I say something wrong?" I asked.

"No," she said, a smile slowly forming on her face once more. "Not at all. Asking a friend out for a drink seems out of character for you, is all."

I considered and then shrugged.

"I guess it is, but I'd still like to go out."

"It's good. I'd love to get a drink. Or two or three," she said. Trisha paused and smiled. "You're different. I didn't see that when you walked in, but I see it now. What happened to you in North Carolina?"

"A lot of things," I said. "I'll call you later. For now, it looks like I've got to visit a young woman in the hospital."

Chapter 3

Nadine's heart pounded against her breastbone, so she drew in a slow breath through her nose and felt it fill her lungs. She held it for a three count before breathing out through her mouth. Charlie had taught her the breathing technique, the same one he had used before going on patrols in Iraq and Afghanistan. He had been a talented soldier. She did this for him.

"Ladies, we have three quadrants," she said, speaking into her phone. "Quadrant A is from Dillard's to the food court. Quadrant B is from the food court to the Brazilian steakhouse's door. Quadrant C is from the steakhouse to the edge of the building. Our target is in Quadrant B. If you see additional targets, call them out."

"The wind is from the west at four miles per hour," said Ursa. "Make your adjustment."

"Understood," said Nadine, doing as her friend suggested. She took another breath through her nose and held it in her lungs, slowing her heart further as the rear door of the armored vehicle swung open. At three hundred yards, she didn't have to worry about the Coriolis effect, but even a hiccup would throw her shot off. Considering her target had a firearm and the training to use it, that could kill somebody she cared about.

A uniformed guard in his late thirties or early forties stepped out of the rear of the armored truck. He had buzzed brown hair, olive-colored skin, and a paunch from too many nights sitting on bar stools and sipping beer. He looked soft, and his belt hung low on his hips, pulled down by the firearm on his right side.

"Target is in sight," said Nadine.

"You're clear," said Ursa.

Nadine squeezed the slack from her trigger. She had only fired the rifle about a dozen times since they purchased it, but it could shoot well enough for her. This would work just fine.

The messenger—a term of art for the person who rode in the back of an armored car—reached into the vehicle and pulled out a pair of ATM cassettes. Each cassette held two to three thousand crisp, new bills. On their best score, Nadine, Ursa, Wendy, and Robin had acquired four full cassettes from a man filling the ATM outside a bank in Kansas City. The guard had died, but they had earned three hundred and fifty grand that day. She didn't expect to earn that much today, but they'd still make out well.

Adrenaline coursed through her system, heightening her senses. She could feel the nap of the rough carpet through her clothes and smell the mulch the owner had recently transported in his little car's trunk. The trigger in her finger felt tight. At this distance, her shot would miss her target by twenty or thirty feet if she was even a fraction of a degree off.

Nadine blew the air out of her lungs and focused on her slowing heartbeat, timing the shot so that it came between beats. A stillness overcame her, as it usually did.

Then she squeezed the trigger.

The heavy rifle kicked hard against her shoulder. Three hundred yards away, the guard went down.

"Go, go, go," she said, sweeping her scope across the asphalt and pulling back the bolt on her rifle to eject the brass. She swung her rifle toward the truck's door. The driver kept the door shut. She lined up the shot, held her breath once more, and squeezed the trigger. The truck's armored window held—which she expected—but the glass broke in a starburst pattern. She pulled back the rifle's bolt and lined up another shot. This round broke through. The driver's blood sprayed on the passenger window.

Nadine ejected the brass again and panned her scope toward the rear of the truck. Ursa and Wendy sprinted toward the messenger's body. Both wore black tactical vests, polypropylene gloves, black jeans, and ski masks. Beneath those ski masks, they wore swim caps that would minimize the amount of forensic evidence they left behind. Once they were far enough away, they'd burn everything.

"People in the mall are running," said Robin from inside the food court. "I am, too. The messenger's got a partner. Take him out."

"Understood," said Ursa. She reached to her belt and pulled out a small cylinder. Nadine almost felt sorry for the man inside the armored truck. An M84 stun grenade, the kind they all had used in the military, would deafen and blind anyone within about ten or fifteen feet. The thermobaric canister Ursa carried wasn't as loud, but it was just as bright, and the overpressure it created would disorient anyone nearby.

Ursa tossed the canister in the rear of the truck and then stepped back. From three hundred yards, the flash when the device blew was like a camera bulb going off and a cannon firing simultaneously. Inside the back of the heavy vehicle, it would have felt like the sun exploded.

A heavyset man stumbled out. Wendy shot him twice in the chest before he could pull a weapon. His body rocked as little puffs of blood exploded through his uniform. Then he fell to the ground.

"We're clear, and we're retrieving the packages," she said through her earpiece. "Watch our six."

"Understood," said Nadine, swinging her rifle toward the front of the truck again. "The driver's down. You're clear."

Wendy holstered her weapon while Ursa jumped into the back of the truck. She tossed two cassettes to Wendy and then emerged with a pair of her own. Nadine couldn't see their getaway car, but it should have been close. Once they reached the car and signaled that they were clear, Nadine would leave, too. They'd meet up again in the parking lot of a truck stop off I-55, an hour south of the city. There, they'd dump their stolen cars and pick up the car they had left. Finally, they'd meet Robin in a little coffee shop called Rise and Grind.

As she pulled her rifle back, Nadine noticed something. The messenger she had picked off was sitting up and reaching for the weapon at his side. She swung her rifle back into position.

"We've got a shooter," she said, already breathing deeply to slow her heart. When she had first shot him, she had aimed for his chest. It should have killed him, but he must have been wearing a vest. "Run, ladies."

The guard's weapon cleared his holster as Nadine blew the air from her lungs. She and the guard fired at the same time. The rifle kicked against her shoulder hard. It didn't break her collarbone, but pain lanced through her side and into her chest, causing her to gasp. She gritted her teeth and cleared the brass. The messenger wasn't moving, but neither was Wendy. Ursa sprinted toward their fallen friend.

"Fuck," said Nadine, her throat growing tight and a knot growing in her stomach. "Is she hurt?"

"Yeah," said Ursa, reaching down to help her friend up. Wendy leaned against her, unmoving.

"Is she alive?" asked Robin, her voice panicky.

"Yeah," said Ursa. "Everybody get away. You know where to go."

"Understood," said Nadine, pulling her rifle from the trunk lid and shimmying backwards. She climbed into the driver's seat, put the car in reverse, and pulled out of her parking spot. Her muscles felt twitchy, and she had to fight her instincts to keep from flooring the accelerator. This was bad.

She squeezed the steering wheel tight and breathed through her nose as she drove toward the exit nearest the interstate.

The mall was enormous, so most people inside had no clue something had happened near the food court's entrance. Nadine slipped her car into the stream of traffic as if she were out for a Sunday drive. Five minutes after she squeezed the trigger for the first time, she reached I-64 and saw half a dozen police cruisers exit the other side of the highway.

"You've got incoming," she said. "I'm on the interstate."

"We're on McCutcheon Avenue, heading north," said Ursa. "I'll meet you shortly."

Her cold tone sent a shiver up and down Nadine's spine.

"Where's my sister?" asked Robin.

"On my backseat," said Ursa. "She's alive. Follow the plan. I'll see you soon."

Nadine turned off the phone. Now that they had finished the job, she'd remove the battery and SIM cards and throw them along with the phone in the first dumpster she could find.

Wendy had understood their job came with risks, but she was hurt because Nadine had screwed up. She should have watched the messenger to make sure his chest wasn't moving. An ache grew in the back of her throat, and her chest felt heavy. She wanted to hit something, but that wouldn't help anyone. For now, she could only hope—and pray—that she hadn't killed her friend.

Chapter 4

St. John's Hospital was a regional medical facility associated with a major Catholic hospital in St. Louis. If I had needed major surgery, I would have gone elsewhere, but for minor emergencies, the doctors at St. John's did wonderful work and saved a lot of lives, mine included. And if they couldn't do something, they stabilized people and sent them to St. Louis. In a time when rural hospitals across the country were closing, we were lucky to have them.

I parked in the patient lot and walked through the main entrance. The hospital had a bright and airy multistory entryway with rich wooden walls, brightly colored furniture, and lots of healthy green plants. It felt like an upscale hotel. I crossed the light gray, polished terrazzo floor to the receptionist's wooden desk and smiled as I unhooked my badge from my belt.

"Morning," I said. "I'm Detective Joe Court with the St. Augustine County Sheriff's Department, and I'm here to speak with Makayla Simpson."

The receptionist, a woman in her early twenties, smiled and typed at her computer before looking up at me.

"The other detective is here already," she said. She paused and narrowed her eyes. "He was a little gruff."

"He's a butthead," I said. "Do you know where he is, by chance?"

"He went to Ms. Simpson's room on the fourth floor, but I'm not sure if he's still there. I can page him if you'd like."

I thanked her but said no and then took an elevator to Makayla's floor. George sat on an upholstered green chair in the lobby outside the elevator. He was in his fifties and had dark hair and an angular, pockmarked face. When he saw me, he sighed and started clapping lightly.

"Glad you could finally make it," he said. "I've been here for half an hour waiting for you."

I forced a smile to my lips and then reached behind me to pull my hair from my face and into a ponytail.

"I didn't have a job half an hour ago, so you only have yourself to blame for your wasted time," I said. "What have you done so far?"

He closed his eyes and started to open his mouth but then seemed to think better of it.

"As your partner," he said, after a pause, "I thought it'd be best to wait for you before doing anything. Ms. Simpson is in room 411 at the end of the hall, but I haven't gone in to see her."

"How's her condition?"

"I don't know," said Delgado. "Her doctor was supposed to brief me, but he's been with other patients all morning."

"Let's find a nurse, then," I said, walking past him to the nurses' desk nearest Makayla's room. It was empty, but a man in dark blue scrubs eventually showed up. He wore a stethoscope around his neck, and he had a pen in the pocket on the front of his scrubs. The badge clipped to his scrubs said he was Cole Forester and that he was an RN. I smiled at him.

"Can I help you?" he asked, stepping behind his desk and then typing at his computer.

"Yeah, Cole," I said, holding up my badge. "I'm Detective Mary Joe Court with the St. Augustine County Sheriff's Department. With me is Detective George Delgado. We're here to investigate Makayla Simpson's injury. Can you talk to us for a few minutes?"

He straightened and blinked a few times as he thought. Cole had pale skin, black hair, and stubble on his chin. He was taller than me and had thick arms and a big chest. Nursing was a demanding field both physically and mentally, and I suspected many of his colleagues appreciated having a big man around to help them with heavier patients.

"I'm not sure how much I can tell you," he said. "She's alive, and her vitals are stable."

I smiled.

"Has she had any visitors?" I asked.

He drew in a breath. His eyes went distant as he thought.

"At about eight this morning, her social worker came by to say hello before work. She wanted to make sure Makayla was doing okay."

I furrowed my brow.

"What about her parents?" I asked.

He shook his head.

"She's in the foster system," he said. "Usually those kids don't get too many visitors."

My smile faltered.

"Tell us about her injuries," said Delgado. "She have any permanent damage?"

Cole looked down and opened his mouth but didn't say anything for a moment.

"We're police officers," I said. "If necessary, we can get court orders to compel the hospital to release her records to us, but we'd rather not do that. If we can get information voluntarily, it'll help us investigate quicker. Do you have kids?"

He considered me.

"Two," he said before pausing. Then he typed for a moment and sighed. "She was brought to the ER unconscious. A nurse in the ER took pictures of her arms because she had bruises on them. They've become more pronounced as time has gone on. They're handprints."

That made this sound like an assault. I looked at Delgado. He drew in a slow breath.

"Are her injuries permanent or life threatening?" he asked.

"You'd have to talk to her doctors," he said. "I'm just reading her chart."

"Tell us about her head injury," I said.

He looked back at his chart and grimaced.

"She woke up on an exam table, and she didn't know where she was. Her memory is fuzzy, and she was very disoriented. Since then, she's had multiple rounds of vomiting as well as slurred speech and some numbness in her extremities. A physician in the ER ordered a CT scan, which found an isolated, linear skull fracture. He called in a neurologist. The neurologist was worried about an epidural hematoma, so she ordered Makayla admitted to the hospital. Since then, Makayla's concussion symptoms have dissipated, but she's still very tired. I will warn you as well that she's not a cooperative patient."

I wrinkled my nose. He seemed like a caring nurse, but the way he described her as noncooperative struck a chord with me.

"Can you blame her for not cooperating?" I asked. "She was shoved down the stairs, cracked her head open, and then woke up in the ER surrounded by strangers. She didn't even have a mom or dad to hold her hand. The poor thing is probably terrified. Does she understand what's going on?"

George grunted.

"Maybe you should calm down, Detective," he said, his voice low. I hadn't even raised my voice, so I rolled my eyes. Cole gave me a sympathetic look.

"Makayla's had it rough," he said. "We've got a lot of moms and dads on staff here, though, and we're taking care of her as if she were one of our own. We're doing the best we can in a crappy situation."

I stepped back and closed my eyes and drew in a breath.

"You're right," I said. "I shouldn't have snapped. Sorry."

"That's all right," said Cole. "It's good to see you upset. Somebody hurt this kid. That should piss you off."

Delgado's expression never wavered.

"Can we talk to her?" he asked.

"If she agrees," said Cole. "I'll ask."

The nurse left, and Delgado turned to me. He raised his eyebrows and then sighed knowingly.

"I appreciate that you came out here, Detective," he said, "but I'm going to send you home now. Given your well-documented experiences in the foster care system, it's clear you're too close to this case to remain objective."

I shook my head.

"Somebody pushed a child down the stairs and cracked her skull open. I'm going to do my job. To remind you, I wear the same badge you do now. You lost the election, so you're no longer the sheriff. You have no right to send me home. If you've got a problem with me, we can get a cup of coffee and talk it out. Or, we can go to Sheriff Kalil. That's up to you. I'm going to work this case, though."

Delgado straightened and narrowed his eyes.

"You're on my shit list, Joe," he said. "Consider yourself on notice."

"Truly, that shakes me to the core," I said, noticing movement out of the corner of my eye. Cole was walking toward us. His lips were tight at first, but he smiled when he reached us.

"No go," he said. "She said she's too tired to talk."

Delgado glowered and closed his eyes.

"We only need to ask one question. Did she see the person who pushed her down the stairs?"

"I appreciate that," said Cole, "but it's not my call. If you'd like to talk to Ms. Simpson, you can contact her social worker. I don't have her name or number, but I'm sure you can find it. Now, if you'll excuse me, I have patients to see."

He walked back to his desk, talked to someone on his phone, and then hurried to a patient's room. I looked at Delgado and sighed.

"That could have gone better," I said. He grunted but said nothing. "We should head to the high school. They might have video, but even if they don't, we can talk to her friends."

Delgado considered me and then shook his head.

"You want this case, it's yours. I'm not interested. Even if Makayla was pushed, her attacker's going to be another kid. We'll spend days working the case, and a judge will just tell her attacker to sit in time-out for a few hours. It's not worth my time."

I lowered my chin and furrowed my brow as I considered him.

"What?" he asked.

"I've known you for a long time, but for the first time, I think I understand you."

He crossed his arms and closed his eyes.

"Oh, do tell," he said, his lips pressed into a thin line.

"Even after twenty-five years in a uniform, you have no idea what it means to carry a badge. It's not about putting people in prison or exacting revenge on wrongdoers. It's about telling people like Makayla Simpson that they're not alone, that somebody cares about them, and that they're worth helping. This young lady lives with veritable strangers, and she was attacked in a place where she should have felt safest. We may never find her attacker, but if we show her that she's worth fighting for, maybe she'll start believing it. Maybe next time she'll talk to us instead of telling us to leave."

Delgado stepped back and looked at me from my feet to my face. Then he scoffed.

"You actually believe that pile of naïve bullshit, don't you?"

"Yeah, I do. And I'm sorry you don't," I said, shaking my head and sighing. "I used to get so mad at you, but now I finally realize what a waste that was. You're not a bad man. You're just a sad loser."

Delgado shook his head and walked away without saying anything. That was for the best. We had nothing more to say to one another, and I had a case to work.

Chapter 5

Nadine's muscles piloted her vehicle to their rendezvous location with little input from her conscious brain. An hour after she left the Galleria, she exited the interstate and pulled into the parking lot of a shuttered truck stop. A canopy covered ten fuel pumps for semitrailers on one side, while a second canopy on the east side covered two dozen pumps for passenger vehicles. Abandoned cars had parked beneath both as if they were fueling up. A gravel parking lot stretched hundreds of feet behind a convenience store and travel center bigger than almost any she had ever seen. It felt like a graveyard.

That station must have done a lot of business at one time, but now the parking lot facing the interstate held about two dozen cars, almost all of which had for sale signs on their front windows. She wondered whether the truck stop's previous owner had leased the spaces out or whether the residents of St. Augustine, the nearest town, had simply begun squatting on what should have been prime real estate.

She parked between a Honda Odyssey minivan and a four-door sedan. Wendy, Ursa, and Robin had different routes to the truck stop, but they should arrive within the next few minutes. Nadine used the time to wipe down the steering wheel, gear selector column, and other bits of hard plastic, metal, and glass inside her stolen car with a microfiber cloth.

Once she finished that, she walked to the black Chevy Suburban they had left in the lot for a portable battery-powered Shop-Vac. After vacuuming the car for stray hairs or fibers, she put a for sale sign in her sedan's front window and unscrewed the license plate.

As she stowed her gear in the SUV, Ursa's black Ford Escape pulled into the lot. They had stolen it from the parking lot of Parkway North High School in St. Louis County that morning. Its owner would have a lousy day when he couldn't find his car, but his insurance would replace it.

The compact SUV skidded to a stop, and Ursa popped out.

"Give me a hand with Wendy," she said. "We need to burn the car. It's got blood all over the backseat."

Nadine's heart started beating fast again as adrenaline coursed through her system.

"How is she?"

"Alive," said Ursa. "Get the trauma kit out of the Suburban. I don't want to move her until we get the bleeding stopped."

Among other things, the trauma kit held a plastic syringe filled with sponges. On the battlefield, a medic would press the tip into an open wound, depress the plunger, and push small cellulose sponges coated with a coagulant and antimicrobial agent into an injury. The sponges would soak up the blood, while the anticoagulant produced almost immediate hemostasis. Those syringes were pricey, but they saved lives.

Nadine got the first-aid kit out of Ursa's Suburban and carried it to the compact Ford SUV. Wendy lay on the backseat. Blood had soaked through her shirt, down her side, and onto the seat. Her skin was pale, and her breath was slow and shallow. Nadine's hands trembled, so she squeezed the sides of the kit hard to make them stop.

"She needs a doctor," said Nadine.

Ursa glanced at her and held out her hand. Nadine gave her the syringe.

"We'll stabilize her first and go from there," she said, pulling up her friend's shirt to expose an ugly wound the size of a golf ball. Wendy's eyes were open, but they didn't focus on anything. Ursa reached beneath the back of her friend's shirt and then looked at Nadine. "The round didn't go through. It's still in there."

Nadine's mouth was dry. She wanted to say something, but telling Ursa and Wendy that she was sorry didn't convey everything she wanted to express. Her stomach roiled, and she kept thinking of that guard she'd shot at the mall. She should have aimed for his head, or she should have shot him twice. At the very least, she should have watched him on the ground to see whether he moved. Instead, she had moved on to the driver immediately. It was a mistake, clearly, and her friend would pay the price.

She couldn't focus on her own worries, though. Wendy needed her help.

"This will hurt, honey," she said, reaching for the seat belt. She pulled it out, wadded it up, and then held it to Wendy's mouth. "Bite down on this."

Wendy did as she asked. Then Ursa counted down from three and pressed the tip of the syringe into her friend's open wound. Wendy's eyes shot open as sponges filled her wound. She spit out the seat belt and gasped and shot her hands to her waist, trying to pull the syringe out. Nadine pulled her friend's arms up over her head so Ursa could finish the job. Wendy screamed and thrashed her feet. Then Ursa pulled away and stepped back.

"I'm done, honey," she said. "It's over."

Wendy gritted her teeth and closed her eyes tight as she groaned. Tears streamed down her face, but then her breath slowed. Finally, she opened her eyes and looked at Ursa and Nadine.

"What happened?" she asked, her voice raspy and tired.

"Someone shot you," said Nadine. "We need to get you to a hospital. You're stable for the moment, but you've still got a hole in your belly."

"No hospitals," she said, clenching her teeth. "Where's my sister?"

Nadine looked at Ursa.

"We're meeting her at a little coffee shop. She's on the way."

"Did we get the money?" asked Wendy.

"Who gives a shit about the money?" asked Nadine. "You need surgery."

"We got all four cassettes," said Ursa, glaring at Nadine before reaching to Wendy's head and stroking her hair. "I went back for them. We got everything."

"Good," said Wendy, drawing in a slow breath. "I'm exhausted."

"We'll move you to the Suburban," said Ursa, looking to Nadine. "Get her shoulders. I'll get her feet."

Nadine nodded, and the two women pulled their friend from the car. Wendy gasped every time Nadine or Ursa stepped, but the syringe had done its job. She wasn't bleeding. They carried her to the back of Ursa's SUV and laid her as gently as they could on the floor. Before shutting the door, Ursa pulled out a red five-gallon gas can.

"What do we do now?" asked Nadine. "We can drop her off at the hospital and run, but they'll call the police."

"We're not doing that," said Ursa, walking to the compact SUV she had stolen. "There's a flare under the Suburban's front seat. Get it. We'll use that to light this thing up. We'll burn your car, too, just in case."

Nadine got the flare from the emergency kit beneath the front seat of the big SUV. Wendy groaned from the back.

"You okay back there?"

Wendy didn't respond, so Nadine opened the rear door. Wendy's eyes were closed. She looked as if she were having a nightmare, but she swallowed hard when Nadine put a hand on her leg.

"Don't worry about me," she said, her voice barely a whisper. "Get the money and do your job."

"Sure," said Nadine. She walked to the smaller SUV and handed Ursa the flare before noticing the ATM cassettes on the ground. If those cassettes held hundred-dollar bills—a high likelihood given the ATM they were destined for—each would have somewhere between two hundred and three hundred thousand dollars. Even if this was their biggest score so far, it wasn't worth it if Wendy died.

As Ursa splashed gasoline on the Ford's interior, Nadine carried the money back to the big black SUV they planned to use as their getaway vehicle. Two minutes later, the Ford was burning. A minute after that, they lit Nadine's stolen Kia Optima. Two plumes of black smoke rose from the parking lot, and already, cars on both I-55 and the highway that led to St. Augustine were slowing. Someone would call the police soon, so they had to get out of there quickly.

The moment Nadine got in the front passenger seat of the Suburban, they pulled out of the lot. The engine droned, and Wendy whimpered in pain in the back, a sound that was barely human. Nadine drew in a slow breath. Her lungs felt tight.

"This is my fault."

"Blame doesn't matter," said Ursa. "I know an ER nurse in Kansas City we can trust. If we can keep Wendy alive long enough to drive there, my friend would help us."

Nadine shook her head.

"She needs a doctor...a surgeon."

Ursa glanced at her.

"You know one?"

"No, but we'll find one," she said. "They take oaths to help people, and Wendy needs help."

Ursa shook her head.

"You're naïve. If we show up at a doctor's house with a woman on the backseat of our car, he'll call the police."

"Then we'll give him a reason to help," said Nadine. "We'll find a doctor with kids and put a gun to their heads."

The moment the words left Nadine's lips, her back straightened, and her fingers stopped trembling. Strength began to fill her again. It was a plan, one that would work. She wouldn't let her friend die. Ursa paused and glanced at her.

"You don't have kids, Nadine," she said, her voice low. "If you did, you'd never consider that."

"Wendy will die without help," said Nadine. "I don't give a shit about anything else right now. We're getting her home alive."

Ursa considered and then sighed.

"All right. We'll find a doctor and see if she'll help."

Nadine looked over her shoulder. She couldn't see Wendy in the back, but she heard her shallow, pained breathing.

"No," she said, shaking her head. "We won't find a doctor and see if she'll help. We'll do whatever it takes to get Wendy home alive. I don't care if that means taking out an entire goddamn orphanage."

Chapter 6

Nadine, Wendy, and Ursa drove the rest of the way to St. Augustine in silence. Fallen leaves covered the ground and filled the drainage ditch alongside the road, billowing in the wake of Ursa's big SUV. Tree limbs swayed in the late fall breeze, while clouds covered the sky to the horizon. It had turned into a gray, dreary day that mirrored the mood inside the vehicle.

By the time the ladies reached Rise and Grind, Robin already stood outside, waiting. She jumped into the SUV's middle row the moment it stopped.

"How's my sister?" she asked, looking over her shoulder to Wendy. She covered her mouth immediately and then reached to hold the injured woman's hand. Wendy barely shifted her eyes.

"We passed a little hospital called St. John's," said Nadine. "We're going to wait in the parking lot, find a doctor, and follow him home from work. We'll make him help us."

"How?" asked Robin, furrowing her brow.

"However we have to," said Ursa. "We'll offer him money. If he doesn't want that, we'll get serious. If we have to, we can hurt his family."

Nadine didn't know how Robin would react, but then she blinked and nodded.

"All right," she said, her voice low.

They reached St. John's Hospital a few minutes later. Nadine hadn't researched the hospital before their arrival, but it had multiple stories, a big awning in front of the emergency room entrance, and a sprawling asphalt parking lot that could comfortably hold two or three hundred cars. Ursa drove through the lot to identify those parking spots reserved for doctors before parking about a block from the building. There, they settled and watched the hospital employees through a pair of binoculars.

At first, they couldn't tell care providers apart, but eventually they saw enough name tags and enough different colors of scrubs to see patterns emerge. Doctors typically wore light blue surgical scrubs beneath white lab coats, while the nursing staff wore dark blue. Nonmedical personnel wore purple scrubs.

Once they knew who was who, it became much easier to pick a target. At five in the evening, a blond woman in light blue scrubs emerged from the back door. A tie held her hair in a ponytail. She shielded her eyes from the sun and then yawned as she headed toward the parking lot. She had probably just finished a long shift, but she looked young and strong. A few more hours of work wouldn't kill her.

"That's the one," said Nadine. "Let's follow her."

Ursa put her SUV in gear and drove. Nadine's heart beat faster. With every mile, Nadine found her throat tightening and her mouth growing drier. The doctor wasn't slowing or turning off into any of the neighborhoods they passed. Finally, she got on the interstate. Instead of following her, Ursa drove past the on-ramp.

"What are you doing?" asked Nadine. "You're losing her."

"We lost her the moment she left the parking lot," she said. "Did you see her license plate?"

Nadine shook her head.

"I wasn't looking at her license plate."

"She's from Illinois," she said. "I was hoping she'd turn into a house, but she's a commuter. We'd have to follow her for an hour to reach her house. There's too good of a chance we'd lose her in rush hour traffic."

"Then let's go to the hospital," said Robin. "We can drop Wendy off in the ER. With the money we've earned from the other robberies, we can go to Canada or Mexico and lay low. I'll have my mom bring my kids. She can bring Charlie, Nadine."

"And you'd be okay abandoning your sister?" asked Ursa. "Once the doctors see a gunshot wound, they'll call the police. She'd go to prison. She might get the death penalty."

"We don't have a choice. This is the only way we all survive."

Ursa pulled onto the side of the road.

"What do you think, Nadine?" she asked. "You want to run?"

Nadine shook her head.

"No," she said, reaching toward the SUV's in-dash touch screen. "Can you search for an address with this thing?"

Ursa hit a few buttons to bring up a search screen. The moment Nadine typed in what she wanted to find, Robin shook her head.

"That's a hard no," she said, her voice flat. "My sister needs a doctor, not a veterinarian."

"A vet will have surgical training, tools, and drugs. They might even have an operating theater."

"My sister's not a cat."

Nadine looked at Ursa for support, but she held up her hands as if she didn't want any part of the conversation.

"Dogs, cats, horses, humans, whatever…we all look the same on the inside," she said, looking back to Robin and then to Ursa. "We're not looking for a brain surgeon. We need someone who can remove a bullet, clean a wound, and stitch her back up. A large-animal vet can do that. Around here, he probably does it a couple of times a week during hunting season. Think about it. Nobody would have to go to prison."

Ursa sighed and drummed her fingers on the steering wheel before looking in the rearview mirror at Robin.

"It's not a bad option," she said. "A vet could patch her up, and then we could regroup. It'd buy us enough time to get her to a real doctor, and it'd keep us all out of prison."

Robin looked from Ursa to Nadine, her jaw tight.

"I can't believe you two are seriously considering this. We're not taking her to a fucking vet."

"What would Wendy want?" asked Ursa. "This is a serious question. You think she'd take the risk?"

"No, it's insane. My sister won't—" began Robin.

"The vet," came a rough, low voice from the back. "I don't want to go to prison."

Robin looked over her shoulder at her sister.

"Honey, you don't know what you're saying. You're delirious."

"No," she said. "I've heard you fighting. I'd rather die than go to prison. If you don't take me to the vet, just let me out here on the side of the road."

"Don't say that," said Robin, shaking her head, her voice quivering. "You're my big sister. I'll protect you. I'll take care of you."

"If you want to help me, do what I ask."

Robin looked toward the two women on the front seat. Ursa looked away, but Nadine held her gaze.

"I'm sorry, Robin," she said. "This is our best option."

Robin clenched her jaw and exhaled through her nose as she blinked away tears.

"Either let me die or take me to the vet," said Wendy. "I'm not going to send my sister to prison and orphan her children. It hurts to talk, so just fucking do it."

Nobody spoke for a moment. Then Robin sighed.

"Fine. Let's get the vet."

Ursa put her car in gear. Nadine breathed a little easier, but in the back of her mind, she wondered how many more of them would die before the day was through.

Chapter 7

The high school was a sprawling brick building surrounded by two football fields, tennis courts, a baseball diamond, and a track. A cold breeze blew across a recently plowed field across the street, carrying with it the scent of fresh, clean earth. The sky was a dull, cloudy gray, making me wish I had thought to put an umbrella in my car. I parked in a visitor spot in the lot out front and stepped onto the asphalt. Though the town of St. Augustine thrived as a tourist destination, the county was still rural and mostly empty. Rolling fields interspersed with copses of trees surrounded the building and grounds. It felt like home.

I walked to the building's entrance. I had, unfortunately, worked several cases involving students and staff from that school, but there had been enough turnover since then that few people should remember me. The glass and steel doors were securely locked, but an intercom system and cameras hung from the awning above my head. I hit a button to alert the office that I was there and held my badge toward a camera.

"Yes?" came a disembodied voice over the intercom.

"Hey," I said. "I'm Detective Joe Court with the county sheriff's department. I'm here to talk to somebody about Makayla Simpson."

"The office is to the right."

The door buzzed and unlocked, so I pulled it open and stepped inside. The school had been built in a T shape with a long, wide hallway straight ahead of me and branching hallways to the right and left. Lockers lined the walls, and pictures of successful alumni hung near the entrance. The smell of old books and tobacco smoke wafted toward me the moment I stepped inside. I smiled and started humming an old song about smoking in the boys' bathroom as I walked to the administration's office suite and smiled at the woman behind the front desk.

"Hi," I said. "I'm Detective Joe Court. I need to talk to somebody about Makayla Simpson."

The receptionist nodded. She had rounded features and black hair that just barely skimmed the red floral print of her cotton blouse. She sat behind a scarred wooden desk with a phone and computer. Behind her, a low bookshelf stacked with documents lined the wall. The nameplate in front of her said Ms. Winters.

"How is Makayla?" she asked.

"She's alive and recovering in the hospital," I said. "I'd like to see the spot where she was found and talk to some of her teachers if possible."

"Give us just a minute," said Winters, already picking up the phone. She spoke to somebody in hushed tones and then looked at me again. "Mr. Walters will be right out. He's the vice principal."

I thanked her. True to her words, a middle-aged man with sandy blond hair and a blond mustache emerged from a hallway on the left side of the office suite. His craggy, pitted face made him look made him look older than he probably was, while his green paisley tie clashed with his checked red shirt in a way that was almost attractive. His green eyes stared at me questioningly as he crossed his arms loosely.

"I was told to expect Detective George Delgado."

"Detective Delgado and I are working the case together," I said, reaching into my purse for an old business card. I took one and handed it to him. "I'm Detective Mary Joe Court. You can call me Joe or Detective Court, whichever you're more comfortable with."

He looked at my card and then slipped it into his pocket before shaking my hand hard enough that I could feel the bones start to rub together. A lot of men did that to me when they shook my hand. In bigger cities, there might have been lots of female police officers and detectives, but in St. Augustine I was still a minority. Some people seemed to find that threatening, I guess, and tried to intimidate me through brute strength. That Mr. Walters would try to do it to me said a lot about him. I almost wished George had come instead of me because the two of them would have gotten along well.

"I voted for him for sheriff," said Walters. "Mr. Delgado."

I forced myself to smile.

"I'm sure your support was appreciated. Can you show me where Makayla Simpson fell?"

Mr. Walters scratched his temple but didn't move.

"So she did fall?" he asked. "It was an accident?"

"She definitely fell," I said. "Whether it was an accident is still an open question. What do you think?"

He hemmed and hawed for a moment and then shifted from one foot to another before crossing his arms.

"I hate to think one of my students would push a girl down the steps and leave her at the bottom in a pool of her own blood without at least telling somebody."

"Is that what happened, you think?"

His mustache twitched as he considered his answer.

"How about I just show you the staircase and let you make up your own mind?"

"Okay," I said. "Show me the staircase."

He led me down the main hall and then to the gym, where we hung a right and entered a smaller branching hallway that led to a secondary gymnasium, weight room, and wrestling room. The concrete block walls were painted white, and the floor was bare concrete polished until it shone. We stopped at a set of dark, concrete steps that led into the basement. There were few overhead lights and no classrooms nearby, but a set of doors led to the track out back. I snapped pictures with my cell phone.

"So what's around here?"

"Athletic facilities," he said. "That's about it."

"What's downstairs?"

He drew in a breath and looked down the stairs.

"Two restrooms, the football locker room, the girls' volleyball locker room, and equipment rooms. You can also reach the boiler down there if you've got keys."

"Was Makayla on the volleyball team?"

He shook his head and closed his eyes.

"She wasn't involved in any extracurricular activities," he said. "At least none sanctioned by the school."

I crossed my arms.

"What does that mean?"

"You can take it any way you want to take it, ma'am," he said.

I didn't know how to take it at all, so I frowned and tilted my head to the side.

"Has she ever been in trouble?"

"Never even received a demerit," he said. "She keeps to herself. I tried to welcome her to the school and introduce her to some of our high-flying young ladies, but she wasn't interested. There's not much I can do to help a student if she doesn't want help."

The way he said it left me feeling cold, but I tried to avoid letting that show.

"She refused to talk to Detective Delgado and me, too," I said. "You know anything about her foster parents?"

He shook his head.

"They brought her in to enroll her, and they seemed like nice enough people," he said before sighing. "There's just not much you can do with some of these kids. They get put in the foster care system when they're three or four years old when their moms go to rehab or prison or whatever, and then they bounce around from home to home until they come here. By the time I get 'em, they're so damaged, there's nothing left."

I clenched my jaw tight but tried to keep my face neutral. My high school principal probably would have said the same thing about me. I showed up to class and did my homework but only because Julia and Doug Green made me. They gave me a home and let me know for the first time in my life what it meant to be loved. They loved me and refused to give up on me no matter how hard I pushed them away. If I lived to be a thousand, I would never be able to thank them enough for all they did.

Makayla probably didn't have a family like the Greens, though. It wasn't a surprise she refused to accept help from anybody around her. In her experience, help probably came with strings attached. Some foster parents expected you to do chores in exchange for room and board. Others wanted you to go to church with them. Other people wanted something else, though, something much more personal. Help in those homes always came with a price. I knew that firsthand.

"It's hard to grow up in foster care," I said. "If no one's ever cared enough about you to pick you up when you fall, you may not recognize help when it's offered."

Mr. Walters smiled bemusedly.

"You sound like our guidance counselors," he said. "I don't believe it, though. These kids get free room and board from strangers just for being alive. When I was fifteen, I pumped gas on the weeknights and cleaned up movie theaters on Friday and Saturday nights after the late shows. Kids these days don't know what work is."

I clenched my jaw and smiled simultaneously.

"Obviously, you're the expert on young people, so you'd know more than me," I said. He straightened and smiled.

"I appreciate you saying that," he said, before drawing in a breath. "We do what we can for students like Makayla, but there's something to be said about not chasing bad money with good. These kids are just bottomless pits. No matter how many resources you pour into them, no matter how many counseling sessions or tutors you arrange, that pit isn't going to fill up. Maybe if we got them when they were in elementary school, we could do something, but by the time we get them, these kids are lost causes."

The longer Mr. Walters spoke, the harder the muscles of my jaw clenched and the tighter my fists became. I wanted to snap at him and remind him that children like Makayla were human beings who had no one in their lives to turn to, but he didn't want to hear it. I had run into educators like him my entire childhood. They loved some of their students, but others, those kids who didn't fit into their preconceived notions of good or bad students, they couldn't wait to discard and throw away.

"When was this stairwell last cleaned?"

Mr. Walters considered.

"The floor was mopped as soon as paramedics took Makayla, and our custodial staff wipes down the handrails every night. We can't be too careful with cold and flu season coming up."

If that was right, there'd be no point in bringing in a forensic team.

"Thank you for showing me your school, Mr. Walters," I said. "I need to get back to my station and fill out some paperwork."

"Sure, of course," he said. "Let me just escort you back."

I looked toward the door to my right. It led to the track, but there should be a way to get back to the parking lot.

"I'll just go out the back," I said, already walking. "You don't need to spend any more time on me."

"You go out there, you'll have to walk around the entire building," he said. "You might as well go out the front."

"I'm fine," I said, pushing open the door. The cold air outside took some of the edge off my anger, but it changed nothing. Thankfully, Mr. Walters didn't follow me. It took almost five minutes to walk back to my car, and I clenched my hands and jaw the entire time. Mr. Walters's casual indifference to Makayla bothered me more than anything. To him, she was an inconvenience and a waste of resources that could have gone to another student, one who mattered, one who was worthy.

Never once had he said anything about her feelings. Was she scared in her new school? Was she scared at her foster home? Was she getting enough to eat? Did her foster parents force her to work long hours for a clean bed? Was that why she didn't do her homework? Did she have to share her bed with anyone? Did she cry herself to sleep at night?

I didn't know Makayla Simpson, but I knew how helpless and tired she must have felt. I had spent most of my childhood in the foster system, but before that, I had lived in the back of my biological mother's car and begged for food from restaurants after they closed. For most of my life, I had felt helpless. I had felt like nobody cared about me. Until I met Doug and Julia Green, maybe nobody had.

But now, I wasn't helpless. I didn't know what had happened to Makayla, but I planned to find out. Because she wasn't a waste of resources or a project to kick down the road to someone else. She was a human being, a young woman.

If no one else in the world cared about her, I would. And I'd make someone pay if they had hurt her.

Chapter 8

Makayla's foster family lived in a picturesque two-story historic brick home with a wide front porch and an American flag flying from a pole in the front yard. In the spring or summer, its mature landscaping would probably have looked pretty, but at this time of year, the hostas were dormant, the trees had lost most of their leaves, and the rose bushes had been trimmed down. I parked on the street out front and followed the broken concrete walkway to the porch. Immediately, a girl called out from a tree in the yard. I hadn't thought to look up and see her.

"Hey, Sam! There's a lady here!"

I looked at her from the front steps. She was probably ten or eleven, and she wore clean blue jeans and a pink jacket. Mud caked her shoes, but that didn't concern me. She looked healthy and well fed.

"Hey," I said, my voice high. I smiled as broadly as I could. "Do you live here?"

The girl squinted at me and then looked toward the house. "She's a cop, Sam!"

I smiled.

"You've got a good eye," I said. "I'm Joe."

"Sam!" she called again. "She's trying to talk to me!"

The home's front door opened a moment later, and a woman with dark, shoulder-length hair stepped out. She had high cheekbones and a thin nose, and she carried a dish towel. When her eyes met mine, she crossed her arms and tilted her head to the side.

"Can I help you?" she asked, giving me a guarded look. I reached for my badge, which was on my belt.

"I'm Detective Mary Joe Court," I said. "I'd like to talk to you about Makayla. Are you her foster mother?"

She considered me before drawing in a breath and looking toward the tree.

"Hey, Danielle, why don't you go inside and start your homework?" she asked.

"I'm good here, Sam," said the girl in the tree. The woman kept the smile on her face, but she lowered her voice.

"That wasn't a request, sweetheart," she said. "It's homework time."

The girl grumbled as she climbed down. Before going inside, she took off her shoes and left them outside on a mat. The woman focused on me and drew in a breath.

"You don't look like a detective."

"I am," I said, smiling. "Like I said, I'm Joe Court. I'm here to talk about Makayla. You have a few minutes?"

She considered.

"I'm Samantha Jefferson," she said. "My husband is Vance Jefferson. He's at work. We're Makayla's foster parents."

"And you have other kids, too, I see." Mrs. Jefferson nodded but said nothing. I forced myself to smile. "I tried to talk to Makayla in the hospital this morning, but she wasn't accepting visitors."

"So we've been told," she said, shifting her weight from one foot to another. "If you try to visit her again, I'd appreciate a phone call first. She's just my foster daughter, but I'd like to be there for the interview."

It was an interesting response considering neither she nor her husband had bothered visiting yet.

"I'll do my best to call if we go over again," I said. "I heard her social worker visited her this morning."

Mrs. Jefferson closed her eyes.

"And I bet you're wondering why my husband and I haven't gone," she said. "Vance works twelve-hour shifts, and I've been taking care of a sick eight-year-old. He's got the flu. Type B. Vance plans to see her this evening."

"It's hard being a parent. I understand."

She flicked her eyes up and down me.

"Do you have kids?" she asked. I shook my head. "Then you don't understand."

My attempts at rapport evidently weren't working. Time to try a new approach. I drew in a breath.

"You're busy, so I'll be direct. It looks like somebody hurt Makayla intentionally. This person, whoever it is, might have even lured her to a disused part of her high school to attack her without anyone else knowing. My job is to find out why this happened and to prevent anyone else from being hurt. You can help by telling me about Makayla. How long has she lived with you?"

Mrs. Jefferson locked her eyes on mine. Her chest rose and fell as she considered the question.

"You could have learned that by talking to her social worker."

I kept the smile on my face.

"True," I said. "Tell me something her social worker couldn't."

Mrs. Jefferson put her hands on her hips and looked down.

"All right," she said. "You want to know about Makayla? It sucks to be her foster mom. She's withdrawn, she's difficult, and she can be mean to everyone around her. It takes a lot to reach her."

I started to hold up a hand and tell her that I hadn't meant for her to speak ill of Makayla, but then Mrs. Jefferson's expression turned wistful.

"But when Makayla smiles at you, it's like she smiles at you with every part of who she is. She's funny, and she's smart, and she can be thoughtful. If you focus on her schoolwork, you'll never see how bright she is, but she could become a doctor if she wanted. She'll have a home with us as long as she wants, but I'm scared I'll never break through the walls she's put up."

Maybe I had misjudged her.

"If you can get her to smile, it sounds like you're doing everything right. It might just take time."

Her wistful smile turned condescending.

"I'm not interested in parenting advice from a woman who's never had children, let alone a teenager."

I wanted to tell her I had spent most of my childhood and teenage years in the same foster system as Makayla and that I had been a sullen and withdrawn teenager, but this wasn't about me or Mrs. Jefferson. It was about a young woman in the hospital with a fractured skull.

"The vice principal at her school said she wasn't involved in any extracurricular activities. Did she do anything outside of school?"

"She babysat for several neighbors," she said. "The kids liked her. She played with them."

"She have any biological siblings or friends outside the family?"

Mrs. Jefferson closed her eyes and then tilted her head to the side.

"I don't know about biological siblings," she said. "Her mother has been in and out of jail for most of Makayla's life. At the moment, she's serving a two-year sentence in the Chillicothe Correctional Center for passing bad checks, but prior to that, she spent time in prison for drug offenses. Makayla's never mentioned her father. We're trying to give her a stable home for as long as we can. She talks to other kids at school, but I'm not sure that she has any real friends. She babysits most Friday nights."

When I was in high school, I had worked in a movie theater and worked every shift I could to build my little nest egg. I had hoped to save enough money to get an apartment and a job as soon as I aged out of the foster care system. That way, I'd never have to live in a shelter or halfway house like a lot of other girls I knew. It sounded like Makayla had her head on straight and understood the world in which she lived.

"Can I see her room?" I asked.

Mrs. Jefferson shook her head without hesitation.

"Not without a search warrant," she said. "My children deserve their privacy."

"She's not in trouble," I said. "You understand that, right? Someone almost killed her. In the future, they might succeed, and I know you don't want that to happen."

"My job is to protect the interests of the children in my care," she said. "That's what I'm doing."

I took a step back and thought for a moment.

"I believe you," I said. "Which makes me wonder what you're afraid I'll find in Makayla's room. Drugs? A gun? Money? What?"

She leaned against one of her porch's support posts.

"Weed," she said. "I've caught her smoking. She's safe in this house. If you search her room and find marijuana, a judge could rule that she's better off in a youth home than here. That's not true, though. My husband and I care about her. I'm not going to let anyone take her."

"I'm not here for marijuana," I said. "If I find any, it won't make it into any written reports I make."

Mrs. Jefferson straightened and shook her head.

"You've heard my answer," she said. "Now have a nice afternoon."

She turned and went inside. I sighed and walked back to my car, where I took a few notes. Mrs. Jefferson seemed to care about Makayla, and she might have genuinely been trying to protect her, but shielding her from me wouldn't help anyone. The person—or people—who hurt her would still be out there, which meant I was far from done with this case.

Once I finished writing my notes, I sat back and tried to think of my next step. The vice principal at Makayla's school knew so little about her that talking to him again would be a waste of time. It'd be nice if I could talk to some of the neighbors for whom Makayla babysat to see what kinds of relationships they had with her. A foster mom might have been hard to talk to, but a young mom next door may have been a little easier. I also needed to talk to her social worker.

Before I did any of that, though, I needed to go home and check on Roy. I had only expected to be gone for a few hours when I went for my interview this morning, so I hadn't filled his water bowl as much as I would have if I had expected to leave for the day. It'd be nice to grab something to eat, too.

So I drove home on familiar, winding roads to my old American foursquare far past the edge of the town of St. Augustine. The house wasn't much, but it was all mine. I had bought it a little over seven years ago. At the time, the realtor had called it a teardown, but I had loved it from the moment I saw it.

The original builder had purchased the plans and materials for the house from a catalog for twenty-two hundred dollars. The home fell into disrepair over time, but for most of its life, moms and dads and kids and grandparents had run up and down its hardwood floors and slept in its bedrooms. I loved that history.

Unfortunately, I didn't love the man with a clipboard peering through its windows as I arrived. I parked in my driveway and clenched my jaw tight. St. Augustine County Councilman Darren Rogers straightened and turned. Rogers was in his sixties and wore a gray tweed jacket, a blue and white striped shirt, and dark pants. The afternoon sun glinted off his balding forehead. When he saw me, his thin lips curled into a tight smile, exposing his eyeteeth and making him look like a jackal. Had I seen him on the street, I would have walked the other way. Since I was at home, I had nowhere to go.

I opened my door and stepped out.

"Any particular reason you're trespassing on my property, Mr. Rogers?"

He considered me before his eyes traveled to the holster on my waist.

"I'd love to talk," he said, "but are you armed, Ms. Court?"

"I'm always armed," I said. "What do you want?"

He considered me again and then turned toward my house.

"I love this old place of yours," he said. "When I was a boy, my friend Paul lived here with his mom and dad. We used to run all through the woods out back. Back then, Paul's family owned about two hundred acres, but they fell on hard times and sold most of that property to the Pennington family. That was before you were born. You know all about the Penningtons."

I knew a few things about the Penningtons, but I didn't care to discuss the matter, so I crossed my arms.

"What do you want, Mr. Rogers?"

"I suppose, before I say anything else, I should congratulate you. Sheriff Kalil offered you the job, didn't he?"

"Yep, and I'm already working a case. I came home to check on my dog. Do we have a problem?"

Rogers drew in a breath and paused.

"I should warn you that I advised Mr. Kalil against hiring you, but he thought you'd be a good addition to his team. He was insistent, so I decided not to overrule him."

My lips curled into a tight, humorless smile.

"Does your position as county councilman allow you to make human resource decisions, now?"

"A lot's changed since you left, Ms. Court. The County Council decided a robust system of government with an executive at its head would better implement policy decisions than the former system had. You are conversing with St. Augustine County's first executive. All county business comes under the executive's purview, and that includes the hiring—and firing—of our law enforcement officials. It's in the new charter."

I uncrossed my arms and dropped my hands to my sides, sure that I had misheard him. I asked him to repeat what he just said. He complied, but it made no more sense after hearing it a second time.

"Did people vote on this charter?"

"Our lawyers didn't deem a vote necessary," he said. My eyes and mouth popped open, but he spoke before I could say a word. "In my capacity as county executive, I'm authorized to call an election if I deem one necessary. So far, I haven't seen the need. Aside from a few angry letters and some minor protests, nobody's even objected. The people want progress. I can give it to them."

I looked down. Then I barked a laugh.

"Were you at least elected to your position?"

He chuckled.

"Transitions between systems of government are always difficult. The council determined—in consultation with our lawyers—that it'd be easier for everyone if we appointed our first executive. It was the council's final act, and they chose me. With the utmost humility, I accepted. It's been a true honor to serve."

Waves of heat began coming over me, but I tried to keep my anger from my voice.

"What are you doing here, Mr. Rogers?"

"I noticed that you applied for some building permits," he said. "You're doing some renovation work, huh?"

"That's the plan."

He reached into the pocket of his jacket for a tape measure, which he then used to measure from my porch to the ground.

"Your deck's thirty inches above grade," he said. "Your porch needs a guardrail."

I shook my head.

"The porch was installed well before the modern building code was implemented," I said. "It's grandfathered in."

"All the same, I'd like you to install a guardrail," he said. "You have a basement?"

"Why?" I asked, lowering my chin.

"Well, I walked around earlier, and I didn't notice any egress windows," he said. "County records indicate you've got an eight-hundred-square-foot basement."

I clenched my teeth before responding.

"There's a window above my washing machine," I said. "That's good enough for my purposes. It lets in plenty of sunlight."

"I saw that one, but it doesn't look like it opens, so it's not a proper egress window."

I counted to five before speaking so I wouldn't say something I later regretted.

"My basement isn't a living space," I said. "My house was built almost a hundred years ago. They didn't have building codes back then, and even if they did, I'm guessing they wouldn't have required an egress window."

"You don't have to get testy," said Rogers, smiling. "I'm here to ensure that you're safe in your home. Sometimes, the county will go by the International Residential Code, but other times, we'll be a little more stringent for the safety of our residents. If this is a problem for you, you can request a variance with the building inspector's office. He works for me, so I can even set you up an appointment right now. I'll warn you, though, that he and I have similar opinions about residential safety. When you apply for your next building permit, I'd like to see your plans to bring the entire home up to the modern building code."

In a hundred-year-old house, that would require me to replace the plumbing, electrical, and heating and air systems and then to look at the windows and structure. I had already done some of that work, but the structural changes would cost me more money than the property was worth.

"I might as well tear the place down and start fresh," I said.

"That's your choice," he said. "If you'd like, I could recommend a good St. Augustine contractor."

One who gave him a kickback, no doubt.

"Get in your car and leave."

He chuckled and allowed his eyes to travel up and down me before sighing.

"Why'd you come back, Joe? You could have gone to St. Louis, you could have gone to Chicago, you could have even stayed in North Carolina. St. Augustine was doing just fine without you."

I tilted my head to the side.

"This is my home."

He sighed before tilting his chin down and giving me a look that was half pity and half scorn.

"Honey, you live here—and even own a house here—but St. Augustine isn't your home. Nobody wants you here."

Though I seethed inside, I kept my face as neutral as I could.

"You might be right, but it's not your call," I said. "Besides, I never would have left North Carolina if not for you."

He brought his hands to his heart and smiled.

"Your interest is flattering, but I'm happily married," he said. "The missus is a jealous woman, so it'd be in your best interests to leave town now before I tell her of your affections."

I didn't even bother scoffing. Instead, I stepped forward. He stepped back.

"I tried to move away and start a life for myself, but you didn't let me. When I lived in North Carolina, you sent a letter to Jeremy Pittman in which you alleged that I had murdered a woman and left to avoid prosecution. I rented a room from Mr. Pittman's ex-wife. She was my friend. Because of your letter, the courts took her daughter."

"I see," said Rogers. "I get it now. You're angry because of that letter I wrote. That makes perfect sense, but you have to understand that I was doing my duty as the county executive. Mr. Pittman's attorney called the sheriff's department asking for information on you, and I told him the truth. That was my duty."

I clenched my teeth and smiled.

"In case you wondered, Ann got her daughter back when I moved out. You also sent the University of North Carolina a letter. They rescinded my admission to graduate school."

He cocked his head to the side and blinked.

"In good faith, I couldn't let you be around all those young people considering your background. You're volatile, Joe. You might have hurt somebody."

Cold spread over me. This time, I allowed it into my voice.

"If I were so volatile, don't you think you'd be dead right now?"

The smile left his lips, and he straightened.

"Are you threatening me?"

"No. I'm making an observation."

He considered me and then looked toward his car.

"I don't like where this conversation is heading," he said. "I'll be leaving."

I turned and watched as he walked toward his car. The moment his hand touched the door handle, I called out.

"Stanley Pennington, the man who bought this property from your friend Paul's father, was a rapist. His wife, Susanne Pennington, murdered him in 1971. You covered that murder up and, as payment, forced Susanne to turn over everything she owned to you and your friends. Her husband's money created the Spring Fair and half the businesses in St. Augustine County. Without her, this place would have nothing. Instead, it's got expensive restaurants, amenities, hotels, bed and breakfasts…even wineries. From the outside, this place is perfect."

He stopped moving but said nothing.

"You built St. Augustine County, but you used poison and lies in place of a stable foundation. I was prepared to turn my back on that, but you showed me I can't," I said. "This town is rotten. I've seen what happens when you let that rot go on too long. Everything dies."

Rogers considered me again and then shifted his weight and smiled.

"If I'm the poison, what are you?" he asked. "The cure?"

"No," I said, shaking my head. "I'm just a cop, and I'm doing the best I can for people I care about. Now please leave my house. If you want to pretend to be a building inspector, call ahead and make an appointment. Otherwise, I don't want you in my life."

He shook his head.

"You've moved back to my county. You made your choice. I'm not going anywhere. This is my town. I've made it what it is."

"That's fine," I said. "If you stay, it'll be easier to find you when I get enough evidence to send you to prison."

He drew in a breath and then shook his head. A smug, condescending smile formed on his lips.

"I'd rather not see a county detective waste taxpayer money, so conduct your investigations on your own time. I'd hate for you to jeopardize your job so soon."

"Sure thing," I said. He got into his car and left. My shoulders rose and fell with every breath as I watched him leave. I knew when coming back that Rogers would be a problem sooner rather than later, but I hadn't wanted to focus on him right away. Now, I guessed I had to. The man just couldn't leave me alone. He'd grow to regret that.

Chapter 9

Once Darren Rogers left, I took a couple of deep breaths to purge him from my mind and walked around my house to get my dog. I wasn't much of a gardener, but I loved my little house and yard and the woods behind it. When I moved in, the yard had weeds everywhere, hedges so overgrown I couldn't see the home's foundation, and dead rose bushes along the road. It took a few weeks, but I tamed the bushes, dug out everything dead, and overseeded the yard. Now, it was comfortable.

Roy barked at me from the dog run. I hated locking him up while I worked, but it kept him safe. He had a doghouse and approximately nine hundred square feet, most of which was beneath an old oak tree. One day, I hoped to fence in the entire backyard so he had room to run and play, but that might take a while.

As I walked toward the gate, Roy jumped and stood on his hind legs with his front legs on the chain-link fence that surrounded his doghouse. Then he barked and wagged his tail so hard I thought he'd throw himself off balance and fall over. I couldn't help but smile.

"Hey, dude," I said, opening his gate. Roy jumped down and then ran toward me once I let him out. He licked my hands, and I patted him on the back. "Mommy got a job. What do you think about that?"

He stuck his tongue out and panted. I took that as tacit approval.

"I've got to do some work, but then you want to go for a run?"

He panted, which I figured was a yes. The two of us went inside. I filled his water bowl and then settled at my kitchen table to track down Makayla's social worker. It only took a few minutes to find her number, but my call went to voicemail. I left a message, but with Makayla still in the hospital, this wasn't an emergency. I'd call again later.

After that, I changed into a long shirt, a pair of leggings, and a bright orange vest that would alert any hunters who had wandered into my woods that I was a human being. Before going out, I put a similar vest on Roy, but I didn't expect him to follow very far. He wasn't big on exercise.

For about an hour, I jogged through the woods. Roy had followed for about five minutes, but, true to form, he had turned back and headed home before I could even finish warming up. The sound of squirrels and other small woodland animals dashing through the fallen leaves surrounded me. I had run through these woods hundreds of times, and yet, every time was different. It felt good to be home again.

When I reached the house after my run, Roy was lying half in and half out of his doghouse, but he sprang up when he saw me. I showered and ordered a pizza and typed some notes on my laptop until dinner arrived. Then, I fed Roy and took my dinner outside to call my parents. Dad answered right away.

"Hey, honey," he said. "Did you get the job? Am I talking to a working girl?"

I smiled and closed my eyes as I leaned back.

"Oh, Dad," I said. "You know the term working girl is a euphemism for a prostitute, right?"

"I feel like I should have known that," he said. "Let's try that again. Did you get the job?"

"Yeah," I said. "Your favorite daughter is now gainfully employed, and she's not selling herself on the street, either."

"I'm glad to hear that," he said.

Dad and I talked for about ten minutes, and then he handed the phone to my mom. Her voice was soft. Mom and I had hit some rough patches over the years, but she had never given up on me, and I had never given up on her. I loved her, and she loved me. Outside my immediate family, I couldn't say that about many people.

"Hey, kiddo," she said. "So those bums saw the light and gave you your job back, huh?"

"The new guy doesn't seem so bad, actually," I said. "He might do good things for this area."

"I'm glad," she said. "Your area needs a good sheriff. Have you seen the old one?"

I grunted and took a bite of pizza.

"Yeah, unfortunately," I said. "The sheriff thought it would be helpful if George and I worked an easy case together as a way of patching things up. So far, it hasn't worked out well."

Mom paused.

"You didn't shoot him, did you?"

I smiled and shook my head.

"No, but I gave my honest assessment of his police work. He didn't appreciate it."

Mom laughed.

"What did you say?"

Mom had been a police officer, so she understood the work and the world in which I lived. I told her about my day and about Makayla Simpson. By the time I finished, my throat felt dry.

"I shouldn't have let Delgado get to me, but he just wrote this kid off. So did the vice principal at her school. She was hurt, and nobody seemed to give a shit."

"She remind you of yourself?"

My lips curled upward, and I stood to get a beer and a second piece of pizza.

"Yeah," I said. "Hard for her not to. I hated school. Other kids had it so easy. They knew they'd graduate and go on to college or get a job or whatever.... I didn't even know if

I'd have a home when I turned eighteen. And Makayla's vice principal was such a dick. He reminded me of a lot of my old teachers. They had all the patience in the world for you if your parents had money, but if you were a foster kid, you were someone else's garbage. If I ever have kids, there's no way I'm sending them to that school."

Mom laughed softly.

"So you're thinking of having kids, huh?"

I smiled and then sighed wistfully.

"Maybe one day," I said. "First, though, I've got to meet somebody worth having kids with."

"If that's what you want, I hope you find somebody," she said. "Kids are hard, but they're worth it."

Mom and I talked for another few minutes, but then my phone beeped with an incoming call. It was my station.

"Hey, Mom," I said, interrupting a story about my brother Dylan. "I've got another call from my dispatcher. Can I call you tomorrow?"

"Sure, of course," she said. "Good luck if you have to go out."

I thanked her and hung up. The caller was Jason Zuckerburg, our station's night-shift dispatcher. He was friendly and conscientious. I had always enjoyed working with him.

"Jason, hey," I said. "What's up?"

"Hey, Joe. Good to hear your voice again," he said. "I wish this was a social call, but it's not. About half an hour ago, we received a call about dozens of shots fired at a cattle ranch way out in the county. It sounded like somebody was target shooting, but I dispatched Katie Martelle and Bob Reitz to make sure things were okay. Upon arrival, they found three bodies on the ground and well over a hundred shell casings scattered around. They called the sheriff, and he asked me to call you."

I drew in a slow breath as I processed that.

"Jeez," I said. "Is it contained, or is our shooter still out there?"

"We don't know," he said. "The Highway Patrol sent us a helicopter with an IR camera. It's scouring the area, but the farm is almost two thousand acres and has almost eight hundred head of cattle. We've got half a dozen barns and four homes to search. I've got every officer on duty on standby, and I've got half a dozen Highway Patrol troopers en route, so we should have the manpower to lock the area down."

"Why does the sheriff need me?"

"It's always helpful to have a detective," he said. "And he wants Roy."

I smiled just a little.

"You know Roy's just a dog, right?"

"He's a trained cadaver dog," he said. "There are hundreds of shell casings on the ground. We don't know what happened yet, but there's a strong possibility there are more bodies lying around this farm. Somebody might even be hurt."

I drew in a breath.

"I get it," I said. "Tell the sheriff I'm on my way."

Jason said he would and then warned me that he had more calls to make. If I needed to talk to somebody in charge, I needed to call the sheriff's direct line. I thanked him and hung up and then looked at Roy. He lifted his head and panted.

"Well, dude, looks like you and I are going to have a busy night."

Chapter 10

I put Roy in the back of my Volvo and headed out. As I neared the farm, I found rolling grass-covered hills and barbed-wire-enclosed pastures that seemed to stretch beyond the horizon. Cows stood in small groups, chewing the grass. The sun had just set, and purples and oranges streaked the sky. The moon had yet to rise.

I followed the barbed wire until I found a gravel road with a cattle guard out front. The gate was open, and a St. Augustine County police cruiser had parked on the side of the road. Officer Alisa Maycock stood outside. She came toward me as I opened my window.

"Alisa," I said. "Where's the sheriff?"

Alisa gave me a tight smile as she straightened and pointed up the gravel road.

"Straight ahead on the gravel road. You'll drive past a barn and then a vet's office. Sheriff Kalil's at the main office. It's about a mile straight ahead. It's a big farm, so stick to the gravel roads or you'll get lost."

If it had a mile-long driveway, it was a big farm. I almost whistled.

"Anything I should know?"

"Radios are a little patchy with the hills," she said. "You might have to use your cell phone."

"I don't have a police radio, so my cell phone it is," I said. She handed me a clipboard with a log sheet on it. I signed my name, the time of my arrival, and my reason for entering the crime scene before handing it back. "Any sign of our shooters?"

She shook her head.

"Not a one. We've run through most of the buildings, but it's a big place," she said. "Good luck. And it's good to see you again."

"Thanks, and you, too," I said. She nodded, and I drove forward. With my window open, I heard a helicopter somewhere to the north, but I couldn't see it. Roy stuck his head out and barked at the cows. He seemed to be enjoying himself, at least.

The gravel road rose at a gradual incline, and once I crested the hill, I found the first barn and a two-story farmhouse with cream-colored clapboard siding and a sign out front with a blue cross on it and an illustration of a cow. Two St. Augustine cruisers and a van from the crime lab had parked in the small lot outside. As I drove past, Kevius Reid, one of our forensic technicians, waved to me and then slipped something—a shell casing if I had to guess—in a clear plastic evidence bag. I waved and kept driving down and then up yet another hill.

THE MEN ON THE FARM

The sheriff had parked at the end of the gravel drive beside a two-story home with white clapboard siding, black shutters, and a big front porch. Kitty-corner to it was a pole barn with six garage bays, four of which held pickup trucks and two of which held golf carts. A van from the coroner's office had parked just outside the pole barn. Its rear door was open, and the two gurneys inside already each held a body bag. Stan Rivers, the county coroner, stood outside. No one spoke to or approached him.

I parked by the sheriff's SUV and got Roy out of the car. He peed on the side of the road and then stuck his nose in the air as if he were smelling something. Then he turned toward the coroner's van. Sheriff Kalil stood outside the farmhouse, talking to two men in jeans and long-sleeved shirts. When he saw me standing on the grass, the sheriff excused himself.

"Thanks for coming out, Detective," he said. "I wouldn't have normally called you out after you put in a whole day's work, but this was an emergency."

"Not a problem. Emergencies are part of the job," I said, nodding toward the two men on the porch. "Are they witnesses or suspects?"

"Neither," said Kalil. "They work for the Henderson family, but they live in a house on the edge of the east pasture. They didn't even hear the gunfire."

"I saw Kevius collecting evidence near a barn."

"That's our first crime scene," said Kalil. "We found one body there and about four dozen shell casings on the ground. The second scene is near the farm's west entrance. Darlene McEvoy with the forensics lab and Sergeant Reitz are there. We found two bodies along with a lot of shell casings there. We also found a Chevy Suburban with stolen plates. It was shot thirty-seven times."

"Jeez," I said, raising my eyebrows. "Have we ID'd the bodies yet?"

"We have," said Kalil. "Near the vet's office, we found Dr. Paul Henderson. He's a large-animal vet. Near the west entrance, we found Jesse Henderson and Wade Henderson. Jesse Henderson is Paul Henderson's brother. Wade Henderson is their father. They all live on the property."

I brought a hand to my mouth as I considered.

"So they're all in the same family," I said. "Could this be a family feud?"

"I doubt it," said Kalil, looking to the two men to whom he had been talking earlier. "Those guys went to school with Jesse and Paul, so they've known the family most of their lives. They both said the Henderson family got along pretty well. Even if they fought, it'd never come to gunfire."

"Are any of them married? Where are the women?"

"They're all married, and they've all got kids, but the ladies and children are at some kind of church event in Branson," said Kalil. "Jesse, Wade, and Paul stayed back to take care of the animals. Jason Zuckerburg is trying to track down the family now."

A cow mooed nearby. Roy wasn't used to livestock, so he picked his head up and looked, but he was trained well enough to stay by my side.

"Sounds like you've got things under control. What do you need me to do?"

"We've got well over a hundred shell casings on the ground. We don't know what happened, but it looks like a gunfight with the Henderson family on one side and unknown subjects on the other. I need you and Roy to find the other shooters."

I put my hand on Roy's side.

"Roy's got a good nose, but he's not a tracking dog."

"But he can smell blood, can't he?" asked the sheriff. I nodded. "Good. See if you can find some."

I hesitated.

"Roy's trained to smell human decomposition," I said. "He can smell fresh blood, but I don't know that he'd think anything of it. It's not what he's trained to find. If we come back tomorrow after that blood has decomposed, he'll be all over it, but I can't guarantee he'll have the same reaction now."

The sheriff scratched his brow.

"Just do your best, then. Start near the veterinarian's barn."

I drew in a slow breath.

"Okay. We'll see what we can find."

The sheriff wished me luck and then turned toward the main farmhouse, while Roy and I followed the gravel road back to the vet's barn and office. Kevius was still outside collecting evidence, so I stayed a good distance away. He bent to bag a shell casing.

"Hey, Detective," he said upon straightening. "Good to see you. Watch your step if you come any closer. I was waiting for Darlene to finish with the metal detector before searching out by the road."

"You find any blood yet?"

He looked toward the barn and sighed before looking at me again.

"I saw what looked like blood near the door, but I can't tell if it's human or if it came from the vet's office. Body was found out here in front. They shot him in the chest. He was unarmed."

I looked at my dog.

"You see any pigs around here?" I asked.

"No," said Kevius, furrowing his brow. "Why?"

"Roy can differentiate between human blood and most other animals, but pigs sometimes confuse him."

Kevius seemed impressed.

"He's that good, huh?"

"He's supposed to be," I said. "He flunked out of the cadaver dog program for being lazy. We'll see how much he picked up. Thanks."

Kevius nodded and focused on his work. Roy and I walked around the barn, and I told him to sit. Once he had calmed down and started paying attention to me, I removed his leash.

"Roy, find it. Find the blood."

The moment I finished the command, he jumped and took off. I could almost see his nose working as he ran first toward the barn and then to the grass beside it and then back to the barn. Every time the wind shifted, he lifted his head and sniffed.

He had something.

"Find it, Roy," I said. "You can do it."

He jogged toward the barn, panting, his tongue hanging out of his mouth. With the sun having set, it was getting dark. I needed to go back to my car and get a light. If he caught the scent of something and ran, I could lose him out here.

"Hey, dude," I said. "Come here."

But Roy didn't come. His nose was about six inches from the dirt near the barn's foundation. Then he sat down and looked at me and stuck his tongue out. I jogged to him and hooked my leash on him before calling out.

"Hey, Kevius!" I shouted. "I need some help back here."

Within seconds, Kevius and Shane Fox, a uniformed deputy, came running. Shane flashed his light at me and then to Roy.

"You okay, Joe?"

"We may have something," I said before calling Roy to my side. He got to his feet and stood, and I pointed to the ground. "Flash your light to where Roy was sitting."

The two men did as I asked. Then we found a bloody outline of a shoe. I looked around. The barn didn't have a rear door. If the footprint's owner had walked around the building, Roy would have caught the scent earlier. Moreover, the grass and dirt he had crossed would have wiped the blood away.

"How the hell did that get here?" I asked.

Shane shrugged, but Kevius flashed his light to the barn. There was a window about ten feet from the ground over the spot.

"Anybody searched up there yet?" I asked, looking to Shane.

He shrugged again.

"I just got here, ma'am."

I looked at Kevius. He, too, shrugged.

"You'd have to talk to the sheriff. We're doing what we can with the resources we've got."

"I will talk to him," I said, already taking out my cell phone. I used it as a flashlight to look at the footprint again. Then I found a second bloody spot on the ground. The pattern wasn't as pronounced, but it looked like a second footprint, and it was leading away from the barn. I called the sheriff's cell and waited for him to answer.

"Hey, boss, it's Joe Court. I'm at the back of the barn by the vet's house. I need a search team to go through the barn's second story, and I need a tactical team. Roy found a blood trail leading to the west. We should follow it."

Chapter 11

No one spoke inside the truck's cab, but Nadine could hear Wendy's labored breathing. They hadn't wanted to move her from the back of the SUV, but after taking fire at the cattle ranch, they didn't have a choice. Robin sat with her, while Ursa sat in the front and Nadine drove. Nadine's shoulders felt tight, and a ball of nausea had grown inside her gut. As she reached forward to turn on the air, Ursa touched her forearm and shook her head.

"Don't. Wendy's shivering already."

Nadine looked in the rearview mirror. Wendy's head lay on her sister's lap. Robin stroked the woman's forehead.

"Drop me off here," said Wendy, her voice slow and labored. "I'm only slowing you down."

"We're not abandoning you," said Ursa. "Just give us some time. We'll figure this out."

"Ursa's right. We're not leaving anyone behind," said Nadine, flicking her eyes to the rearview mirror and then back to the road. "We'll find a doctor or nurse. You'll be okay."

The lie sounded hollow the moment she said it. They didn't have plans for this. Her mouth felt dry, and she worked her fingers against the steering wheel as her mind raced to come up with something—anything—that could help.

She still didn't understand what had happened at the farm, but they had gone there because Dr. Paul Henderson was a veterinary surgeon, and he had a nice website that showed pictures of clean, modern operating theaters. The man advertised. He should have expected that customers might come to his office after hours.

Instead of welcoming them and asking what they needed, though, the moment they drove onto the property, two crazy men had opened fire on them with hunting rifles. They weren't warning shots, either. The first round hit the SUV's engine block, and the second shattered their front window. They meant to kill. For all Dr. Henderson and his buddies knew, Nadine and the ladies in their SUV could have been a family hoping to get their injured puppy help. It was insane.

They tried to retreat, but the Hendersons kept firing at them. To save their lives, Nadine and Robin fired back. Old instincts, picked up on multiple combat tours in Iraq and Afghanistan kicked in, and the ladies killed everybody. Nobody had needed to die. The Hendersons could have prevented the entire massacre with a NO TRESPASSING sign. The loss of life was pointless and stupid.

Unfortunately, the cattle ranchers shot the SUV so full of holes the wind had whistled through it even when it stood still. Nadine and the ladies couldn't drive that without drawing attention, so they stole the first vehicle they could find: a pickup truck with a cattle trailer on the back.

As they left, Nadine drew in a breath and looked at Ursa.

"We can try the hospital again," she said. "Maybe we can find a doctor."

"In this thing?" asked Ursa, opening her eyes wide. "It's too conspicuous. We'll ditch the truck and figure out our next move." She paused and looked over her shoulder. "How are you feeling, Wendy?"

"Cold," she said.

"You think you can make it to Kansas City? It's about four and a half hours from here."

"I'll try."

Ursa looked at Nadine.

"Take us by the truck stop where we parked earlier," she said. "If the cops are still there, we'll drive past and get on the interstate. If they're not, we'll get a new car."

At least it was a plan, even if it wasn't a good one. Nadine drove. The heavy pickup shimmied on rough roads. Wendy gasped on big bumps, but twenty minutes after they left the farm, they pulled into the same parking lot in which they had burned two vehicles earlier. Both cars were gone, but there were scorch marks on the asphalt and oily puddles in low spots on the ground.

Nadine parked and pointed toward an old Ford Crown Victoria with a POLICE INTERCEPTOR badge on the trunk. It probably came from a sheriff's auction. There was a FOR SALE sign in its front window.

"That should have a big backseat," said Nadine. "Since it's a former police cruiser, it'll have a big engine and upgraded shocks."

"Then get it," said Ursa. "Robin and I will take care of Wendy."

Nadine opened her door. This day had gone on too long already. Everybody needed to rest, but first they needed a car.

The moment Nadine stepped foot outside, though, she knew sleep would be a long time coming. She reached for the pistol on her hip.

"Ursa, Robin, get out now. We've got a problem."

***

Cassie and Lily had been watching TV in the living room when someone tripped the alarms. Floodlights had popped on throughout the farm, and a buzzer had started blaring in every building. Lily's father—Paul Henderson—was in the veterinary barn with his girlfriend. No one was supposed to know Paul had a girlfriend, but it wasn't hard to put two and two together when an attractive young woman showed up at the veterinary barn every time Paul's wife left for the night.

Cassie had babysat Lily for years, so the lights didn't bother her. They had probably made Paul shit some bricks, though. Lily's mom—Jennifer Henderson—had probably come home early and set off the sensor on the front gate. Paul deserved it. He was a nice guy, but he had two daughters and a beautiful wife. If he couldn't keep his penis in his pants for them, he deserved to get caught philandering.

She had watched out the window, expecting to see Jennifer's minivan any moment. Her smile had disappeared, though, when Jesse and Wade appeared with hunting rifles. Then she noticed a black SUV with its lights off coming up the driveway from the west entrance. It just stopped and then began backing up.

Then the gunfire started.

Cassie didn't know who fired first, but both sides opened up. She hadn't known what the hell to do, so she had grabbed Lily and dove to the ground. When the gunfire subsided, she looked out the window to see Paul Henderson running from the veterinary barn with a pistol. Becky Parish—his twenty-four-year-old girlfriend—came out a few steps behind him wearing a long-sleeved men's T-shirt but no pants.

Then another gunshot rang out, and Paul fell forward. He didn't move again, but two women came running. One checked on Paul and then pointed toward the veterinary barn, where Becky stood. Becky had a gun, too. She fired at the two ladies, and the two ladies fired pistols back at her. Then Becky ran inside. One lady chased her, while the other started coming toward the house Lily and Cassie hid in.

Cassie picked up Lily and ran out the back door. She hadn't known how many bad guys there were, but she didn't think she could make it over the hill to the big house—and even if she did, she didn't know whether she'd be safe there. The next closest solid structure was the stock trailer.

So that's where they went.

She and Lily had hidden in the back and prayed that the bad guys wouldn't look for them there. Then they heard footsteps, and the truck's heavy diesel engine roared to life and took off. Cassie would have jumped out the back, but she didn't want Lily getting hurt by falling out the back of a stock trailer at thirty miles an hour.

The driver left the farm and drove for about twenty minutes. That whole time, Cassie never stopped praying. She didn't have any weapons, and the trailer was empty—save for the two of them. They had to escape, but as long as the truck kept moving, they were stuck.

Then, about twenty minutes later, the trailer stopped moving, and the truck's engine stopped. Every muscle in Cassie's body felt rigid, and a heavy knot had grown in the pit of her stomach. With each sound, her heart jumped.

"We have to run, honey," she whispered to Lily. "If we're quiet, they won't even see us."

Lily may not have understood, but she nodded. The two crept toward the rear of the trailer. Cassie opened the rear gate with trembling fingers and stepped onto broken asphalt. Despite the tension in her muscles, her legs felt weak, and her chest felt so tight it was like trying to breathe in water. One of the pickup's doors opened. Without thinking, Cassie gripped Lily hard enough that the little girl yelped.

"Run, honey," she whispered. Panic edged her voice. Lily buried her face in Cassie's chest.

"Ursa, Robin, get out now," said a woman's voice. "We've got a problem."

Cassie ignored the shout and shot her eyes around the parking lot. She didn't recognize the area, but it was a big lot. A dozen cars had parked facing the highway, but they'd all be locked, and even if they weren't, none would have keys. The truck's other door opened, and two women emerged from the pickup. Both of them had guns. Cassie felt the blood rush from her face and gut as if she had just crested the hill on a roller coaster.

"Don't move, honey," said one woman, pointing a pistol at her. Cassie hesitated and put Lily on the ground.

"Run, Lily," she whispered. "I'll distract them. You run to the highway. Flag somebody down."

She turned and tried to run toward the three women with guns, but Lily held on to her leg, stopping her.

"I'm scared," she whispered. Cassie put a hand on her back and looked toward their assailants. One of them walked toward her.

"Hands in the air!"

"I can't," said Cassie, straightening and keeping a hand on Lily. "I'm holding a little girl."

The women hesitated. They were all blonde, and they all looked young.

"Are you armed?" said the second woman. Cassie shook her head. The woman lowered her weapon. The others did, too. Then one woman called out.

"You work at the vet's office?"

Cassie hesitated.

"Yeah, but I'm just the technician. I babysit on the weekends when needed. We won't hurt you. Just let us go. Please."

That seemed to get their attention.

"Do you assist in surgeries?"

Cassie, again, hesitated.

"Yeah. Dr. Henderson's a talented surgeon. We do a lot of surgical work."

The ladies looked at one another. One of them mouthed something. The other two nodded. A woman stepped forward.

"I'm Ursa. You and the girl are coming with us. We've got a job for you," she said before looking to another lady. "Nadine, forget the Crown Vic. It's too small. Get the Honda minivan. We've got to get out of here."

Chapter 12

We didn't have the manpower for separate search and tactical teams, so Sheriff Kalil sent me every officer he could, and we got to work, starting with a search of the barn. It was a two-story building with four stalls for animals and two finished exam rooms on the first floor. The second story held offices and a bedroom.

Two uniformed officers had already gone through the building, but they had been looking for threats. Now, we were here for bodies. Roy led us straight to the second-story bedroom, where a dead woman lay huddled beneath the bed. She was in her mid-twenties, and she wore a maroon T-shirt but no pants, shoes, or socks. Blood pooled beneath her. By the smears on the ground, it looked as if she had been injured elsewhere and then had crawled under the bed. The poor woman was hunted down like an animal and then cornered. That anyone could do that to someone else was disquieting.

I took a picture of her face, forwarded it to Sheriff Kalil, and asked him to show it to the two farmhands with whom he had been speaking when I arrived. Hopefully they could ID her.

We finished clearing the floor but, thankfully, didn't find any more bodies. Our killers had murdered four people, at least three of whom were from the same family. This was awful.

Once we finished searching the building, Roy and I walked outside and found the sheriff talking to Sergeant Bob Reitz near the gravel road. I walked toward them.

"I'm glad to see you back, Joe," said Bob, before looking down to Roy. "I hear this guy's a hero. I read a story about him in USA Today that said he took out a drug dealer in North Carolina."

I petted the dog's back.

"He also helped us find a body inside and some blood behind the barn," I said. "It's Roy's world. We all just live in it."

The men smiled but said nothing. I asked the sheriff about the girl upstairs, and he drew in a breath.

"The farmhands identified her as Becky Parish. She's twenty-three or twenty-four, and she does not live on the farm."

"But she was upstairs while the doctor's wife was away," I said. "That's awkward."

"Yep," said the sheriff. "We're still trying to get in touch with the rest of the Henderson family. In the meantime, get your vest. We need to see where that blood trail leads."

I didn't have a bulletproof vest in my Volvo, but that didn't matter. I had seen the shell casings on the ground. Our perps had rifles, and their rounds would punch through my vest as easily as they would my shirt. I checked the magazine in my pistol and looked at the sheriff.

"You going with us?"

He shook his head and then spoke into his radio.

"No. You've got Bob Reitz, Shane Fox, and Alisa Maycock. The Highway Patrol's helicopter is refueling, but we've got six more troopers on their way."

I looked at Bob.

"You want to wait for them?"

He frowned and looked toward the barn.

"I think we'll be okay with four officers plus your dog," he said. "You're rated to shoot the M4, aren't you?"

The M4 was the primary infantry weapon used by soldiers in the US Army. It was accurate, light, and fun to shoot at the range, but it had been a while since I last picked one up. I hesitated.

"Yeah, but I can't carry a rifle and hold Roy's leash," I said. "I'll be fine with a pistol."

"Bob, you watch her back," said the sheriff, looking to Bob. The sergeant nodded, so Kalil looked at me. "And if somebody starts shooting, I want you out of the way. You'll be badly outgunned with just a pistol."

"Will do," I said. "I don't plan to get shot."

I got my flashlight from my Volvo and checked to make sure the batteries worked. I had been in gunfights before—more often than I cared to think about if I were honest—but most of them had happened so quickly I didn't have time to consider what was happening. Here, it felt different. If I stopped to scrutinize the situation, my legs would probably start feeling weak, and my fingers would tremble. I couldn't slow down. If I did, I'd never start up again.

So I walked around the building with Roy while the rest of our team got ready. Then, once the four of us were together, I patted Roy on the back. My hands shook just a little.

"Roy, find it," I said.

He lifted his head, and I could see his nostrils flaring. Then, the wind shifted, and he took off across a grassy field. We jogged to keep up with him. It was dark, but we had enough flashlights to illuminate the ground ahead of us. Occasionally, we came across groups of cattle, but otherwise, nothing moved.

Eventually, Roy led us to a tree line and then to a field and wooden fence beyond it. The dog shimmied beneath the fence, while my team and I climbed over. I didn't know whether we had just crossed onto somebody else's property or whether we were still on Henderson Angus's ranch, but there was a barn in the distance. Its sliding front doors were open, and a light illuminated the interior. Roy was leading us straight to it. I called him to my side to make him stop.

"You guys ready?" I asked, looking to my colleagues. They nodded, so I took a breath and patted Roy's side again. "Find it, Roy. Find it."

He took off once more and continued heading straight to the barn. As we approached the building, Sergeant Reitz took point, while Roy and I shifted toward the back. A gravel road led to a house in the distance. A silver pickup truck with rusted wheel wells and a cracked front window sat outside. The closer we got to the barn, the faster my heart beat. About thirty feet away, Sergeant Reitz looked at me.

"I'll go in first with Shane behind me and Alisa behind Shane. Joe, I want you and Roy to stay near the truck in case our bad guys run. You can use the truck for cover and call in backup. Sound like that'll work?"

We all nodded. As much as I appreciated Roy following the blood trail, I much would have preferred a shotgun at that moment. My heart thumped against my rib cage, and my skin felt almost itchy. As we walked toward the truck, I forced my breath to slow. Roy and I knelt in front of the truck, putting the heavy engine block between us and the barn. The rest of my team continued.

When Bob reached the barn's door, he knelt and then peered around the corner before looking back and holding up two fingers. Two bad guys. Our team should be able to handle two bad guys.

I wondered whether the Hendersons had thought the same thing.

The muscles of my shoulders twitched as I raised my pistol toward the barn. I couldn't give my team much cover, but if they came under fire, they'd run toward me. I was all they had.

Bob counted down with his fingers from five to one. I held my breath as he counted off the last finger, and the three team members vaulted forward.

"Police!" shouted Bob. "Hands in the air now!"

There was a brief scuffle, and then Alisa repeated the command.

"We didn't do anything! Just don't shoot us!"

I didn't recognize that voice, but it sounded like a kid.

"Hands in the air!" shouted Bob again. My entire chest moved with every beat of my heart as I waited. "We're clear!"

My shoulders relaxed, and I holstered my weapon and stood. Roy and I walked toward the barn. Dim overhead lights hanging from chains attached to the ceiling rafters illuminated the interior. There was a firepit full of embers near the door. A young couple lay facedown on a sleeping bag big enough for two in front of the fire. Their arms were extended above their torsos. I didn't see any weapons. The barn had enormous round bales of hay stacked against every wall and square bales in the loft on the second floor. The fire cast flickering shadows on the bales of golden yellow hay. The air smelled fresh with just a hint of smoke.

"Slowly lower your hands to your backsides," said Reitz. "My officers will cuff you."

The young couple did as Bob commanded, and Shane and Alisa secured the prisoners. My breath slowed further. The boy and girl were young, fifteen to eighteen if I had to guess. They probably had snuck off to the barn for a romantic evening away from their parents. I doubted that evening included mass murder, but Roy wouldn't have led us to the barn unless he smelled blood.

Shane patted the boy down, while Alisa focused on the girl. Bob, meanwhile, walked outside to call Sheriff Kalil, but his radio only spit static. I leaned down to whisper to Roy.

"Find it, buddy," I said. "Find the blood."

Immediately, Roy lifted his head and sniffed. Then he ran toward a hay bale. About halfway there, he stopped and turned toward the young couple and held his nose low to the ground as he sniffed the air. Then he darted forward and promptly lay down beside the boy's shoes. I flashed my light at them. I couldn't see anything on the soles, but the kid's eyes opened wide.

"I didn't shoot anybody," he said.

"Roll over and sit up," I said. I looked at the girl. "You, too, miss."

They did as I asked. Sergeant Reitz crossed his arms. I knelt in front of the couple and looked from the boy to the girl.

"As you guys can tell, you're in some trouble," I said. "We've found four bodies so far at Henderson Angus. Why did my dog find a blood trail that led from the bedroom in Dr. Paul Henderson's office to this barn, and how did you get blood on your shoes?"

"We were over there," said the boy.

"Why?" I asked.

The girl blinked glassy eyes. A tear fell down her cheek.

"We heard the gunfire," she said. "Then, when it went quiet, we ran over. I wanted to make sure my sister was okay."

I cocked my head to the side and narrowed my eyes.

"Did you call the police?"

They shook their heads. I ground my teeth but tried not to react otherwise.

"Who's your sister?"

"Cassie Prescott," said the girl. "I'm Julie Prescott."

I looked at Bob. He shrugged, so I narrowed my brow and focused on Julie again.

"And your sister, Cassie, was at the farm tonight?" I asked.

"Yeah. She works for Dr. Henderson as a veterinary technician during the week, but she watches Lily—Dr. Henderson's daughter–on the weekends when Dr. Henderson and his wife go out."

"So Lily and Cassie should have been there tonight?" I asked.

"Yeah," said Julie. "We looked for them, but we couldn't find anybody. I figured that was good, right? If we couldn't find them in the house or the barn, they must be okay, right?"

"You two, stay where you are," I said, already heading out of the barn and trying to keep my thoughts from racing ahead of the facts. I called the sheriff's cell phone. My breath came in short, fast bursts, and my head felt light. My skin tingled as sweat began to form on my lower back and forehead. "Hey, boss, it's Joe Court. We followed the blood trail and found two teenagers in a barn. You guys find a little girl named Lily or a young woman named Cassie yet?"

Before answering, the sheriff paused. I started pacing the length of the truck and praying he wasn't about to tell me they had found more bodies.

"No," he said. "Were they at the farm?"

I closed my eyes and swore under my breath.

"Supposedly, yeah," I said, forcing my voice to stay slow and even. "Lily is Paul Henderson's daughter. She's a child. Cassie is her babysitter. They're supposed to be at the farm. Get the Highway Patrol's helicopter back as soon as you can. We need its infrared camera. Cassie and Lily are probably still hiding out somewhere on the farm, but if they're not, we need to know now."

"I'll make the call," said Kalil. He paused. "I'll call the day shift back in. We'll get some boots on the ground."

"Good idea," I said. "I'll call you soon."

I hung up before the sheriff could respond and walked back into the barn and looked at Julie and her boyfriend.

"You two, stand up," I said. "I need you to tell me everything you know about Henderson Angus and the Henderson family."

Chapter 13

After securing the kids, we searched the barn. If we had found any firearms, the kids would have gone straight to holding tanks in our station, but since we didn't, we walked them back to Henderson Angus, where we could interview them in relative comfort in the back of the sheriff's SUV.

According to Julie and Brett—Julie's boyfriend—the gunfire had begun right before seven in the evening. The sun had been up, so the gunfire hadn't worried either kid. A dozen people lived at the farm, and they all had firearms. Sometimes they hunted, and sometimes they set up targets across their fields and used the hills as backstops. That was common in rural areas.

But the gunfire increased in intensity, and it stopped sounding like target practice. Julie tried to call her sister, but Cassie didn't answer. That worried her—but not enough to call the police, apparently. They went to the farm, found the bodies, and then ran home, too shellshocked to do anything.

Unfortunately, neither Julie nor Brett had any idea who would have shot up the farm. Both teenagers knew the Henderson family, but they didn't know of anyone who wished the Henderson family ill. Brett described them as good people who raised healthy animals. Brett's father shared a property line with the Hendersons and liked working with Wade Henderson. Wade, according to Brett, didn't put up with bullshit and didn't cheat his business partners—no matter how big or small they were.

When Sheriff Kalil asked about Henderson Angus's security and surveillance systems, Brett said they had expensive bulls, including one they had purchased at auction for almost half a million dollars. The sale made several industry newsletters, so people—including thieves—would have known they had valuable property around the farm. I had never worked a case involving stolen cattle, but money was money. If our perps could get even a quarter of the bull's market value, they'd have a very large payday.

So now I had a theory. Some bad guys came to the farm, expecting to steal a bull. Unknown to our perps, the farm had an extensive security system, which alerted the Henderson family to the intruders. They came out with firearms to defend their property. A firefight broke out, and four people died. Somewhere along the way Cassie Prescott and Lily Henderson disappeared. If I had to guess, they were still hiding on the farm somewhere.

I wished the Henderson family had just called the police. They may have lost some animals, but their insurance company would have reimbursed them, and they would have survived. It was a pointless tragedy. At least the rest of the family wasn't at the farm when the shooting began. If they had, this tragedy may have been a bigger disaster.

I left Brett and Julie with Sheriff Kalil near the farm's main house and started walking toward the veterinary barn, outside of which Kevius was still collecting evidence. Before I could get there, my cell rang. I answered without looking at the screen.

"Hey," I said. "It's Joe Court."

"Joe, it's good to hear your voice. I hear you're back in St. Augustine."

The speaker was an FBI agent with whom I had consulted on several cases. I smiled despite the situation.

"Bryan Costa. It's good to hear from you, too," I said, stopping on the side of the gravel driveway. "This is a bad time, though. Can I call you tomorrow?"

The land sloped downward in front of me, giving a sweeping look over a massive field as well as the veterinary barn and Dr. Henderson's home. Somewhere in the distance, a dog barked. Roy looked in the direction but didn't run off. I wrapped his leash around my hand anyway.

"Unfortunately, no," said Costa. "Your dispatcher told me you were back in town. I'm in the parking lot outside Club Serenity right now."

"And I'm at the scene of a quadruple homicide at a cattle ranch," I said. "I can't talk."

Costa paused.

"Is that cattle ranch called Henderson Angus, by chance?"

My skin tingled, and the hairs on the back of my neck stood on end.

"How'd you know that?"

"Because I'm looking at a pickup and cattle trailer," he said. "The trailer has Henderson Angus painted on the side, and the pickup's got two bullet holes in the passenger door."

My mouth popped open. I cleared my throat before speaking.

"Anyone inside?"

"No," he said. "I'm working an armored-car robbery in St. Louis, and the bad guys dumped and burned a pair of vehicles near here earlier today. My forensics people towed those cars away as soon as your fire department got done hosing them off. What are the chances my bad guys would dump a car in the same lot as your bad guys?"

I shook my head.

"I don't know," I said. "What does Vic Conroy say? He runs Club Serenity, and he's got surveillance cameras all over his property."

Costa, again, paused.

"You've been out of town a long time, Joe."

"I know that," I said, turning around and walking toward the sheriff again. "Get that video. I'm on my way."

I hung up before Costa could reply. Then Roy and I jogged toward the sheriff's SUV. He opened the front door just as I arrived.

"What's going on?"

"I just got a call from Bryan Costa with the FBI. They found a pickup with bullet holes in the side and a stock trailer in the parking lot outside Club Serenity. The trailer had Henderson Angus painted on the side."

"That explains how our bad guys got away," he said. "Is Costa there now?"

"Yeah," I said. "He's working some kind of armored-car robbery in St. Louis, but he said his bad guys had dumped two cars there earlier."

"I heard about the cars, but the feds have jurisdiction on armored-car robberies," said the sheriff. "I didn't call in any of our people."

"I get that," I said, "but these murders are ours, and it looks like our shooters dumped their getaway vehicle outside Club Serenity. If the club has surveillance video, we can close our case tonight."

The sheriff crossed his arms and drew in a breath.

"The club's closed, Joe. There won't be any video."

I stopped moving and cocked my head to the side.

"Why would Vic Conroy close the club? It's a gold mine, especially when combined with his other businesses."

"Vic Conroy's dead."

At first, I didn't react. Then I brought a hand to my face and felt muscles all over my body stiffen. Vic Conroy had been a vile human being. He owned multiple businesses around town and used them all to exploit young women.

First, he owned a truck stop with an enormous lot where trucks could park overnight. He profited from gasoline and diesel sales, but the real money came from the parking lot in which young women—and more than a few boys—worked as prostitutes.

Once the girls turned eighteen, they moved to Club Serenity, his strip club, where they danced on stage. The strip club, like his truck stop, made money on its own, but it also served as an advertisement for his flesh-peddling hotel across the street. Dancers would pick up men at the strip club, sleep with them at the Wayfair Motel, and send Vic half their profits for providing security and a venue in which to ply their trade.

Once the girls became too old to dance or sell themselves, Vic hired them to work as bartenders, clerks, cooks, and whatever else he needed. We had investigated him for years, but every time we drew close to him, something went wrong...a witness would die, evidence would disappear, or a lawyer would intervene. We knew Conroy had somebody inside our department—and probably in the Highway Patrol and the St. Louis County Police Department—but we never discovered them.

I stared at the sheriff another moment, expecting him to elaborate. He didn't.

"How'd he die?" I asked.

"Does Vic Conroy's death affect your investigation into these murders?"

I straightened and drew in a breath.

"No, sir," I said.

"Then go to the club. I'll hold down things here."

I started toward my Volvo, but then stopped.

"If you find Cassie and Lily, send me a text."

"Will do," he said. "Good luck, Detective."

"You, too," I said.

As I got Roy settled on my backseat, I couldn't help but feel that my entire world had changed. Vic Conroy had been a cancer on this county and its people. He was one reason I returned. I wasn't a vicious person, and I didn't want anyone to die, but a big part of me was glad he was gone. He wouldn't hurt anyone anymore. Another part of me, though, wondered what the hell had happened. Even if he died, someone should have taken over his business.

I had a case to work, though, so I'd worry about that later. I put my seat belt on and headed out.

Chapter 14

Nadine knew they couldn't keep the minivan forever, but out of all the vehicles they had stolen, she liked this one the most. It was roomy, and it absorbed the bumps on the road without protest. The owner should have replaced the tires months ago, but he likely didn't want to spend the money before selling the car. As long as it didn't rain, they'd be fine. This time, Ursa drove, while Nadine sat in the front seat. Cassie Prescott and Lily Henderson sat in the middle, while Robin and Wendy sat in the back.

As much as she hated to admit it, Nadine had stopped worrying about Wendy. Her skin was so pale the minivan's dim interior lights made her look almost green, and she shivered despite the sweaters and jackets Robin had placed on her. If the blood loss didn't kill her, she'd die of infection soon. Nothing would change that.

Nadine looked over her shoulder.

"How's she doing?"

"She's breathing," said Robin.

Before, their plan had been to get out of town and track down a trauma nurse Ursa knew in Kansas City. Now that they had Cassie—who sort of had medical training—they'd go back to the home they had rented near Grant's Farm in the St. Louis suburbs.

They drove an hour north in relative silence and hit the outskirts of the city. Then, as they neared their rental home, Ursa dropped Nadine off at a Wal-Mart, where she picked up plastic painter's tarps, tape, black trash bags, and a lot of first-aid supplies. She then took an Uber to the entrance of the neighborhood where they had rented the home and walked the remaining two blocks with her purchases. Ursa opened the front door and took the bag from her.

"We're setting up in the dining room," she said. "Robin's boiling water now. Did you find a scalpel?"

Nadine shook her head.

"They didn't have scalpels or other medical instruments, but I got gauze, bandages, and alcohol. I also got some kitchen tongs, scissors, and razor blades. That was the best I could do."

"It'll be enough," said Ursa. "Take the kitchen stuff to Robin and then help me put up plastic. We don't want to get Wendy's blood everywhere."

Nadine swallowed and did as Ursa had asked. While Robin boiled their "surgical instruments," Nadine and Ursa covered the walls, floor, and furniture with multiple layers of plastic. They'd operate on Wendy while she lay on the dining room table and use reading lamps with flexible arms as surgical lights. The setup wasn't perfect, but it worked.

After securing the plastic, they wiped everything down with a mix of bleach and water. Their work wouldn't kill every germ, but it should eliminate a lot.

About an hour after Nadine arrived at the house, Ursa and Robin carried Wendy to the dining room. The patient wore a clean bathrobe that could open at her abdomen but otherwise afforded her some privacy. Her face was pale, and her breath was shallow. She didn't move. In a hospital, they would have given her propofol or something similar to knock her out, but since they didn't have those, they had doped her up with enough opioids to put her to sleep. Hopefully it wouldn't kill her.

After getting her on the table, nobody moved for a few minutes. Robin's eyes were closed, and her lips moved as she prayed. It looked like Ursa was doing likewise. After a few minutes, Robin cleared her throat.

"I'll get Cassie."

Nadine gave her friend a soft smile.

"No," she said. "Stay with your sister. Hold her hand. She needs you here. I'll get Cassie."

"And I'll get the instruments from the kitchen," said Ursa.

Robin nodded. Cassie and Lily were in the home's finished basement. They didn't have any toys, but the house had a big-screen TV with a bunch of movies. As Nadine entered, she saw that Lily and Cassie had started watching Moana, a Disney movie about a young Polynesian woman, but it looked like Lily had fallen asleep on her babysitter's lap. Cassie stroked the little girl's head.

"They're ready for you upstairs, Cassie."

Cassie cleared her throat but didn't move from the couch.

"This is a terrible idea," she said, shaking her head. "I'm not a doctor. I'm not even a vet."

"You're the best option we've got," said Nadine. "As long as you try your best, nobody will hold what happens against you. You'll be fine."

A tremble passed through her. Her eyes stayed glued to the TV.

"You're going to kill us, aren't you?" she asked, her voice a whisper. Lily stirred but then settled.

"We won't kill anyone unless you refuse to help us," she said. "Then, it's out of my hands. I promise that if you do your best, no harm will come to either you or Lily."

Cassie's eyes were bloodshot, and her cheeks looked hollow.

"I've never done anything like this."

"But you've assisted surgeries," said Nadine.

"Well, yeah, but I've not performed them," she said. "I helped with anesthesia, and I've even sewn a cow's wound up, but I've never pulled a bullet from a woman's abdomen. It's best to leave the round inside, anyway. That's what Dr. Henderson usually does. Unless the round's in danger of piercing her colon or something similar, it's better to leave it in until you can get her to a hospital."

"Fine," said Nadine. "Examine her and tell us what we should do."

She hesitated.

"I already know what you should do. Take her to the hospital. No matter how much trouble she's in or what you've done, that's your safest option."

Nadine forced a smile to her lips.

"If we take her to the hospital, they will call the police. She may survive the night, but then she'll die in prison. That's a fact. If you help her, though, there's a chance she'll live."

"No, there's not," said Cassie. "If I go digging around in her wound, her chance of surviving is as close to zero as you can get."

"Then tell her sister that."

Cassie shifted her weight and pushed Lily onto a pillow. The little girl, once more, stirred but didn't move. Cassie didn't stand. Nadine sighed.

"You care about Lily, don't you?" Nadine asked.

Cassie blinked a tear from her eye.

"Yes."

"If you don't go upstairs and help my friend, I'll kill Lily in front of you," whispered Nadine. "I don't want to do that, but I will place my gun against her temple, and I will squeeze the trigger. She'll die in your arms, but she won't feel anything. Then I'll gag you before shooting you in the abdomen. You'll bleed and then probably turn septic. You'll be in so much pain you'll pray God takes you quickly. Is that how you want to go? All you have to do is try to help my friend."

Cassie clenched her jaw and narrowed her eyes. Her skin turned pink.

"You're evil," she whispered.

"Evil doesn't exist, honey. We're all just people with our backs against the wall," said Nadine. "Now go upstairs. I'll stay with Lily."

Cassie stood. Lily opened her eyes and looked around, confused, but then Cassie knelt in front of her.

"Hey, honey," she whispered, smiling. "I've got to go upstairs for a minute. I'll be back as soon as I can."

Lily blinked and then swallowed.

"I'm hungry. I want chocolate milk."

"Do you have any chocolate milk?" asked Cassie, flicking her eyes to Nadine.

Nadine ignored her and focused on Lily

"How about a cookie?" she asked. "Do you like Oreos?"

"I'm not allowed to eat snacks after I brush my teeth," she said, her voice and face serious. "That's a rule."

Nadine winked.

"Then it'll be a secret," she said. "We'll eat Oreos and drink orange juice, and I'll braid your hair."

"Friends don't make secrets, and secrets don't make friends."

Nadine smiled.

"You're adorable, honey," she said. "We'll tell your mom when we see her next. It won't be a secret then. Okay?"

She considered and then drew in a breath.

"Okay."

Nadine looked at Cassie.

"Go upstairs," she said. "I've got this."

Cassie stood and climbed the stairs to the second floor, where Robin and Ursa were waiting for her. Nadine scooted toward Lily. The little girl smiled and then focused on the TV. They watched Moana for a little while, but then Lily fell asleep again. Nadine held her and wondered how different her life would have been if her husband had survived his tours in Iraq without injury. Maybe they would have had a little girl Lily's age.

About half an hour after Cassie left, she returned. Ursa followed a few steps back. Cassie now wore a blood-stained kitchen apron, but her hands and forearms were clean. Her skin was pale. She looked tired. Ursa did, too.

"Is Wendy alive?" asked Nadine.

Ursa looked at Cassie.

"Yeah," she said. "But I left the bullet inside. If I tried to get it out, I'd do more damage than the bullet ever did."

"What did you do, then?" asked Nadine.

"I cleaned and packed the wound," she said, her voice soft. "I don't think the round pierced her intestines. If she were a cow, I think she'd be okay. If the wound turns white or black, though, or if it starts to smell bad, it means she's got a serious infection. She needs to see a doctor, anyway. A CT scan could tell you more about the wound than I ever could."

"That's not going to happen," said Ursa.

"I figured," said Cassie.

The room fell into a heavy silence. Nadine drew in a breath.

"Can we move her?"

"You shouldn't," said Cassie. "Her wound needs time to heal. The more you move her, the more likely she'll start bleeding again."

Ursa looked at the ground and sighed.

"I don't think we'll have a choice. There's an ironing board in the laundry room. We can use that as a makeshift back brace. At the very least, it'll let us put her in the car."

"Yeah. I guess you could do that," said Cassie. She paused. "If you want her to live more than a few days, she needs antibiotics. I don't have those."

Ursa crossed her arms.

"What antibiotics?"

"The kind you get in the hospital," said Cassie.

Nadine had thought she'd say that.

"Would a vet's office have them?"

Cassie shrugged.

"Some might," she said. "But you'd have to get the dosages correct. And there's no guarantee antibiotics meant for a horse would help a human. They might kill her."

"But if she doesn't have them, she'll die," said Ursa. "Looks like you'll be with us a little longer, Cassie. We'll need you to tell us what to get."

"I'll write some suggestions down," she said.

Ursa shook her head.

"No," she said. "You're going with us to the office. We can't risk leaving empty-handed if they don't have something on your list."

Her lips moved, but no sound came out. Then she closed her eyes.

"What about Lily?"

"She'll be safe here with Wendy and Robin," said Ursa. "Now go to the bathroom and clean yourself up. We've all got work to do."

Chapter 15

Roy and I drove to Club Serenity and the truck stop beside it, but we didn't pull into the parking lot. Instead, we parked alongside the road out front behind a big black SUV so we wouldn't contaminate a crime scene. None of the pumps at the truck stop had hoses, and a big sheet of plywood covered the front door of the strip club. In the summer months, weeds would have likely begun sprouting from cracks in the asphalt parking lot, but for now, it was still barren. I had driven past that club and the truck stop beside it two or three times in the past week, but I had paid them so little attention I hadn't realized they were closed.

I got Roy from my backseat and then snapped pictures of the parking lot and shuttered businesses. Roughly a dozen cars had parked beneath the metal awning that covered the pumps at the once thriving truck stop. More cars had parked alongside the road, and almost all of them had FOR SALE signs in their front windows. The gravel parking lot for trucks had about a dozen big rigs inside. Some were on, but most were quiet.

As I put Roy's leash on, Special Agent Bryan Costa walked toward me with a tight smile on his lips. Agent Costa had thin black hair buzzed close to his scalp and a narrow chin that seemed almost to come down to a point. He reminded me of Dracula from old movies. I had worked with him on a couple of cases, and I had come away impressed every time. He was intelligent, meticulous, and honest—a rare combination in any field. I liked working with him.

"Hey, Joe," he said. Roy sat beside me and waited patiently. "Glad to see you. I was dreading working with George Delgado. He's abrasive."

"Can't blame you. George is a dick," I said, looking toward the pickup. "So what do we have?"

Costa raised his eyebrows and nodded toward a big red pickup and gray stock trailer parked at the edge of the lot. Officer Lee Hernandez stood outside.

"A big old truck," he said. "I came by earlier to take some pictures of the parking lot for my own investigation, and I found this with bullet holes in the side. I thought you might be interested."

"We are," I said, crossing my arms, "but tell me about your case first. You were here for an armored-car robbery?"

"Yeah. Nasty work, too," he said. "As best we can tell, they're a team of four. First, they steal cars. In one, they drill a hole in the trunk through which they can aim a rifle. The other cars are their getaway vehicles.

"When the armored vehicle arrives, they wait until the guard steps out. Then their sniper kills the guard. If the driver steps out, they kill him, too. The guards don't even have a chance to draw their weapons. They're dropped without warning. It's brutal. So far, they've hit eleven armored cars and killed fourteen guards in four different states."

I raised my eyebrows.

"Jeez. And you think they're in St. Augustine?"

He shrugged.

"They were here," he said. "By now, I suspect they're long gone. They hit an armored car at the Galleria in St. Louis this morning and killed three armed guards but not before one of those guards shot a perp in the abdomen."

"I assume you're watching the hospitals," I said.

"We are," said Costa. "We've also reached out to urgent care centers and clinics. After hitting the armored car in St. Louis, they drove here and torched their stolen vehicles. Somebody called your fire department, and they came and put the fire out. The fire department called your sheriff to let him know of a suspected arson. The arson investigator saw a notice one of my agents wrote and called us to let us know the vehicles we were looking for were on fire in his jurisdiction."

"And your forensics people took the cars," I said. It wasn't a question, but Costa nodded. I looked around and then lowered my voice. "Why are you really here? We're an hour from your office, it's late, and you've already taken the evidence you needed for your case."

The corners of Agent Costa's lips curled upward.

"Your mind never stops working, does it, Joe?"

I smiled.

"If you'd rather deflect my question than answer it, we've got a problem."

"We don't have a problem," he said, shaking his head. He sighed. "This area was a hot spot for prostitution in times past. Your sheriff tells me that's changed, but I wanted to see for myself."

"I wouldn't have believed it, either, unless I had seen it. Vic Conroy's dead, though. I don't know what happened, but his truck stop, strip club, and hotel are closed."

Costa looked down and then sighed.

"He was murdered by a customer at his strip club who didn't appreciate the high price of a two-minute lap dance."

I almost laughed.

"I hadn't heard that."

"Yep. The biggest pimp in the state was taken out because he accidentally overcharged a hot-headed drunk with a pistol."

"That's so ridiculous it's almost funny."

Costa tilted his head to the side and shrugged.

"Some people don't consider human life worth much. It's sad."

"Isn't that the truth?" I asked, looking over the parking lot again before focusing on Agent Costa. "We've got a few truckers in the lot. They might not have seen anything, but I'm going to talk to them. You want to stick around and interview them with me?"

"I'm here," he said. "I might as well."

He didn't seem overly enthusiastic, but that was probably because he knew he'd find little for his case. I checked in with Lee Hernandez to tell him our plan, and then Costa and I started knocking on doors and talking to long-haul truckers who had bedded down in the parking lot for the night.

Most drivers cooperated once they saw our badges. I suspected more than a few had come hoping to pick up one of Vic Conroy's underage prostitutes, but we couldn't arrest people for their intentions alone.

After an hour of getting nowhere, we knocked on the door of a blue Peterbilt semitrailer with a big sleeping compartment in back. The guy who opened the door had greasy, unkempt hair, and he wore a sleeveless T-shirt. Tattoos covered his exposed forearms. On the street, he would have looked scary. With sleep in his eyes and a dazed expression on his face, he wouldn't have intimidated a five-year-old.

"Hey, honey," he said. "It's a little late for visitors, but come on in."

"This isn't a social call," I said, showing him my badge. He straightened. "I'm Detective Joe Court with the St. Augustine County Sheriff's Department. You know where you are right now?"

He raised his eyebrows and lowered his chin.

"I'm guessing St. Augustine County."

Both Costa and I smiled.

"Yeah," I said. "You're also in a parking lot notorious for being a place to pick up underage prostitutes. Have you been here before?"

He shook his head quickly.

"Nah," he said. "I just drove by and thought it seemed like a good place to stop for the night."

"Good," I said. "How long have you been here?"

"A few hours."

I pointed across the lot toward the stock trailer.

"Was that here when you arrived?"

He squinted and then shrugged.

"I couldn't say. When I got here, I just pulled right into my spot, ate a sandwich, and went to sleep."

"Where'd you get the sandwich?" asked Costa.

The trucker looked at him as if for the first time.

"You NTSB? You've got to tell me if you are."

Costa reached for his wallet and flashed his badge. The trucker straightened.

"My daughter made it before I left home this morning. I just drive. Whatever's going on, I'm not a part of it. If you want, I'll leave now."

"No, you're not leaving," I said. "There's a rest area about fifteen miles north of here. It's lit, it's got clean bathrooms, it's got vending machines, and it's convenient to I-55. If you needed diesel, you could have gone to the Love's station in Bloomsdale. It's clean, and it's got showers. You could have gotten a hot meal there, too. Instead, you parked in this lot. It doesn't have any facilities or amenities. Hell, it doesn't even have overhead lights."

He drew in a breath and puffed out his chest.

"I'm light sensitive."

I laughed and shook my head.

"No. You came here to pick up a girl," I said. "Unfortunately for you, their pimp died a while back and they disappeared."

"That's not true," he said, shaking his head.

"Yeah, it is," said Costa. "I'd advise you to look really hard at that stock trailer. Was it here when you arrived or not?"

The trucker brought a hand to the back of his neck and drew in quick, shallow breaths.

"I guess not," he said.

"Don't guess," I said. "Was it here or not?"

"No," he said. "It wasn't here."

"When did it arrive?" Asked Costa.

The trucker looked at him and closed his eyes as he shrugged.

"I don't know. I didn't look at the clock."

"What can you tell us about it?" I asked. "If it would help, I can put you in a warm holding cell for the evening. You'd get some food and a quiet place to rest while we process you for attempting to solicit an underage prostitute."

I couldn't actually do that, but I suspected he wouldn't know. The trucker's eyes blinked rapidly, and his Adam's apple rose and fell as he swallowed.

"No," he said, shaking his head. "I can't go to jail. I'd lose my kid."

"Then talk to us," said Costa. "What'd you see?"

"The truck parked there. I don't remember if the sun was down or not," he said. "I wouldn't have paid any attention to it except that two people got out the back. One was a kid."

My breath caught in my throat for a second, and my back straightened.

"What'd the other one look like?"

"Skinny," he said. "She was probably college-age. Had brown hair. She was pretty, but not so pretty she'd be stuck up."

I didn't have pictures of Cassie or Lily on me, but that could have been them. My heart started beating faster, and muscles all over my body tightened. I held his gaze.

"So the truck parked, and the little girl and the young woman got out. What happened next?"

"Three women got out of the cab of the pickup," he said. "They were all blonde, and they were real pretty. Two of them had ponytails. I didn't get a good look at 'em, so I don't know how old they were. They were in good shape, though. They looked like they exercised."

"Okay," I said, leaning forward. "What'd they do?"

He licked his lips.

"The women who got out of the cab had guns. They raised them toward the girls. They talked for a minute, and then they broke into a minivan and drove off."

I closed my eyes and cocked my head to the side.

"Let me get this straight," I said. "You saw three women pull firearms on a child and another young woman, and then you saw these women steal a minivan, and you didn't call the police?"

"It was a Honda Odyssey," he said, holding up his hands. "I just drive a truck. I don't know the law."

I brought a hand to my face and rubbed my eyes before sighing.

"Get down from there. I'm taking you to my station so we can get your statement on the record."

He straightened.

"I didn't do anything wrong."

"You did a lot wrong," said Costa, putting a hand on my elbow and gently pulling me away from the truck. "Now get your wallet and keys and shut your rig down."

The trucker did as we asked. I smiled at Costa as he took his hand from my elbow.

"Getting a little touchy-feely in your old age, Bryan?"

He smiled sheepishly and mouthed an apology. I looked toward the truck.

"Looks like we got lucky," I said. "I don't know if he would have been as ready to talk if he weren't staring at an FBI agent's badge."

Agent Costa shifted and looked down at the concrete but said nothing.

"Something wrong?" I asked. Costa sighed and looked at me.

"I hate to do this to you, Joe, but your farm murders are now a federal case," he said. "If that trucker's description is accurate, your shooters are my armored-car robbers."

Chapter 16

I had thought it was too much of a coincidence that Costa's armored-car robbers and my murderers would dump their cars in the same lot, but I groaned anyway. Pieces of my puzzle began to fit together. Our perps had abandoned and burned their getaway vehicles here because they'd known they could pick up another car, and they'd gone to the farm hoping that Dr. Henderson would work on their friend who'd been shot in the abdomen. Unfortunately, they'd run into a buzz saw there.

"Have your perps abducted anyone before?" I asked.

Costa shook his head.

"Not that we know of."

"So this is new," I said, sighing. I waved Lee Hernandez over and asked him to drive the truck driver to our station for a formal interview. Hernandez agreed and led the trucker away before I looked at Costa again. "A little girl and a young woman are missing from a farm in the county. The woman was a veterinary technician named Cassie Prescott. She was babysitting the vet's daughter—Lily Henderson. We were hoping they had run away or hidden somewhere on the farm."

Costa crossed his arms and considered.

"If that was them in the back of the trailer, the good news is they were still alive as of a few hours ago," said Costa. "These ladies aren't afraid to pull their trigger when they want someone dead. Hopefully they'll just let Cassie and Lily go."

I shook my head.

"Hoping they'll let Cassie and Lily go isn't good enough. We've got to find them. So what do we know about our shooters so far?"

Costa shifted his weight.

"They're organized, methodical, and efficient," he said. "They use new weapons and new vehicles for every robbery. Each weapon, so far, has been purchased from private individuals. Their sniper tends to favor bolt-action rifles. She's used a different Remington 700 for seven robberies. She's also used a Springfield M1A, two Browning X-Bolt rifles, and four rifles we couldn't identify from the rounds alone.

"The weapons were purchased at gun shows in the South by straw buyers. There's no paperwork, and the weapons were all purchased at least two years ago. We've recovered several of the firearms, but we have yet to find a usable fingerprint."

"If they purchased the guns years ago," I said, narrowing my eyes, "they must have been planning this for a while."

"Looks like it," said Costa. "Or maybe they just like collecting weapons."

That was a possibility, too.

"Do they burn all their cars?"

"Some, but not all," he said, shaking his head. "They've abandoned at least two in high-crime areas with the keys still in the ignition. Both were taken for joyrides. One was eventually pushed into the south branch of the Chicago River. A second was rammed into a bridge pylon outside Indianapolis. We also suspect they stole a car from the long-term parking garage at O'Hare International Airport in Chicago and then returned it after their robbery. The owner realized there was a problem when he returned to find his car significantly cleaner than it had been when he left. The return ticket on his dash also had a different date on it than it should have had."

I narrowed my eyes.

"How do you know they were involved in the theft?"

"An airport police officer reported seeing four attractive blonde women in the garage the day the car disappeared. Unfortunately, the car was so clean we couldn't even lift any viable prints from it."

I crossed my arms.

"So you've got almost nothing," I said.

"These ladies are good, but they're not perfect," said Costa. "We got lucky twice and found hairs in the back of two vehicles that they had tried to burn. In one case, the fire department arrived shortly after the car was lit. They took care of it before the interior could burn too badly. In the other case, we found the hairs in the trunk, which hadn't caught fire. One set of hairs was light brown, and the other was auburn. Both, though, had been dyed blonde. The hairs didn't have roots, so we couldn't extract nuclear DNA, but mitochondrial DNA indicates that the women had the same mother. They're sisters."

"Has any of the money they've stolen shown up in circulation?"

Costa shook his head.

"Not yet."

"So they're smart and patient," I said. "That doesn't bode well for us."

Costa looked toward the pickup and stock trailer.

"Like I said, they're good, but they're not perfect," he said. "One of the ladies has been shot, which means we're going to find blood. We'll collect that, isolate the nuclear DNA, and start using genetic genealogy databases to track down her relatives."

I narrowed my eyes.

"You can do that? Legally?"

He tilted his head to the side.

"It's a gray area, but these ladies have killed a whole lot of people. Not only that, it seems they've abducted a little girl and her babysitter. Privacy matters, but at this point, it's not my primary concern. You okay with that?"

I hesitated.

"If this is a federal case, you're in charge. What do you want to do?"

"Everything we can," he said, already taking out his cell. "I'm going to call in a forensics team. We'll process the pickup and trailer. I need you to tell your boss what's going on. I haven't talked to him since this afternoon." Agent Costa paused. "The circumstances are lousy, but I'm glad to work with you again."

"Me, too," I said. "Let's hope it turns out better than last time."

***

The vet's office looked dark from their position in the strip mall's parking lot, but surely it had an alarm system. Cassie wondered whether it would go off if she broke a window. That'd bring the cops. Nadine would shoot at them, but that might give her the chance she needed. She could run and get help. The cops were trained to deal with armed assailants, so they'd know what to do.

Then again, Nadine would probably shoot her in the back at the slightest excuse. She had to get out of this somehow—if not for herself, then for Lily. Nadine and her friends didn't know it, but they had abducted a diabetic. Unless they let Lily go or gave her the correct dosage of insulin, she would get very sick very quickly.

Cassie shifted on her seat and then swallowed before looking to Nadine. She was fit and strong and well armed. Cassie exercised regularly, but she had little doubt that Nadine would kick the shit out of her in an actual fight. If she tried to steal Nadine's pistol, she'd end up in a body bag. Lily would die, too. She didn't know what to do, so she shivered and hugged herself tight and tried not to cry.

"Suck it up, buttercup," said Nadine, not turning her head from the vet's office. "We've got a job to do."

Cassie swallowed the lump in her throat.

"I don't want to be here."

"I wish you didn't have to be here, either, but we need you," said Nadine. "And if my friend dies because you refuse to help her, you'll regret every moment of the rest of your life. You help her, I'll help you."

Cassie shuddered and hugged herself tighter.

"Let's just get this over with. There's nobody here."

Nadine looked around again and drew in a deep breath. This was the third vet's office they had considered robbing. Nadine didn't explain why the first two offices they went to wouldn't work, but it didn't matter. Cassie had no choice in anything that happened.

Nadine opened her door and walked to the back of the van to let Cassie out. The night air was cold and so dry Cassie's nose hurt the moment she stepped onto the hard asphalt. Before she could move, Nadine gripped her arm tight and then reached into the van to turn off the dome light. Then she scowled.

"You want to get caught, honey?"

Cassie thought it was a rhetorical question, so she said nothing. Nadine tightened her grip on Cassie's triceps.

"That hurts," she said.

"It's supposed to," said Nadine, yanking her arm and then pushing her toward the vet's office. "We're in and out in five minutes. Any longer than that, and I'll shoot you and leave your corpse behind."

"If you kill me, who will help your friend?"

Nadine drew in a slow breath.

"I love Wendy like a sister, but she's dead. We both know that."

She was probably right, but agreeing with her didn't seem like the best choice given the situation.

"Why are we doing this?"

Nadine drew in a breath through her nose. Her eyes were flinty as she held Cassie's gaze.

"You're doing this because I'm telling you to," she said. "And I'm doing this because Wendy deserves everything we've got—even if it's futile. Now shut up and walk."

Nadine pulled Cassie toward the storefront. The vet's office had a wall of glass facing the street. Black miniblinds—now shut—prevented Cassie from seeing inside, but none of the lights were on. As they approached the glass front door, Nadine pulled a metal cylinder with a point on the end from her bag.

"What's that?" whispered Cassie.

Nadine ignored her and held the cylinder to the door. The moment it touched, the glass shattered. Cassie gasped and brought her fists to her chin. Nadine pocketed the device and used the butt of her firearm to clear the broken glass from the frame. No alarm sounded, but they had likely set one off.

"It's an automatic center punch," said Nadine. "If you don't have one in your car for emergencies, you should. It'll save your life if you ever have to break your window. Now get in."

Nadine roughly shoved Cassie forward. Glass crunched under her feet as she stepped through the now-broken door. It felt oddly surreal to step into that office, like she was floating. Nadine hurried through the waiting room down the hall. The office had three exam rooms, a break room for the staff, a small office, and then a wooden door with a brass deadbolt and the word PHARMACY on its nameplate.

Cassie stood back, her heart pounding, as Nadine kicked the locked wooden door near the handle. It didn't budge, so she kicked again. Once more, it didn't budge.

"Shit," she said.

"If we can't get in, we should leave," said Cassie. "The police are probably on their way already."

"I'm sure they are," said Nadine, turning. "If you're not here when I get back, I'll call Ursa and tell her to kill Lily."

Nadine started jogging down the hall. Cassie started to follow, but Nadine told her to stay put.

"What are you doing?" she asked, her voice quivering.

"You'll see."

Cassie stopped moving and took deep breaths. There was an emergency exit at the rear of the office. She thought about pushing the door open to set off the alarm, but she suspected Nadine would kill her. That'd leave Lily alone in a house full of monsters. Cassie couldn't risk it, so she stayed still and breathed deeply to keep herself calm. Within thirty seconds, Nadine came running back into the office. This time she held a shotgun.

"Cover your ears," she said, pointing the weapon at the door. The instant Cassie raised her hands to her head, Nadine fired. Even with her hands over her ears, the intensity of the sound made Cassie's ears ring. She stumbled back. Nadine seemed unaffected. The door, however, had a hole in it where the deadbolt used to be. It opened on well-oiled hinges. "Get the drugs. Let's go."

Cassie hesitated and crouched low. Her head swam, and everything sounded as if she were underwater.

"Move!" said Nadine, grabbing her arm and pulling her forward. Cassie hurried inside. The room had metal shelves full of white and brown pill containers and boxes full of anti-flea and heartworm medications. She browsed until she found the antibiotics. Then she frowned at what she saw.

"I don't know if I can do this," she said.

"Reconsider," said Nadine, lifting the shotgun so that it pointed at her abdomen.

"That's not what I mean," she said, shaking her head and trying to force her hands to stop trembling. "These aren't the kind of drugs I'm used to seeing. I work with cattle and horses. These are antibiotics for ferrets and lizards and birds. I've never used these."

"Then find some that are familiar," said Nadine, her voice harsh. "You've got about a minute."

Nadine didn't need to specify what would happen in a minute if Cassie failed. She swallowed the lump in her throat and turned toward the shelves. Her hands and arms trembled so much she pushed more pill containers on the ground than she pushed aside. Nadine scowled but said nothing. Cassie hadn't lied. She had heard of these drugs, but she had never administered any and didn't have their dosages memorized. If she gave Wendy the wrong drugs, she'd die. Then Ursa, Robin, and Nadine would probably kill her. Her vision began to swim in front, and her head throbbed as if she were getting a migraine. It was her blood pressure. It always rose when she was stressed. She closed her eyes and took a couple of breaths.

"Move, buttercup," said Nadine. Cassie's breath caught in her throat as she felt the shotgun against her spine. She gasped and straightened.

"I can't do this if I can't breathe," she said. The weapon left her back.

"Hurry."

Cassie pushed aside pill canisters until she found a broad-spectrum antibiotic used for dogs who contracted tick-borne diseases. She recognized it because Dr. Henderson kept a limited supply on hand for his family's Labrador retrievers.

"I need a pen and some paper," she said. "I need to do some calculations."

"We'll do them at home," said Nadine. "Grab the drugs, and we'll go."

"I need to make sure there's enough," said Cassie. "This is made for twenty- and thirty-pound dogs. If I give your friend too little, she'll die."

Nadine growled and then shot her eyes around the pharmacy. Then she tossed Cassie a prescription pad and a pen she had found on a nearby counter. Cassie's hands trembled as she began scratching numbers. Then she stopped and straightened.

"I think I heard something."

Nadine shook her head.

"You didn't."

"I did," said Cassie, forcing a measure of panic into her voice. It wasn't hard. Her heart pounded, her chest felt tight, and muscles all over her body quivered with adrenaline. "If it's the police, they'll shoot us."

Nadine growled again and then stepped into the hallway. Cassie started scribbling.

Cassie Prescott. Help. Brick house. Grantwood Lane.

She tore the note from the prescription pad and tossed it to the ground. Then she reached to the shelf, pulled off the pill container she needed, and knocked over the rest of the drugs. They clattered to the counter and then the ground. Nadine ran back into the room.

"What the hell did you do?"

"I just knocked some things off the shelf," she said, holding up her hands as if she were under arrest. Her voice wavered. "It was an accident."

"Did you at least get what you need?"

"I got the drugs for your friend," said Cassie, "and now I need to get some insulin and syringes for Lily."

Nadine cocked her head to the side.

"Excuse me?"

"You heard me," said Cassie. "You abducted a child with type 1 diabetes."

Nadine's eyes opened wide, and she lowered her chin.

"You didn't think to mention that earlier?"

Cassie clenched her teeth before speaking.

"I didn't get the chance," she said.

Nadine scowled.

"Then fine. Get what you need."

Cassie looked at drawers until she found one labeled SYRINGES. She grabbed a box of ultra-fine syringes for dogs. They'd have to do. Then she grabbed the only two ten-milliliter vials of insulin from a fridge. The insulin was meant for dogs and cats, but it should work for human children, too.

Afterwards, Nadine grabbed her arm and yanked her forward.

"The cops will be here soon. We've got to go."

The two ran out of the vet's office and sped away. All the while, Cassie hoped and prayed the police would see her message. It was her only hope to survive.

Chapter 17

Jason Zuckerberg put two towels on the floor behind his desk for Roy, giving him a comfortable, out-of-the-way spot to sleep while Agent Costa and I worked. It was a long night, but I interviewed the trucker—Lionel Holcomb—on the record and then re-interviewed Julie Prescott and her boyfriend, Brett Colten. None of them said anything that would help my case.

At a little after midnight, Agent Costa and I notified Becky Parish's parents that she had died in a shootout at Henderson Angus. Becky was having an affair with Dr. Henderson, but she was an innocent woman with her entire life in front of her and a family who loved her. I wished we could tell her mom and dad that she had died for some greater purpose, but we couldn't. All we could do was promise to do our best to find her killers. It was a minor comfort.

At about three in the morning, Costa sent me and Roy home for a few hours to sleep and recharge. I would have worked all night, but I appreciated the break. As soon as I reached my bedroom, I crashed on the bed and slept a deep, dreamless sleep.

Unfortunately, my sleep only lasted until eight when Roy woke me up. I let him outside to use the restroom and then made coffee. While that brewed, I called Agent Costa to ask what he needed me to do, but his phone went to voicemail right away. I left him a message, showered, changed, and then drank some coffee before putting Roy in the dog run out back and heading to work.

Sheriff Kalil had called in earlier to say he wouldn't be in until later, but Trisha had keys to my new office on the second floor. The room was fifteen feet by fifteen feet and had a big wooden desk, two bookshelves, a gray sofa, and a picture window with a view toward downtown St. Augustine. Two walls were blank off-white drywall, but someone had already installed hooks for pictures. I could put up posters or something. My wall to the hallway was floor-to-ceiling glass with closable wooden shades. The sheriff's office was bigger, but this was nicer than any office I had ever had.

I pulled my desk chair out and sat down. At first, I filled out paperwork that explained what I had done last night, who I had spoken with, and why I thought my actions were necessary given the situation. I doubted anyone would see those reports, but they helped me organize my investigation and thoughts. As I wrote about the pickup truck and stock trailer at Club Serenity, though I couldn't help but also think of Vic Conroy.

Once I finished my paperwork, I called up our department's internal records and reports database. Even a simple murder investigation would generate hundreds of reports from uniformed officers, detectives, and our civilian support staff. Many departments consolidated those reports and put them in bankers' boxes for easy storage, while other departments created murder books—binders that contained written reports, photographs, and an index to whatever evidence a detective or technician might have collected.

My department stored our reports digitally on the cloud. Every case received its own unique identifying number, which we then attached to every report filed for that case. If I knew a case number, I should be able to find a record of everything done on that case from the initial call to its final disposition in or out of court.

I searched for Vic Conroy's death investigation but then grunted when my computer told me someone had sealed the file. That happened on active cases involving victims or witnesses whose identity needed protecting, but Conroy's case was closed. I pushed back from my desk and took my phone from my purse to call the sheriff, but he still didn't answer. I left him a voicemail and then turned back to my computer when my cell phone rang. The caller ID said it was the local high school, so I answered right away.

"Mary Joe Court," I said, pinning the phone between my ear and shoulder and calling up our files on Makayla Simpson. "What can I do for you?"

"Detective, this is Allen Walters. We spoke yesterday at the high school."

I gritted my teeth but then forced myself to smile.

"It's good to hear from you, Mr. Walters. What can I do for you?"

"First, I'm calling to make sure I didn't offend you yesterday," he said. "You left suddenly."

I'd left because I hadn't wanted to snap at him and call him an asshole for writing off a young woman's life without knowing who she was or giving her a chance to succeed. Saying that wouldn't have helped my present investigation, though.

"I apologize if it seemed that way," I said. "Sometimes when I'm on a case, I get an idea and need to act on it right away or risk running into problems later on."

"What kind of idea did you have?" he asked, his voice brightening.

"This is still an active investigation, so I'm limited in what I can say," I said. "Do you have something to tell me?"

He grunted.

"A young man came to my office this morning to show me a video that's been circulating amongst the student body. Usually, when students come to my office with videos, it's something sexual. This was a video of Makayla's attack."

I sat straighter.

"Okay," I said. "Do you know who assaulted her?"

"They wore ski masks like they planned to rob a bank," he said. "There were two of them, but a third filmed it. Makayla's attackers arrived at the stairwell first. When she arrived, they spoke for a few moments, but then Makayla tried to walk away. They fought, after which somebody threw her down the stairs."

That the attackers came to the school with masks showed that they had planned the assault—or at least something criminal. It wasn't an accident. Makayla knew her attackers, too. Otherwise, she wouldn't have spoken to them or met them away from prying eyes.

"Do you have any other video of the attack?"

"No. Our surveillance cameras focus on the school's exterior."

I leaned back from my desk.

"You think the attackers are students?"

"I'd hate to think one of my kids could do this."

I raised my eyebrows.

"Some of the most chilling criminals I've ever arrested have been under eighteen," I said. "It's hard to think those innocent-looking faces could belong to a monster, but they can."

"It's not a student," said Walters.

"Okay," I said. "Who is it?"

He paused and then chuckled.

"I don't know," he said. "Isn't it your job to find out?"

I forced the smile to my lips again.

"If it wasn't a student, someone slipped into your school unnoticed to commit an attempted murder," I said. "Sounds like you've got some liability issues, Mr. Walters."

He paused.

"Are you threatening me?"

"That's a fact, not a threat," I said, shaking my head. "Start looking through the surveillance footage taken the day Makayla was injured. If you see a single face you don't recognize, I want to hear it. Maybe it was a student, and maybe it wasn't. Either way, I'd hate to discover you were so negligent in your duties that a criminal could walk inside your secure building and push a young woman down the stairs. It'll come out if that's the case. Now's your time to get in front of it."

"I don't care for your tone," he said.

"I don't care," I said. "Send me the cell phone video. My email address is on my business card. I expect to hear back from you about the surveillance video by the end of the day."

He hesitated.

"Fine," he said. "If it's that important, I guess I can do that."

The smile left my face, and my annoyance crept into my voice.

"Don't guess," I said. "Either you do it, or I walk through your doors with a court order and half a dozen officers. We'll interview every student, faculty member, cafeteria worker, maintenance worker, administrator, and coach in the building. We'll even interview the school nurse."

He paused.

"We don't have a nurse."

"That's unfortunate for your students. Watch the video and call me with your findings."

I started to hang up, but he spoke before I could.

"Before you go," he said, "I searched Makayla's locker this morning and found a bag of marijuana. Detective Delgado already came by to pick it up."

I closed my eyes and swore under my breath. It would have been nice if Delgado had told me that.

"Okay," I said. "Thank you for keeping me informed."

I hung up before Walters could say anything else. St. Augustine had an excellent school system, and they wouldn't have hired Mr. Walters if he didn't have an extensive track record of success in other positions. I had no doubt talented young people across the state owed at least part of their success to his work, but his past success wouldn't knit the bones of Makayla Simpson's skull together. He hadn't just let her fall through the cracks; he had discarded her like garbage. She deserved better than that.

After that phone call, I was so angry I had to get up and move, so I went for a walk. George Delgado wasn't in his office, so I sent him a text message asking about the marijuana he had confiscated. He didn't return my message right away, so I walked down to the evidence room to see what he had picked up.

Mark Bozwell, our lecherous evidence clerk, pretended to search through the database, but his eyes kept flicking to my chest. I was used to that. Eventually, he told me Delgado had found an ounce and a half of marijuana in a Mylar bag. Makayla hadn't packaged it for resale, but she could have sold it for three or four hundred bucks if she had. At least I knew where her babysitting money went.

I thanked Bozwell and walked back to my office, where I found Detective Marcus Washington. He gave me a tight smile.

"Hope you don't mind me dropping by," he said.

"Not at all," I said, motioning toward a chair in front of my desk. "You want to sit and talk?"

He shook his head and stayed still. I walked to my chair and sat. For a moment, he held my gaze, but then he sighed and looked down.

"You're a good cop, Joe," he said. "I've always thought that even when I didn't agree with you."

"I've thought the same about you."

He closed his eyes as he looked up.

"My office is next door," he said. "It says detective on the nameplate. Same as yours."

I forced myself to smile.

"I didn't realize I had a nameplate. No one's ever given me one before."

He shook his head.

"No jokes," he said. "I'm here to tell you it's rude when you question my work."

The anger I had felt toward Mr. Walters disappeared, replaced by confusion. I furrowed my brow and crossed my arms to match his posture.

"What are you talking about?"

"Vic Conroy," he said. "That was my case. I closed it. If my judgment isn't good enough for you, George Delgado and Sheriff Kalil both signed off on my reports. I don't need anyone else looking over my shoulder."

"I'm not looking over your shoulder, Marcus, and I'm not questioning your work," I said. "In fact, I'm glad you worked the case. You're a good cop."

"Then why did you look it up?"

I blinked and cocked my head to the side.

"Curiosity. Vic Conroy was my white whale. I wanted to send him to prison. Now that I know he's dead, I wanted to find out what happened," I said. Then I paused. "How'd you know I tried to look it up?"

"Darren Rogers called and told me."

I considered Marcus for a moment.

"Someone sealed the case. I couldn't access any of your reports."

Marcus softened his expression. His gaze looked distant.

"That's odd," he said. He gestured to the chairs near my desk. "If you're just curious, you want to hear about it?"

"Please," I said. He crossed the room and sat. Then he sighed. "Conroy's case was open and shut. A man named Dale Wixson walked into Club Serenity, drank two Long Island iced teas, and ordered three lap dances from a woman named Janice Brown. Her stage name was Cinnamon. The dances should have cost Wixson a hundred and twenty bucks, but he claims the club charged him two hundred. When he asked to speak to the manager, Vic Conroy came out and asked him to leave. Mr. Wixson pulled a nine-millimeter pistol from his waistband and shot Vic in the chest. The bouncers rushed him to St. John's, but he died on a surgery table."

I shook my head and sighed.

"That's not how I expected Vic to go."

"It's not how any of us expected it to happen," said Marcus. "We caught the shooting on three surveillance cameras, and we have half a dozen witnesses. We've also got the firearm."

"Did you give Wixson a medal for taking Conroy out, or did you actually send him to prison?"

"Neither," said Marcus. "After shooting Vic, he ran out of the club while the bouncers tended to their boss. We found him dead two days later of a self-inflicted gunshot wound. He used the same gun to kill himself that he used to kill Conroy."

"Jeez," I said. I paused. "What happened to Conroy's employees?"

"The old chef at Club Serenity now works at The Barking Spider, and three of his old bouncers got together and now they renovate houses across the county. His dancers and prostitutes have moved on," said Marcus. "We caught some trying to go independent in a bed and breakfast by the river, but the owners drove them out."

"What about the hotel and truck stop?" I asked. "That truck stop was always busy. His family could have found new owners."

Marcus shrugged.

"Once Conroy died, his wife left the area," he said. "I assume she still owns the properties, but she's not running anything. We figured Vic had made enough money that she could retire in style."

I leaned back in my chair.

"So Vic Conroy is over and done," I said.

"Yep," said Marcus. "You said he was your white whale. Would you have come back if you had known he died?"

I considered but then tilted my head to the side.

"He's not the only bad guy in town. I've got a lot of white whales. Or at least I tilt at a lot of windmills." I paused. "How did Darren Rogers know I tried to access your report?"

Marcus looked at the ground.

"He's around a lot," he said. "More than I'd like. He says he's making sure we're using taxpayer dollars well."

"But he's a civilian," I said, lowering my chin. "He shouldn't be able to access police records, and he sure as hell shouldn't be able to limit my access to my department's records or to know when I've accessed something necessary for my job."

"It is what it is. Darren Rogers is the county executive now, so he controls the purse strings. You piss him off at your own peril."

"Yeah. I guess you're right."

Before leaving, he wished me luck with my cases. I thanked him. Afterwards, I spun around in my chair, thinking to myself. Marcus was a great cop. If he thought Wixson killed Vic Conroy and then committed suicide, he was right. Still, I couldn't help but feel the story was incomplete. In life, Vic Conroy had seemed untouchable. We had tried investigating him and his various businesses, but we had consistently gotten nowhere. Even on those rare occasions when we had arrested his girls for prostitution, they'd never turned on him. He had protected them, and they had protected him—even as he was exploiting them.

His shooting was random and pointless, like most of the murders I had worked. And now, he was just another victim. Death had absolved him of his sins. That bothered me most of all.

Vic Conroy had turned young, vulnerable girls into prostitutes because he knew no one would stop him. He had hurt people to make money. For the things he had done, he didn't deserve the dignity of a quick, painless death. He deserved to sit in prison and to feel as powerless as the people he had hurt, and it pissed me off that he hadn't.

Chapter 18

As I sat and stewed and thought of Vic Conroy, my phone beeped, telling me I had an email. Mr. Walters had sent me the cell phone video of Makayla's assault. It was short and violent and just as Mr. Walters had described. Two people met Makayla by the staircase; they spoke for two or three minutes; and then Makayla tried to walk away. One of the masked persons grabbed her and flung her down the stairs. She tumbled down, and, even though I knew it was coming, I still gasped when her head smacked into the ground. Afterwards, one of the assailants walked down the steps, ran his hands over Makayla's body, and took something from her pocket before joining his friends.

I watched the video four times, but it never became easy to see. My training told me to remain objective and to focus on the facts, but that was hard to do when watching a thug throw a young woman down a staircase and then walk away while she bled. The video had no sound, but my brain filled it in anyway. When I closed my eyes, I saw Makayla falling, and I heard the hollow thump of her head smacking the concrete. And then I heard the braying of jackals as the thugs who hurt her laughed and left her to die. It left me sick to my stomach and angry.

As I pushed back from my desk, my entire body felt flushed and hot. I balled my hands into fists and sucked in two deep breaths to slow my heart. Getting angry wouldn't help anyone. I needed to work the case, and that meant talking to Makayla. I called St. John's to ask whether she was available for an interview, but the neurologist in charge of her care had already discharged her. Her complete recovery would take a few months, but as long as she refrained from playing sports and took it easy, she could recover at home.

I thanked the nurse with whom I had been speaking, hung up, and got in my car to drive to the Jefferson's two-story historic home. Unlike on my previous trip, no children climbed the trees out front, so no one was outside to announce my arrival. I climbed the concrete steps to the front porch and knocked. Within moments, Mrs. Jefferson opened the door. She blinked when she saw me.

"Detective," she said.

"Morning," I said. "I called the hospital, and they told me they had discharged Makayla. If she's awake, I'd like to talk to her."

Mrs. Jefferson stepped back but not to let me in. Instead, she positioned herself in the doorway to prevent me from seeing inside.

"She's resting. It's important to minimize her stress right now."

"I understand," I said, "but I need to talk to her. A video of her attack has surfaced, and it's clear that she knows the people who attacked her."

Mrs. Jefferson furrowed her brow.

"If you've got video, why do you even need to talk? Just arrest her attackers."

"They wore masks," I said. "That said, Makayla met them in a disused part of the school and spoke to them for several minutes. She wouldn't have done either unless she knew them."

Mrs. Jefferson brought a hand to her face and rubbed her eyes.

"All right," she said. "Wait here."

She shut the door before I could respond. Hopefully the kid would talk to me this time. I considered and then sat on the patio set to my right. The door opened again about five minutes later, and a young woman strode toward me. She had curly brown hair, olive colored skin, and brown eyes, and she wore light blue pajama pants and a white long-sleeved top. The moment I saw her, the video of her falling down the stairs came to my mind unbidden. I forced myself to smile anyway as I stood.

"Hey," I said. "I'm Joe Court. Thanks for talking to me."

"Sam said I didn't have a choice."

I tilted my head to the side.

"You've always got a choice," I said. She said nothing, so I pointed to the lounge chair across from me. We sat, and I reached into my purse for my cell phone. "I'd like to record our conversation."

"That's fine," she said, her voice soft. I turned on my recording app and then put the phone on the coffee table to my right.

"Okay," I said, drawing in a breath. "For the record, I'm Detective Joe Court, and I'm interviewing Makayla Simpson, a minor in the custody of Vance and Samantha Jefferson. This is a voluntary interview, and I'm here to talk about a recent assault. Does all that sound right to you?"

Makayla looked at me and nodded, so I asked her to speak aloud for the record. Then she leaned forward.

"Yes," she said. "But I don't remember what happened. My doctor says that's common in head injuries."

It was true, so I picked up my phone again.

"Would you like to see what happened?" I asked. "Your attackers filmed it."

She straightened.

"Why would they film it?"

"So they could share it with their friends," I said, thumbing through my files until I found the right ones. "People are stupid. I don't know."

I turned the phone toward her and let her watch. She flinched as her attacker pushed her, but then she looked at me and shrugged.

"So there's no sound?"

"No," I said, turning my phone toward me again and making sure I hadn't just turned off the recording app. "Your vice principal, Mr. Walters, told me that part of the school is empty most school days."

She shrugged.

"Okay."

"Why'd you go there?" I asked. "You weren't there for class."

"I don't know," she said.

"Do you remember what you talked about?"

She shook her head.

"No. Sorry. That entire day's a blank."

"You went through some serious trauma and almost died," I said. "How are you feeling now? You dizzy or anything?"

"Maybe a little," she said. "I'm tired."

"You'll go back inside in just a minute," I said. "Before you do, though, can I see your phone? I'm guessing your attackers contacted you beforehand and asked you to meet them back there. Otherwise, you would have been walking to your geometry or English class, right?"

She looked down. Her right foot tapped on the ground, and she worked her fingers together nervously. Then she looked up and swallowed.

"I don't think my phone is—"

"Be careful if you plan to lie to me," I said, interrupting her. "I'm here to help you. The people who attacked you could have killed you. If you don't help me find them, they might try again, and they might succeed next time. And if they're willing to throw you down the stairs and leave you to die, they'll be willing to do the same to others. Think about that and tell me about your phone."

She licked her lips and then closed her eyes.

"Um," she said before pausing. I let her think through her answer. Then she looked at me and narrowed her eyes. "You asked for my permission to see my phone."

"That's right," I said.

"You can't just force me to hand it over?"

I looked at her without blinking.

"I could get a court order," I said. "To do that, the court would appoint a guardian ad litem to look after your interests, and I'd fill out a lot of paperwork to prove that I had cause to look at your phone. Then, once I had jumped through the correct hoops, a judge would issue the order, and you'd be forced to turn it over. Barring that, I'd contact your cellular provider and have them turn over a list of your last couple hundred calls and any text messages. I'd then work with the courts to look at your emails. If you force me, I will invade your privacy and learn every secret you have to keep. I don't want to do that. Please don't make me. Just tell me who attacked you. I'll take it from there."

She considered and then stood.

"I don't want to help you."

She started to go back into the house, and I swore under my breath.

"Before you go, there's something else we need to discuss," I said. "Detective Delgado confiscated an ounce and a half of marijuana from your locker at school."

She stopped walking and faced me.

"So?"

"Possession of thirty-five grams or more of marijuana is a felony," I said. "The law says that anyone with that much marijuana likely intends to sell it. The penalty is seven years in prison and a ten-thousand-dollar fine. It doesn't help that you kept it at school. That adds an enhancement to the charges, which means you're facing thirty years in prison for trafficking."

She narrowed her eyes.

"That's bullshit."

"I don't write the law," I said. "I'm guessing you kept the weed at school to keep it away from your foster siblings, and that's admirable, but I can't help you if you don't help me. Do you want to go to prison?"

She looked down.

"No," she said, her voice soft.

"Then talk to me," I said. "If you tell me who assaulted you, I can work with the prosecutor on the weed. You're a minor, and this is a first-time offense. Mr. Deveraux, the county prosecutor, and I get along well. I might be able to get you community service. Think about that. Community service—that means picking up litter at a park for a couple of Saturdays—or thirty years in prison. Who attacked you?"

Instead of answering, she blinked and shook her head.

"Prison."

I softened my voice.

"If you're scared, we can protect you," I said. "I'll station an officer outside your house. Hell, if you want, we've got cots in our police station. I can find you a safe place to stay until we arrest the people who hurt you. All I need is a name."

She looked down.

"I'm not talking."

I sucked in a breath through my nose and felt my skin grow hot. The muscles of my jaw hurt from clenching, but I forced myself to sound calm.

"Okay, then," I said. "Pack a bag. It's too late to arraign you today, so you'll be spending the night in jail."

She nodded and went inside without saying a word. I closed my eyes and shook my head as I sighed.

"What are you hiding, honey?"

Chapter 19

The client would only pay if Peyton made Dr. Hines's death look like a suicide. Recently, he had killed Dale Wixson and made it look like a suicide, but he hated suicide jobs. They dictated the methods he could use and increased the risk. Still, it was work, and he wasn't at the point in his career where he could turn down paying jobs.

He shifted on his chair. He had rented the house on Airbnb a week ago. It had cost two hundred and fifty-two bucks a night and had far more bedrooms than he needed, but it was half a block from his target's home. If he hadn't rented a place so close, he would have had to hide in someone's garden shed. This was much more comfortable. Peyton sipped his coffee and watched on his iPad as the Hines family went about their morning routine.

Nico Hines, the family patriarch, was an anesthesiologist who specialized in the management of acute and long-term pain. He had earned his M.D. at the University of Oklahoma and then had done a residency in anesthesiology at a Catholic hospital in St. Louis. He had completed his formal education with a fellowship in pain management at yet another university and hospital in the region.

With his training, he could have been a good doctor, and he could have earned three or four hundred thousand dollars a year. But three hundred grand a year wasn't enough for Dr. Hines. He had kids, a million-dollar mortgage, and a very attractive bride fifteen years his junior to care for. As long as Dr. Hines kept her happy and their children fed and clothed, he had nothing to worry about from her.

Kira Hines was a beautiful Russian expat, and she loved her children. Every morning, she made their lunches and included little notes and drawings in their lunch boxes. She cut the crust off her son's sandwiches, and she peeled apples for her daughters. She showed her love and devotion to them every day.

Dr. Hines and his beautiful young wife slept in separate rooms most nights, but twice a week, she paid her debt to him by slipping into his bedroom after the children went to sleep. Afterwards, she shuddered in the hallway, showered, and called her boyfriend from her bedroom. She and her personal trainer boyfriend would stay up for hours talking, and she'd wake up the next day exhausted but with a smile on her face. Dr. Hines flattered himself and joked that he must have tired her out the night before, and Kira never contradicted him. As long as he cared for their children, Kira would never leave her husband, but her heart belonged to another.

THE MEN ON THE FARM

Peyton didn't enjoy violating the Hines family's privacy, but the information he gleaned from the wireless video cameras he had installed in their home was vital to his efforts. Murder was easy, but suicides were hard to fake. The staging was always imperfect. A good detective could recognize the irregularities and mistakes and realize something was amiss. The key to a proper suicide job was to convince the mark to commit suicide. That took effort.

Peyton fast-forwarded through video footage and flipped through pages of his spiral-bound notepad until he found his most recent entry. Dr. Hines had gone to bed at ten the night before, while Kira had gone to bed at eleven after giving her boyfriend a private striptease on her cell phone. He had woken before her at seven this morning, but she had gotten up shortly after that. Whenever she turned her back to him, the doctor allowed his eyes to linger on her. They did that often. His gaze wasn't lecherous. It was soft and kind. He loved her. Kira rarely returned the look.

If the doctor understood the situation, he'd thank Peyton. By killing him, Dr. Hines would never know the one person in the world he loved more than all others didn't love him in return, and the world would never know he illicitly prescribed opioids to a parade of addicts and drug dealers.

The doctor and his family didn't know how drastically their lives would change in just a few short hours. Peyton hoped the kids, at least, had enjoyed their morning. It'd be the last morning with their father they would ever have.

***

Cassie prepped an insulin injection for Lily. Without proper testing supplies, she didn't know what the little girl's blood sugar levels looked like, but she could smell the sugar on her breath and see her lethargic mannerisms. This was bad.

Lily shifted as Cassie cleaned the injection site on her abdomen.

"Hush, honey," whispered Cassie, praying the stress didn't enter her voice. Her fingers trembled, and she had to try twice to fill her syringe with two units of insulin. Before injecting her, Cassie held her breath and closed her eyes and prayed she was doing it right. Then she looked at the little girl she loved like a younger sister and smiled. "This is going to sting, sweetheart."

Lily's eyes flew open as Cassie gave her the shot. Like most kids with diabetes, Lily had grown used to needles, but they still hurt—especially if she was asleep and unprepared. Lily cried for a moment, but the drugs would keep her alive. Afterwards, Cassie held her on the couch and rocked her back and forth as she sang a lullaby and tried to avoid crying herself.

Cassie was nineteen years old and lived in her childhood home with her mom and dad. At night, she attended classes at the University of Missouri-St. Louis. By day, she worked at the same vet's office where she had worked when she was in high school. She wasn't ready to care for a little girl. She could hardly take care of herself.

It was only a matter of time before Ursa or Nadine shot them both. Cassie tried to be strong, but more than anything in the world, she wanted a hug from her dad or a kind word from her mom. For now, she could only pretend she wasn't terrified.

The joists and wooden floor on the first floor creaked as someone walked around. Cassie held her breath and waited. The muscles in her shoulders twitched, and her fingers trembled, so she balled her hands into fists. The noise changed as Nadine walked down the carpeted steps to the basement. She stopped about ten feet from the couch on which Cassie and Lily sat.

For a moment, Nadine said nothing. Then she blinked and looked down.

"Thank you for what you did last night," she said. "At the vet's office. We couldn't have done that on our own. We didn't know enough."

Cassie swallowed hard.

"No...no problem," she said, trying to force strength into her voice. Lily stirred and then fluttered her eyes open before squinting. She whined just a little, so Cassie rubbed her back. Then she settled down as she blinked and woke up.

"Wendy's still alive, if you're curious," said Nadine.

"Good," said Cassie, focusing on Lily.

"I'm hungry," said Lily. "I want my mom."

That she was talking at all indicated the insulin was working. The knot in Cassie's stomach untangled a little, but then the worry grew as she looked at Nadine.

"Do you have any food?" she asked. "Lily hasn't eaten breakfast yet. She likes scrambled eggs, but she'll eat cereal."

"We've got granola," said Nadine, walking forward to kneel in front of them. She smiled at Lily. It was tender and genuine. It made Cassie hold her all the tighter. "Do you like granola, honey? We can put some sugar on it."

Before answering, Lily looked at Cassie, who nodded.

"Okay," said Lily. "I want my mommy."

"I know, honey," said Nadine, her voice singsong. "We'll get you to her as soon as possible. You want to watch some cartoons?"

Lily nodded, but she didn't have much enthusiasm. Cassie turned on the TV and flipped through the channels until she found Nickelodeon. Lily settled in to watch PAW Patrol.

"Can you come with me, please, Cassie?" asked Nadine, raising her eyebrows and smiling.

"I don't want to leave Lily."

The smile left Nadine's lips.

"I won't hurt you unless you make me," said Nadine. "Just come upstairs. That's not a request."

Cassie's heart beat faster, but she tried to keep her nervousness from her voice as she leaned toward Lily.

"I love you," she whispered. "You stay here."

"Okay," said Lily.

Cassie's knees trembled as she stood and followed Nadine up the stairs. The home's blinds were open, and the sun shone so brightly outside that Cassie had to squint as her eyes adjusted. The kitchen and dining room both smelled like bleach. Cassie didn't know where her captors had put all the plastic tarps, but they were gone from the dining room. So was Wendy.

"Can I get that granola for Lily?"

Nadine considered and then closed her eyes.

"In a moment," she said. "For now, I need you to talk to me. Wendy's still alive. Her temperature is down a degree from last night, and she seems to be breathing okay. She's asleep."

"Good," said Cassie. "If her temperature's down, it means the antibiotics are working. You've bought some time, but she still needs to see a doctor."

"We know," said Nadine. She looked down. "We have one more job planned, and then we're done. After that, we'll leave the country, and we'll take Wendy to a real doctor."

Cassie shook her head.

"Unless your job is today, I doubt you have that much time," she said. "The antibiotics are working, but the bullet's still inside. It could move and tear open her colon or rupture her spleen. She was shot with a pistol, right?"

Nadine nodded, so Cassie continued.

"If she was shot with a jacketed hollow-point round, the bullet will have expanded inside her like a mushroom, and it'll have edges as sharp as-"

"I know what a hollow-point round does," said Nadine, interrupting her. "That's why you'll be staying with us. Keep her alive."

"This is a really terrible idea," said Cassie, crossing her arms.

"Your opinion is noted," said Nadine, her voice sharp. "Now get her ready to move. We've stayed here too long already. I'll get Lily some granola."

Cassie's eyes popped open, and she shook her head.

"No," she said. "If we move her, the wound will break open. She'll bleed out in the back of the van."

"Then dress her wound with hemostatic gauze. Wendy's alive, and we plan to keep her that way. Get to work before the police arrive."

Every muscle in Cassie's body tightened at once. She must have flinched because Nadine narrowed her eyes.

"The police are coming?" she asked.

"They will eventually," said Nadine, crossing her arms and narrowing her eyes. "And that seems to scare you. Why?"

Cassie licked her lips and forced her mind to focus so she could come up with a believable lie that didn't involve her leaving a message in the vet's office with their street name on it.

"Because if the police come, Lily and I will become expendable," she said. "You'll kill us. And even if you don't, we'll get caught in the crossfire when you try to escape."

Nadine drew in a breath through her nose and looked thoughtful.

"We won't kill you," she said. "And you're not expendable. The police won't come anywhere near us as long as we hold a gun to your head."

Cassie swallowed hard as her throat threatened to tighten shut.

"I don't want to die."

"And I don't want to kill you," said Nadine. "Take care of Wendy. If she dies, you will, too, and Lily will never see her home again."

Chapter 20

I put Makayla in handcuffs and sat her on my backseat. Mrs. Jefferson, her foster mother, yelled at me from the front porch and told me I had better call my lawyer because she planned to sue me and everyone with whom I worked. People yelled at me a lot, so it didn't bother me. Still, I hated what I was doing. Makayla should have been in bed, resting, and I should have been arresting the assholes who'd hurt her. Nobody won today.

Once I had her settled on the backseat, I sat in the front and looked at her in my rearview mirror.

"You okay back there?"

"Fuck you," she said.

I drove her to my station and walked her inside. Trisha sat behind the front desk, but she vaulted to her feet the moment she saw us, her eyes wide.

"You need some help, Joe?"

"Do me a favor and check to see whether we've got a free holding cell," I said, speaking so that my voice carried throughout the lobby. "If not, I'll put Ms. Simpson inside an interrogation booth. We'll transfer her to the Juvenile

Detention Center in St. Louis County as soon as she's arraigned."

"Okay," said Trisha, drawing the word out. She considered me and then bit her lower lip. "Is this the young woman assaulted at the high school?"

"Yep. Detective Delgado found an ounce and a half of marijuana in her locker this morning. We're booking her on trafficking charges."

Trisha motioned me forward. I told Makayla to sit on a chair in the lobby and walked closer to Trisha's desk.

"I don't mean to tell you how to do your job," she whispered, "but are you sure this is wise?"

I looked back to Makayla. She was sitting straight in the chair. Her eyes were defiant, but her lower lip trembled. I had probably looked the same way when I was her age.

"Nope," I said. "But it's what I'm doing. This girl knows who attacked her. I'm trying to solve a very serious assault, and she's not helping."

Trisha looked at Makayla and then at me.

"Okay," she said, her voice a regular volume once more. "If you leave her here, I'll have her transferred to a cell."

"Sure," I said before leaning forward and lowering my voice. "I don't plan to charge her with anything, but she needs to realize how much hot water she's in. Go through the motions but keep the paperwork light."

Trisha's shoulders relaxed a little.

"Gotcha," she said.

I thanked her and then walked back to Makayla.

"Ms. Simpson, I'm going to go upstairs to fill out the paperwork on your arrest. We'll put you in a cell very shortly. Officer Marshall behind the front desk is here if you need anything. Since we don't have the facilities to house juveniles, we'll transfer you to a detention center in St. Louis. That sound okay with you?"

"You're a bitch."

I took that as a yes, so I walked toward the stairs that would take me to my office. About ten minutes after I sat down behind my desk, Detective Delgado and Sheriff Kalil knocked on my open door. They walked in before I could even turn to look at them.

"What the hell are you doing with that girl?" asked Delgado. "She has a goddamn head injury. She should be in the hospital. Are you out of your fucking mind bringing her here?"

"No, Detective, I'm working a case," I said, standing. "And I'm doing it alone because you quit."

Delgado started to retort, but the sheriff held up a hand, stopping him.

"Tell me you didn't pick her up from the hospital," he said. I snorted and shook my head.

"I'm not stupid," I said. "Her doctors discharged her. I arrested her at her house for the ounce and a half of marijuana Detective Delgado found in her locker at school."

The sheriff considered us both.

"That's a fair bit of marijuana, but she's still a juvenile with a serious head injury. The prosecutor will offer her a plea deal and release her to her foster parents."

"She doesn't realize that, though," I said. "I've got her convinced that she'll spend the next seven to thirty years in prison for that much marijuana. I've also told her I can make it go away if she tells me who assaulted her. She won't. She's terrified."

Delgado crossed his arms but said nothing. The sheriff gave me a neutral expression.

"Go on," he said.

"I don't care about the weed. I'm worried about this kid," I said. "She's in trouble, and she seems to think the best way out of it is to spend the next thirty years in prison. That's a problem. Instead of fighting with me, we need to find out what she's hiding."

Delgado scoffed and shook his head.

"You know what your problem is, Joe?" he asked. "You think you're the only detective in this station gifted with a brain. I talked to Mr. Walters at the school. He reviewed the school's surveillance footage from before Makayla's assault. A sophomore named Sean Kirby shot the video. Fifteen minutes before Makayla's assault, he let two men through a side door. We're still trying to identify them.

"I've already got Sean in an interrogation booth. He's not talking, but it doesn't matter. Officers Scott Hall and Emily Hayes searched his car and found cash, marijuana, methamphetamines, opioids, sleeping pills, and several prescription drugs we have yet to identify. He's a dealer. My guess is Makayla is, too. That's the secret she's willing to go to prison to keep. He and his buddies went after her to eliminate a competitor. Case closed."

The room went quiet as he finished speaking. It felt like someone's hidden hand had reached into my chest and squeezed my heart and lungs. The theory made sense. We'd need evidence to make it stick, but that wouldn't be hard to find. First, we'd subpoena phone records to see who Sean Kirby had called. Then, we'd use those contacts along with the video of him letting our suspects into the school as leverage.

Sean Kirby was a minor, but he and his buddies had attempted to murder a young woman. We'd charge him with assault in the first degree. Normally, that'd be a class-B felony, but because Makayla was under seventeen, Missouri law classified her as a child. That made her a special victim, which kicked the felony up to a class-A. That carried a potential sentence of life in prison. He was screwed. Delgado could use that in an interrogation to get him to turn on his friends and on Makayla.

I flopped into my chair and looked at Delgado.

"I left you a text message," I said. "You should have called me back."

"I was busy working the case," said Delgado, crossing his arms. "Should I have stopped just because you got your panties in a twist?"

The sheriff held up a hand before I could speak.

"That's uncalled for, Detective Delgado," he said. "You both have taught me something here. I won't put you on a case together. That's my fault. Your inability to put aside your personal grievances is yours. I'm disappointed, and now I've got to drive a little girl home so she can sleep in her own bed tonight. George, keep working the case. Bring it to fruition. Joe, you've got other assignments."

He left the room. Delgado looked at me and then at my desk and chuckled.

"Better luck next time, Sherlock," he said, starting toward the door. "Assuming you still have the job."

I almost told him to fuck off, but he was right. I had screwed up. Once he left, I stood up and shut the door. If I'd had a bottle of vodka, I would have poured myself a shot. Thankfully, I didn't have any in my office. Liquor had been my escape since I was old enough to drink it. At the end of a bad day, I could drink myself to sleep, and my bad day would be over. Then my bad days merged, and I found myself drunk most nights of the week. I had cut back since then. My life hadn't gotten better, but I had decided that I didn't want to run from things—even from my mistakes.

I sighed and spun around on my desk chair. Sheriff Kalil would drive Makayla home, but maybe I could go by later and apologize. Then again, if she dealt drugs as Detective Delgado thought, I wouldn't need to go to her. She'd end up in a holding cell soon anyway, so maybe I could bring her some cookies or something while she awaited trial.

Still, Makayla's unwillingness to even talk about her assault bothered me. I had all but offered to make her drugs disappear. Makayla should have jumped on that deal, but she didn't. That told me she didn't care about the drugs—or at least that they weren't her primary concern. Delgado might arrest Sean Kirby and his friends, but Makayla was mine. There was something else going on here, something we needed to find before it blew up in our faces and somebody else got hurt.

Chapter 21

Shortly after the sheriff left, I opened my department's database and searched for references to Sean Kirby, the young man who had filmed Makayla's attack. Unfortunately, I didn't find much. He had no arrest record, but our officers had questioned him a couple of times about minor offenses. Delgado had yet to request his cell phone records or emails, but he would in time. Since the assault case against Kirby was already so strong, future work would focus on providing evidence useful to the prosecutor.

Once Delgado had more information to work with, I'd dive into that case again. In the meantime, I had received an email from an FBI agent in St. Louis with login information so I could access the Bureau's reports on the armored-car robberies.

I skimmed the Bureau's documents but didn't dive into the forensics or ballistics reports. Instead, I focused on the big picture. Agent Costa had emphasized how dangerous these ladies were, but he hadn't mentioned how quickly they worked. Each robbery came within a week of the one prior, and each individual attack lasted under two minutes.

The perps didn't even bother going inside the armored cars. Instead, they stole only what the guards carried. In each case, the local police arrived within seven minutes, but, by then, the perps were miles away. It was professional, clean work. They shouldn't have impressed me, but they did.

I read for a while, but at about eleven, my cell rang. I answered without looking at the caller ID.

"Hey," I said. "This is Detective Joe Court."

"Joe, it's Bryan Costa. I just got a call from a lieutenant in Mehlville, Missouri. His officers were responding to a break-in at a vet's office and found a note on the ground. It had Cassie Prescott's name on it, and she was pleading for help. It said she was in a brick house on Grantwood Lane. It's near Grant's Farm. We haven't found the specific house yet, but we're looking."

Grant's Farm was a three-hundred-acre animal park owned by the Busch family, the former owners of the Anheuser-Busch Companies. It was a beautiful property, and the family kept it open for public tours. When my siblings were young, my family and I had gone there often, so I knew the area well.

"I'm on my way," I said, already pushing back from my desk.

"Not so fast," said Costa. "I've got a team en route to Grant's Farm, but you're closer to Mehlville than we are, so I need you to get out to the vet's office. I want surveillance footage. If we can get a picture of these ladies, we'll be that much closer to identifying them. Look at gas stations, traffic lights, convenience stores, banks... any business you can find with a camera."

"I can do that," I said. He gave me the address and wished me luck. I thanked him, hung up, and then called Sheriff Kalil to let him know where I was going. He told me to keep him informed of any developments. Within five minutes of my phone call, I was in my car, heading north.

Mehlville was a sprawling middle-class suburb south of St. Louis. I hit the outskirts in about forty-five minutes and found the strip mall that held the Southside Animal Clinic within an hour. As I parked, a familiar man in a navy suit stepped out of the front door. I closed my eyes and felt myself sink into my seat.

"Fuck."

The detective must have seen me because he waved and began walking toward my vehicle. I sighed again and reached for my purse to make sure I had a notepad. Mathias Blatch was a St. Louis County detective assigned to the South County Precinct on Sappington Barracks Road. He was a good detective, and I had once cared deeply about him. He had hurt me, though. I had forgiven him, but I didn't trust him or his judgment.

I opened my door and gave him a tight, forced smile.

"Detective Blatch," I said.

"Hey, Joe," he said, smiling. "I didn't realize you were still in the area."

"It's a long story," I said. "Tell me about the robbery."

The smile left his lips, and his shoulders fell as he stepped back.

"Can we talk for a minute first?"

I closed my eyes and crossed my arms.

"Okay. Fine. Talk."

"You're still mad, I take it," he said.

"It doesn't matter. We're both professionals, and we've both got a job to do here. Let's work the case."

Mathias said nothing. Then he looked down.

"There's something you should know, and I wanted you to hear it from me," he said. He wouldn't say anything more until I met his gaze.

"Fine. Go on," I said.

He cleared his throat.

"I'm engaged. My fiancée and I are having a baby in two months. A little boy. I'm going to be a dad."

At first, some little part of me felt almost jealous. Then it passed, and I softened my voice.

"Good for you," I said. "I always thought you'd make a good father."

"You thought about me having kids?"

"That was a lifetime ago," I said, walking toward the vet's office. "Now tell me what we've got."

Mathias hurried to keep up with me. Southside Animal Clinic had a wall of glass facing the parking lot. Two uniformed officers stood outside. One held a clipboard with a log sheet, while the other simply stood there. Broken glass covered the sidewalk in front of the door. I signed the log sheet and looked at the officer who was doing nothing.

"What's your name?"

"Vince," he said. I raised my eyebrows, hoping he'd continue. He straightened his back. "Vince Feldman, ma'am."

"Okay, Officer Feldman," I said, looking around the strip mall. The mall had about a dozen stores. "I need surveillance video. Visit every store in the mall and see what they've got. Once you finish that, I want you to go by every gas station within a two-block radius and see what surveillance video they've got. If there are any neighborhoods nearby, I want you to knock on doors and see if anyone's seen an unfamiliar Honda Odyssey minivan lurking about."

He smirked.

"Is that it?"

I smiled, but I didn't allow it to reach my eyes.

"I'm in a bad mood, Officer Feldman. Please do as I ask. If you can't, I'll call your commanding officer and have him send me someone who can."

Feldman looked at Mathias.

"She's in charge," said Mathias.

The patrolman sighed and then left. I mouthed a thank you to Mathias before stepping through the front door and into the office. The waiting room looked clean and neat. More glass littered the ground, but it didn't look as if our perps had spent much time in there. I looked at Mathias again.

"Tell me what we've got," I said. He pulled a notepad from his pocket and started reading.

"The St. Louis County dispatcher received a call from the office's alarm company at 1:09 AM. They didn't have details, but their system said someone had tripped a sensor on the door."

"Do we know how they broke the glass?" I asked.

Mathias shook his head.

"They took their tools with them when they left," he said. "They planned this robbery. It wasn't a spur-of-the-moment decision."

"Good," I said. "Go on."

He looked back at his notes.

"The alarm company called my station, and we sent a pair of officers. They arrived at 1:17 AM and observed the broken door. After determining that the building was empty and that there was a significant quantity of pills on the ground, they left the office and called for assistance. We've had officers sitting on the office since then.

"I arrived at 9:14 AM and walked through with Dr. Alexa Hays. She couldn't tell what the perps had taken, but narcotics are kept in a safe. Only she and one of her assistants have access."

"I was told you found a note."

"Yeah," he said. "It was written on the back of a prescription form. It said Cassie Prescott, help, and gave a street name near Grant's Farm. When I called that in, my lieutenant recognized Cassie Prescott's name from a notice that came in last night and called the FBI. The agent he spoke to said a detective from St. Augustine County would come up. And now you're here. What's going on, Joe?"

I considered what to tell him and figured I might as well go with the truth.

"Cassie Prescott and a little girl named Lily Henderson were abducted from the scene of a quadruple homicide last night. Agent Costa believes they were taken by four ladies who have robbed multiple armored cars and have now murdered at least eighteen people in multiple states."

Mathias straightened.

"Wow. What can I do?"

"Just do your job," I said. "I want every surface they could have conceivably touched searched for prints, I want surveillance footage from every camera in the area, and I need every bit of forensic evidence you can collect."

"I'll call in a forensics team," he said. "If I had known what was going on, I would have called them in already."

"Good," I said. "Anything else I should see?"

"They blew the pharmacy's door open," he said. "If I had to guess, they used a breaching shotgun."

"I'll take your word for it," I said, already pulling my phone from my pocket to call Agent Costa. He answered quickly. "Hey, Bryan. It's Joe. I'm at the vet's office. Where are you?"

"We're getting set up now on Grantwood Lane. We think we've found the house. It's a short-term rental, so guests come through often. Neighbors thought nothing of it when four women moved in. We're evacuating the area around it and are preparing to go in. I've called in a tactical team from St. Louis County."

"Good. I'm on my way," I said, already heading out. Mathias followed, but I ignored him. "There's nothing worth my time here."

Chapter 22

Grantwood Lane was a beautiful street with expansive lawns, mature trees, and nice homes. I parked in the circular driveway of a ranch-style home with minimal landscaping and an American flag flying on the front lawn. Agent Costa and his team had already kicked down the door of their targeted house and found the place empty, so now he was focusing on the neighbors, several of whom had begun congregating on the lawn of a quaint stucco home with Japanese maple trees in front. When Costa saw me, he excused himself from an interview with a middle-aged woman and walked toward my car.

"Did you find anything interesting?" I asked.

Costa shook his head.

"Not yet," he said. "A witness walking his dog said he thought he saw their minivan leave about an hour before we arrived. They cleaned the house pretty well before they left, but there's residue from tape on the walls and windows in the dining room. A neighbor also reported finding a suspicious trash bag in his garbage can already."

I looked toward the house.

"How was a trash bag suspicious?"

"It wasn't his," he said. "His family used white trash bags. This one was black. An evidence technician checked it out and found plastic painters' tarps inside. They had blood on them, so we took them back to our lab for processing. I've asked the other neighbors to check their trash cans and dumpsters for other surprises, but so far, we haven't found anything."

A cold chill passed over me as I crossed my arms.

"Let's address the elephant in the room," I said. "Did we find Cassie or Lily's body yet?"

He shook his head.

"No."

"That's something, at least," I said, my voice low. "The vet's office was a bust aside from the note Cassie Prescott left. I asked the detective in charge to make sure they dusted for prints and that they searched the surrounding area for surveillance cameras, but I don't know what'll turn up. We still think they're driving a Honda Odyssey minivan, right?"

"At the moment, yes, but if their pattern holds, they'll dispose of it and steal a new car soon," he said. He paused. "We have another problem. While searching the house, we found a vial of canine insulin and a used syringe in the basement."

"Okay," I said. "How is that a problem?"

"I talked to Lily Henderson's mother. Lily is a type 1 diabetic," he said. "Her insulin and testing supplies are at home."

My shoulders fell, and my stomach tightened.

"Shit," I said, closing my eyes. I paused and let that sink in before speaking. "Best-case scenario: will insulin designed for a dog keep Lily alive?"

"I don't know," said Costa. "I read an article about diabetic adults using cheaper animal-grade insulin, but nobody seems to know what'll happen here. It's not ideal. That's the best anybody'll tell me."

I gave myself another moment to process it.

"What happens if she runs out of insulin?" I asked. "Can she exercise and drink lots of water to control her blood sugar?"

"I asked her mom about that, but since Lily is a type 1 diabetic, exercise isn't enough," he said. "Without insulin, she'll go through diabetic ketoacidosis. I don't know the entire process, but it's life-threatening, and it can happen quickly in children. The bottom line is that we need to find her sooner rather than later."

I uncrossed my arms and adjusted my feet as I considered what to ask.

"What do these ladies do usually after finishing a job?"

"We think they leave town and stake out their next target in their next city," said Costa. "Everything is different now, though. One of their own is hurt, and they've got Cassie and Lily. Given the circumstances, I don't think we can assume their next moves will look anything like what they've done in the past."

I swore under my breath and looked down.

"So we've got nothing."

"We've got a babysitter willing to risk her life for the little girl in her care," said Costa. "That's hardly nothing."

I brought a hand to my face, thinking.

"You're right," I said, looking toward a crowd forming nearby. "Let's work and make sure this babysitter's heroics aren't in vain."

***

Modern cars were easy to steal. Thirty years ago, a car thief would have had to remove part of the dash panel to expose the ignition wiring system and then splice wires together to bypass the ignition lock. A competent thief could do it in five or six minutes, but in that time, he was vulnerable and easy to spot. Nadine had stolen her present car in about thirty seconds using equipment she had purchased on the internet for three hundred bucks.

As she drove, the sealed bottles of Clorox Clean-Up, ammonia, and vinegar on her backseat tipped over, crinkling their plastic bags. While her partners and their captives established a new, temporary home at an empty warehouse near the airport, Nadine would clean their rental home. The plastic tarps had caught most of Wendy's blood, but she needed to wipe down the woodwork and door handles to remove fingerprints and to clean the basement where Lily and Cassie had slept.

As she turned on to Grantwood Lane, though, her skin began tingling, and her heart started beating faster. Two police cruisers had parked on the shoulder just out of sight from the main road.

"Damn," she said, braking and then putting on her turn signal to turn into a nearby driveway. One of the police cars flashed its lights, and she swore again. If she had known the area better, she would have run. Nothing here was familiar, though, and these little neighborhoods had so many dead-end roads that she could turn down one without realizing it, leaving her nowhere to go. Instead, she kept her hands on the steering wheel and tried to look nonchalant.

The cop parked on the road in front of the driveway, blocking her in. As he stepped out of his car, Nadine tossed her purse over the pistol on the passenger seat and rolled down her window, hoping her car's original owner hadn't called it in stolen yet.

"Hey, sugar," she said. "Something going on?"

"Yes, ma'am," said the officer, smiling. He was forty-five or so, which made him ten years older than Nadine. He was young enough that she could flirt with him without making him feel patronized. She could use that. "Can you turn off the car?"

"Oh, of course," she said, putting the car in park and then reaching for the starter button. "You want me to get out, too?"

"You're okay inside," he said, looking at her backseat before focusing on her face again. "Do you live in the neighborhood?"

"No, sir," she said. "I just clean houses."

"Which house?"

"None yet," she said. "I was hoping to knock on some doors and drum up some business. I've got cleaning supplies in the back. You own a house, Officer?"

She leaned forward and wished she had thought to unbutton the top few buttons on her blouse. The officer smiled.

"I do, but my wife and I do most of the cleaning ourselves," he said. He sighed and straightened before looking down the road. "I can't let you in the neighborhood today. We've got a situation at a residence, and we're keeping everyone out for their own safety."

Nadine's throat tightened, but she tried to keep nervousness from her voice.

"What happened?"

"I can't get into it, ma'am," he said, stepping away from her car. "I'll move my car, and you head out. This'll be taken care of by tomorrow."

"Thank you so much for keeping me safe," she said, forcing the biggest smile to her face she could muster. He winked.

"Just doing my job, ma'am," he said, already turning and heading toward his cruiser. Once he got in and pulled out of her way, she reversed out of the driveway and waved out the window before heading back toward Grant Road. From there, she drove north for a few blocks before pulling into the parking lot of a QuikTrip gas station, where she pulled out her phone and texted Ursa.

Problem at the house. Cops everywhere. I'm driving.

Before Nadine could even put her car in gear, Ursa called.

"What do you mean there were cops at the house?"

"I mean just what I said," said Nadine. "There were cops at the house. They wouldn't let me anywhere near it. I thought they were going to arrest me."

"How'd they find it?"

"It's a good question," said Nadine. "I plan to ask about Cassie it when I get there."

Ursa paused.

"How would Cassie have alerted them?"

"At the vet's office last night, she said she needed a pen and paper to calculate Wendy's antibiotics dosage. I gave it to her, and she started scribbling numbers. I think the brat might have written the police a note."

Once again, Ursa paused. When she spoke again, her voice was ice.

"We'll both talk to her."

Nadine hung up and put the car in gear. The drive to their warehouse took about twenty-five minutes. It was a clean building in an industrial park. The FOR SALE sign out front had faded in the sunlight, and one of the rear windows had broken and never been replaced. No one had been there in a while. She parked out back and knocked four times on the door. Ursa opened and let her in.

"We've got a problem," she said.

"Other than the police?" asked Nadine. Ursa nodded.

"Lily's running out of insulin."

"Peachy," said Nadine, closing her eyes and wishing she had never stepped foot in this town. "What do we do?"

Ursa sighed.

"I don't know. Robin and I tied Cassie to a chair. She denies telling the police anything, but I don't believe her."

"I don't, either," said Nadine. Ursa lowered her voice.

"Cassie's not our big problem, though. I read about diabetics who can't get insulin. If we don't get Lily some drugs soon, a bullet will be a mercy."

Nadine clenched her jaw and sighed.

"We'll do what we can," she said. "For now, let's talk to Cassie. It's time she learned what happens when she lies to us."

Chapter 23

Dr. Hines rented an office suite in a brown brick building on a sloping piece of property near St. John's Hospital in the town of St. Augustine. A brick retaining wall held dirt from the parking lot and created a nice planting bed for shrubs and other perennial plants, while a pair of jack pine trees planted alongside the walkway gave his patients privacy as they entered the clinic.

Peyton had watched Dr. Hines for a week, so he knew his schedule. At three every afternoon, the doctor called his wife while sitting at a picnic table behind the clinic. Afterwards, he almost had a glow to him. Peyton didn't know what Kira looked like after those conversations, but he doubted her talks with her husband filled her with the same joy.

Peyton parked at the edge of the lot and waited for the doctor to emerge from the clinic's side door. Hines wore a white lab coat, khaki pants, and a white button-down shirt with a red tie. A stethoscope wound around his neck like a chain, while an unconcerned expression formed on his face. Not for the first time, Peyton wondered if Hines abused the same drugs he sold to his patients.

Hines sat at the table and placed his call. He and Kira only spoke for a few minutes, but it seemed to cheer the doctor up. Assuming she was home, Peyton should have video of Kira's end of the conversation waiting for him if he needed to view it.

Once Dr. Hines slipped his phone into the pocket of his lab coat and stood, Peyton opened his car door and hurried past the cypress trees planted around the break area. The doctor straightened and smiled.

"The entrance is in front," he said. "This is just the break area."

Peyton looked to his right. A concrete walkway led to the clinic's closed rear door.

"I'm Detective Peyton Weldon with the St. Augustine Police Department. I need you to come with me. We've got a problem at your kid's school."

The doctor furrowed his brow.

"I didn't think St. Augustine had a police department," he said. "I thought we had a sheriff."

Peyton tried to hide his grimace.

"There's a problem at the school. Ben's in some trouble."

The doctor furrowed his brow again.

"What'd you say your name was?"

"Detective Weldon," said Peyton, stepping to the right in case the doctor ran for the clinic. Hines held up a hand.

"I'd feel more comfortable if you stayed where you are," he said. "I run a pain management clinic, so I hope you understand my hesitation to believe you. People have tried to rob us in the past. Is that what this is?"

"No," said Peyton, sighing. "I'm trying to be gentle, Doc, but I've got a pistol in a holster behind my back. If you don't come with me, I'll shoot you in the kneecaps and drag you away. If you come with me, everyone will live happily ever after."

The doctor stepped back.

"If you're after drugs, threatening me won't help."

Peyton considered him.

"What would help?"

"Make an appointment like everyone else," said Hines. "I understand that you're in pain. If you're going through withdrawal, it seems like that pain will never go away, but it will. Just make an appointment. I've got sixties and eighties in the office right now."

"Just to be clear," said Peyton, lowering his chin and narrowing his eyes, "you're offering me eighty-milligram OxyContin pills?"

"If you've got the money, I'll get you what you need," said the doctor, a sly smile on his face. "I can even bill your health insurance if you've got it."

Peyton snickered and shook his head.

"You're a piece of work," he said, reaching behind him for his pistol. "Follow me and get in my car, or I'll go to your house and pick up Kira. She's young and pretty, so she'll have a couple of good years left in her. There are dozens of brothels in Bogota that would love some fresh meat."

The doctor's back straightened.

"I could call 911 and you wouldn't be able to stop me."

"If you call 911, you'll die well before they arrive. So will Kira. Now take off your lab coat and drape it over the table. If you reach into your pocket, I'll make good on my promise and kill you, abduct your wife, and sell her as a slave. They love Russian women in Colombia."

The doctor considered and then removed his lab coat and put it on the table. Then he stepped back with his hands in the air.

"Walk toward the parking lot," said Peyton, motioning with the barrel of his pistol while he took the coat and draped it over his hand that held the pistol. "Then get in the red car. We'll drive, and then you'll write a letter for me. If you do as I ask, you will be fine."

"What if I don't want to write a letter?" asked Hines.

"Then I'll kill everyone you love. Now walk."

***

I stayed at the house on Grantwood Lane for about an hour, but the Bureau didn't need me. There were no signs of Cassie or Lily, and none of the neighbors to whom I spoke had seen a little girl or a young woman. Most of them, though, had seen our perps. Apparently, the local men had a hard time forgetting the four attractive blonde women who had rented the house, and their spouses had a hard time forgetting their husbands' wayward gazes.

While I spoke to the neighbors, Agent Costa had arranged for two agents to look into the rental house itself. A Nevada-based holding company called Western Investments held the title, having purchased it at a foreclosure auction six years ago. According to their vice president, the company had intended to renovate the home and then resell it, but then their analytics department persuaded them to try using it as a furnished corporate rental. It had done well enough that they kept it on their books.

Our perps had rented it with a prepaid Visa card in the name of Triad Industries. The company's registered address was an abandoned storage shed a few miles from the US-Mexico border. The ladies had used the same card to rent two other homes in two other cities, but the owners had rented and cleaned both homes multiple times since then. Costa sent out agents to search, but he didn't expect to find anything. In a bit of luck, we got surveillance footage from a neighbor's doorbell camera, and it showed the ladies piling into a Honda minivan that morning. We put out an APB on it. Hopefully it'd show up.

Agent Costa had things in hand, so, after interviewing some neighbors, I drove home. Roy and I walked alongside my road for about a mile. He wasn't a great runner, but he seemed to enjoy our walks. He stopped and sniffed every tree we passed and then disappeared into the woods for a moment before re-emerging about a hundred yards ahead of me.

About half an hour after we left, the dog and I arrived home. Marcus Washington sat on a rocking chair on the porch, but he stood and waved when he saw us. I waved back and walked toward him.

"Hey, Marcus," I said. "Did we have an appointment scheduled?"

He gestured to my other rocking chair and held up a pair of manila file folders.

"Nope, but this is everything we've got on Vic Conroy's murder and Dale Wixson's suicide."

I climbed the steps and took the files from his hands.

"Thank you, but I don't need this," I said. "I trust your investigation."

"And I appreciate that," said Marcus. "Once I left your office, I started thinking, though. I don't trust Darren Rogers, and I don't know if I trust our new sheriff."

I tilted my head to the side.

"Okay," I said. "I'll bite. What's the sheriff done?"

"It's what he's not done," said Marcus. "When Delgado was sheriff, he pushed back on Rogers and kept him out of our business. The new sheriff has practically invited him in. He's monitoring our computer usage, for crying out loud. The moment you checked out Vic Conroy's file, he called me. A civilian shouldn't have access to our file system."

"I agree," I said. "But I'm not sure the two of us have much say in it."

"George Delgado agrees, too."

"Kalil beat George in an election," I said, raising my eyebrows. "He's hardly unbiased."

"Still, Rogers is amassing a lot of authority in a very short amount of time. Oversight's one thing, but this is meddling."

"Not much we can do about it," I said.

He nodded toward the files in my hands.

"Look at the Dale Wixson investigation," he said. "Our coroner declared it a suicide based on the gunshot wound's location on Wixson's skull and the amount of GSR on his hands."

I glanced at him and browsed the file. At one time, we'd had a board-certified forensic pathologist on standby whenever the county needed him. We had shared him with several counties around us, but Dr. Sheridan had helped us break a lot of cases. Unfortunately, Dr. Sheridan, his assistants, and his lab cost more money than our county councilmen wanted to pay, so they fired the doctor and hired a mortician who may or may not have even had a college degree. They should have known better.

I looked at the summary report for Wixson's death and confirmed what Marcus had just told me.

"It's good evidence," I said.

"Yeah, but the GSR was on Wixson's right hand," he said. "He was left-handed."

I straightened and drew in a breath. Statistically, few people shot themselves while holding a pistol in their nondominant hand. That was a problem.

"Did the coroner know that?"

"He didn't bother asking," said Marcus. "Look at the particulate count, too. It's very low."

I closed the file.

"I trust your judgment," I said. "Bottom line this for me."

"Neither George Delgado nor I believe this was a suicide," said Marcus. "We talked to Sheriff Kalil, who said he'd look into things and talk it over with the coroner. The next day, Darren Rogers invited George and me to a lunch meeting. He told us to mind our own business and reminded us that being part of the law enforcement community was like being on a football team. If a player doesn't do what the coach needs him to do, he'll get cut."

"You think it was a threat?"

"I know it was a threat," said Marcus. "George backed off. He's just trying to coast until he can retire with a full pension. I can't afford to lose my job, either, but I figured you could do some digging without too much worry."

I smiled.

"You think I don't need the job?"

"The way I hear it, you could retire today and live better than anybody I know."

The smile slipped from my face. He was right. My biological mother had left me a very large trust fund when she died, and then my friend Susanne had left me her home and property when she died. At one time, I had owned well over a hundred acres of some of the prettiest real estate in Missouri. I had sold that property to a nice couple from St. Louis for more money than I would have earned in two decades of work as a police officer, but I would have traded it in a second to have my friend back.

My eyelids fluttered as I thought.

"I'll look into it."

"And you'll leave my name out of it?"

"If anybody asks, I'll say I stole the files from your office."

"That'll work just fine," said Marcus. "Good luck, Joe."

I thanked him for stopping by. Then he walked to his truck. I looked at my files and whistled for the dog. At least I had something to keep me occupied for the night.

Chapter 24

I read Marcus's reports for the next few hours. Dale Wixson had killed Vic Conroy, but that shouldn't have closed the case. First, Wixson had lived in an abandoned cabin deep in the county and didn't have a cent to his name, yet he had somehow shown up at a strip club with a prepaid credit card worth several hundred dollars. He could have walked the eight miles to the club, and he could have earned the money doing a job for somebody off the books, but none of the reports mentioned evidence of that.

The weapon was an anomaly, too. Wixson had shot Conroy with a SIG Sauer P220 chambered for a .45-caliber round. Guns were easy to get, but they cost money—SIG Sauer pistols more than most. Most drug dealers and other criminals stuck to cheap firearms they could dispose of with little financial pain, but Wixson's gun would set the average gun owner back a week's salary. Someone had purchased the weapon fifteen years at a gun store in New Mexico, but then it had disappeared until resurfacing in our case. Prior to Conroy's shooting, no one had used it in a crime, as best I could tell.

Officially, Conroy's murder investigation was closed, and Wixson's death investigation never got off the ground. Unfortunately, that left me with more questions than answers. Something was going on there.

At about seven, Roy sat beside his empty dinner bowl and started whining to get my attention. I looked up at him and smiled as I stood.

"Sorry, dude," I said, picking up his bowl to fill it with his kibble. He gorged on his food and then sat beside his bowl again, panting and seemingly hoping that I'd fill it up again. I shook my head and smiled as I searched through the pile of takeout menus beside my phone. I ordered Chinese food and picked it up a few minutes later.

I ate alone at the breakfast table in my kitchen while a Thelonious Monk album played in my living room. It was pleasant but a little lonely. Roy lay beside me at the table. He was the best friend I could ask for, and I loved spending time with him, but I wished I had a human companion instead of just a dog.

For most of my life, I had pushed away everyone who had tried to get close to me. It was a defense mechanism. If I kept the world at arm's length, no one could hurt me. At one time, I had needed that layer of protection. I hadn't been strong enough to care about someone—or to risk being hurt. In the past couple of years, I had gone through more shit than most people endured during their entire lives. I had been shot at, fired from a job I loved, and accused of murder.

I had seen friends die, and I had seen my nightmares come to life. Through it all, though, I had survived.

I wasn't the same person I was a year ago. I was stronger. Somewhere along the way, I had even made—and lost—friends. I missed them. Roy snored at my feet. I watched him before getting my phone and sitting beside him on the ground. He raised his head at first, but then he put it back down and yawned. I patted his side and searched through my phone's address book until I found the number of Audrey Green, my little sister. She answered after two rings.

"Hey, Joe," she said, almost squealing. "I'm glad you called. Mom said you got the job!"

"Yeah," I said, smiling. "They gave me a badge again, and I haven't stopped moving since. How are you?"

"I am fabulous. Work is kicking my ass, but I love my apartment. The building has a gym for residents, and the manager bakes cookies every afternoon and leaves them in the lounge."

I looked down to Roy.

"You're living large," I said. "My roommate steals my food the moment I turn my back."

She paused.

"Who's your roommate?" she asked.

"Roy," I said. "He's an asshole, but I love him."

She laughed. We talked for about an hour, and I hung up feeling better than I had all day. My relationship with Audrey had been easy from the moment I met her. When she was a little girl, I used to braid her hair at night and drive her to and from soccer practice. Now that she was an adult with a life of her own, I had feared that we'd drift apart. We hadn't, though; our relationship had changed, but she was still my sister, and we still loved each other.

My brothers were harder. Dylan—my adoptive brother—and I had a few issues to work through, but we talked once or twice a month. Ian, my biological brother, was the hardest. He and I got along well, but the family who had adopted him was protective and didn't appreciate the baggage that came with my job. I hated to admit it, but I couldn't blame them. My work was a huge part of my life, and it had a habit of creeping into my private life. Ian and I exchanged text messages, but we hadn't spoken on the phone or in person in almost a year. I missed him, but I knew I'd see him again. He was family.

At about nine that evening, I let Roy into the backyard. Then he and I watched an absolutely bonkers Netflix true-crime documentary about a guy who owned a private zoo. Afterwards, I went to bed. The next morning began for me at six when Roy woke up, stretched, and licked my face. I pushed him away, and he scampered onto the hardwood, panting.

"If I close my eyes again, will you let me go back to sleep?"

He cocked his head to the side and furrowed his brow. Then he panted and barked. I took that as a no, so I let him into the yard so he could go to the restroom while I made coffee and dressed. It was a cold morning, so I stretched for a few extra minutes before going for my morning run. As he usually did, Roy followed for about two or three minutes before going home. My vet said he got enough exercise on our daily walks, so I wasn't too concerned. He was just lazy. After my run, I showered and dressed again before going to work.

Once I got to my office, I checked my messages. Agent Costa had been true to his word and kept me looped in on everything related to the murders at Henderson Angus and the abductions of Cassie Prescott and Lily Henderson. Unfortunately, he had learned little worth reporting.

The Bureau's technical teams were still trying to figure out who had rented the home on Grantwood Lane, but they were running into serious problems. The bad guys apparently used a virtual private network when reserving the home. That VPN acted as a relay for their internet traffic, obscuring their identities. Unfortunately, their VPN provider didn't keep logs of anything its users did online, and the company refused to release its customer data. DOJ lawyers were already working on getting the information, but it'd take time we didn't have.

The Bureau's forensic teams were running into problems of their own. They had hoped that the blood evidence found in the pickup in Club Serenity's parking lot in St. Augustine would allow them to narrow down who our perps were. To a degree, it did. At least one lady we sought was of northern European descent and had brunette hair. Unfortunately, that was all they learned. None of her relatives had ever tested their DNA.

I read reports for about an hour but learned very little new. Rather than waste more time, I went down to the basement and followed signs to our new forensics lab. The heavy steel door was locked, but there was an intercom button beside the handle and a camera suspended from the ceiling. I hit the intercom button and smiled for the camera. Within thirty seconds, Dr. Darlene McEvoy stepped out with a smile on her face.

"Hey, Detective," she said, holding open the door. "Come on in."

I stepped inside and whistled. Before the building's recent renovation, the county crime lab had been functional but dull. Now it was about three times the size it had been and looked like the set of a TV show.

"Wow," I said. "I like the new digs."

"They're nice, huh?" said Darlene. "We're state-of-the-art. We've even got a new mass spectrometer. This one works. And you should see the gym next door if you haven't. It's nice."

"I've heard about the gym," I said. "Unfortunately, I've been working so much I haven't had the chance to check the building out. How are we on the evidence from Henderson Angus?"

She sighed.

"We're working on it," she said, nodding toward an open door at the far end of the lab. "Let's go to my office."

I said hello to Kevius as his boss and I walked past his workstation. Dr. McEvoy's office was small, but it had a big desk piled high with papers and a pair of chairs. I sat in one, while she sat behind the desk and began pulling out papers from a drawer. Then she read for a second before looking to me.

"So we collected almost two hundred shell casings from the property," she said. "Most appear to have been fired by AR-15 type rifles, but we've also got shell casings from a nine-millimeter pistol and five casings from a .30-06 rifle. Kevius is still processing everything, but so far, we've not found matches in our ballistics database on any round fired."

"Any fingerprints?"

"Two," she said. "They belonged to Wade Henderson. It's rare to find fingerprints on spent shell casings, so it didn't surprise me that we didn't find more. We don't know who your perps are, but they're well-armed. The St. Louis County crime lab has the blood evidence collected from the pickup at Club Serenity, and the bodies found at Henderson Angus are with the St. Louis County Medical Examiner's Office. Those labs are processing the bodies and blood evidence on behalf of the FBI."

"I don't know if they've gotten anywhere with the bodies yet," I said. "The FBI agent in charge of the case has been sending me updates."

Darlene told me she'd call me if she found anything interesting. I thanked her and pulled out my phone as I left the lab. Agent Costa answered after three rings.

"Bryan, hey," I said. "I just visited my crime lab. They're still processing the shell casings found at Henderson Angus. So far, they've found two fingerprints, both of which belonged to Wade Henderson. Have you guys gotten anywhere on the credit card used to rent the house on Grantwood?"

Costa sighed.

"It's a prepaid card purchased at a convenience store in Inglewood, California, by a young man named Reggie Castonzo. Agents in the Los Angeles office brought him in. He says he bought it for a pretty redhead six months ago. He asked for a blow job but settled for a hundred bucks."

I took the stairs two at a time but then stopped in the lobby when Trisha, our dispatcher, motioned me toward her desk. An attractive woman about my age stood near her. I nodded to them both and then held up my index finger to let them know I'd be there momentarily before focusing on my phone call.

"Did he know her outside this transaction?"

"Nope," said Costa. "She bought some weed from him and then asked him to do her a favor. He's seventeen. Just a stupid kid."

"It's a prepaid card, though," I said. "How'd the redhead get money on it?"

"Online," he said. "It's an open-loop prepaid debit card backed by a company in Hong Kong. They let the redhead start an account under a fake name and load it with money from a bank in Bahrain."

I shook my head and sighed.

"These ladies knew what they were doing," I said. "If they got the card six months ago, they've been planning this for a while."

"Looks like it," said Costa. "They're good."

"Well, keep me updated. It looks like I've got something to take care of here," I said. He wished me luck before hanging up. I crossed the lobby and smiled at Trisha and then to the woman across from her.

"I'm Detective Joe Court," I said. "Can I help you?"

"I hope so," said the woman. She had a slight accent, but I couldn't place it. "My husband is missing. He disappeared from work yesterday and never came home."

"Okay," I said. "Who's your husband?"

"Nico Hines," she said. "He's a doctor."

I recognized the name. Hines may have had an M.D., and the pills he dispensed may have been legal with a prescription, but he was a drug dealer, nonetheless. Still, I kept the smile on my face.

"Let's go to my office and talk."

Chapter 25

As we walked to my office, we stopped by the break room, where I poured coffee into two paper cups. I didn't want stale, burned coffee, but the cup would give Mrs. Hines something to hold. When she needed a break from our conversation, she could sip her drink, blow on it to cool it off, move it from hand to hand, spin the cup around…whatever she wanted as long as she didn't spill it. Without that cup or something similar, she'd have nothing to shield her from my questions.

The environment mattered during interviews and interrogations. Sometimes, I preferred to make my witnesses comfortable. Other times, I learned more from an uncomfortable, vulnerable witness. It all depended on the situation. Here, I didn't know what I had, so I figured I might as well give her every chance to speak to me honestly before I put the screws to her.

She sat on the chair in front of my desk with her coffee in front of her. Kira Hines had pale but flawless skin, wavy brunette hair, and deep green eyes. Her arms held more than a hint of muscle tone, and the skin on her cheeks stretched taut over high cheekbones. She was beautiful, but her beauty was inaccessible. She was a piece of art. Her eyes were cold, and her lips were thin and straight. She held the world at a distance. I could respect that.

"Okay," I said, sitting behind my desk. "Your husband is Dr. Nico Hines, and he's missing. We'll talk about that in a minute, but first, I need your contact information."

She introduced herself as Kira Vladimirovna Hines. The middle name was a patronymic formed from her father's name. He must have been Vladimir. Clearly, she was educated and had likely spent a significant amount of time in the United States. I didn't ask her for details, but I would if they became necessary.

"So your husband is missing," I said. "Tell me about that."

"He went to work yesterday and called me in the afternoon. We spoke for ten minutes, and then we hung up. Half an hour later, a nurse at his office called me to ask if he had come home. He hadn't, so I called him. His phone went to voicemail, so I called him again half an hour later, but once more, the phone went to voicemail. He didn't come home last night. This morning, I called his office, but he didn't stay the night there. I also called his cell phone, but it was still off."

I jotted down some notes. I'd nail down the specific times later, but for now, I just wanted a big-picture overview.

"Did you call the police last night?" I asked.

"Why would I have done that?"

I raised my eyebrows and lowered my chin.

"Because your husband didn't come home."

She crossed her arms.

"My husband is an adult. To file a missing-persons report, he needed to be missing twenty-four hours. I read that on the internet."

That was true, but if she had called earlier, we could have looked for his car. I smiled.

"What'd your husband do for a living?"

She narrowed her eyes.

"He's a physician. I believe I made that clear."

"Is that all he did?"

Mrs. Hines considered me.

"I don't care for what you're implying."

I leaned back in my chair.

"I don't mean to imply anything," I said. "Your husband is missing, and I'm asking questions that will help me find him. He's a physician, which means he has some money. I'm asking if he has other business interests that might have gotten him in trouble. For instance, I once worked a case involving an accountant who owned a bar. Unfortunately, the bar put him in contact with some dangerous people. They killed him. Does your husband have business interests outside his medical practice?"

She shook her head.

"No."

"He doesn't own a pharmacy?" I asked.

She considered and then drew in a slow breath.

"He dispenses pharmaceuticals through his clinic to his patients. It's a common practice."

I didn't know how common the practice was, but the Highway Patrol had put Hines's pharmacy under surveillance twice after finding significant quantities of opioids in the cars of patients who had visited his clinic.

"Has his pharmacy had problems lately?" I asked. "Missing drugs, missing money, anything like that?"

"I wouldn't know," she said. "My husband prefers to keep his business life separate from our personal life."

"Tell me about your day yesterday," I said. "Where were you when your husband went missing?"

She hesitated.

"Why does that matter?"

I forced a smile to my lips.

"It's standard procedure," I said. "In cases like this, I have to consider every possibility. If someone has hurt your husband—and I don't have any evidence to indicate that yet—I'd like to eliminate you as a suspect right away. So tell me about your day yesterday. Where'd you go, who'd you talk to, what'd you do?"

She closed her eyes.

"I spent the day at home. My husband went to work at 7:30 AM, and my children got on the bus for school at 8:15 AM. They came home at 3:25 in the afternoon."

I wrote down the times and then glanced at her.

"This is great," I said. "I appreciate the detail. What'd you do at home?"

She closed her eyes and then tilted her head to the side as she sighed.

"Is that necessary?" she asked. I nodded. "I was exercising."

"All day?" I asked, lowering my chin.

"My personal trainer came at nine. We had a very thorough workout that lasted until 2:30."

Five and a half hours. That would have been a thorough workout.

"Did your husband know about your workouts?"

She didn't answer, but it didn't matter. Her trainer didn't stay there for five and a half hours for the exercise. Mrs. Hines and I spoke for another twenty minutes to fill in details, but I learned little new. Forty-five minutes after sitting down, I escorted her from the building. After that, I drove to Hines's clinic. The doctor wasn't in, but the nurse practitioners and two physician assistants were, and they were seeing patients. I didn't stay long, but they confirmed that Dr. Hines had gone in yesterday morning and then disappeared at 2:45 in the afternoon. They had tried calling him, but he hadn't answered his phone.

When I asked the office manager whether she suspected a patient might have hurt him or whether the clinic was missing any drugs or prescription pads, she referred me to the clinic's general counsel and suggested that I'd need a warrant if I pursued that line of questioning. It wasn't the first time someone representing a shady business had stonewalled me during an investigation, and it wouldn't be the last. I didn't care. Secrets had a way of coming into the open during missing-persons cases, so I'd find out what I needed to know soon enough.

Dr. Hines's Lexus was still in the parking lot out front, so I snapped pictures of that. The interior looked clean, none of the windows were broken, and it didn't look like anyone had disturbed the car. Wherever he had gone, someone had given him a ride. After that, I drove to the Hines family's home and talked to his neighbors. They all agreed that the Hines family had adorable children, but nobody said they knew the couple well enough to speak about them personally. One neighbor mentioned, though, that Mrs. Hines had a frequent male guest while her husband was away. I figured that was her very attentive personal trainer. Nobody reported seeing the doctor since he left for work yesterday.

After checking out the house, I drove back to town and stopped to fill up my Volvo at a gas station. If I had found reason to suspect foul play, I would have written affidavits in support of search warrants for Dr. Hines's house, office, and financial records, but it looked as if he had just disappeared. There were no bloodstains or signs of struggle at his office, none of his neighbors had reported stalkers or signs of trouble at home, and the office manager at work had seemed to think everything was fine.

Nico Hines may have been a physician, but he sold prescription opioids to drug addicts. That was the story here. If I had to guess, he found out his wife was sleeping around on him and conducted a cost-benefit analysis. Depending on whether they had a prenuptial agreement, a divorce might have cost him millions. If he disappeared, though, he could take his fortune with him. He'd keep everything he had earned and hurt his duplicitous wife. From his perspective, that was a win-win.

The kids were the only problem. The family's neighbors implied that Dr. Hines was a devoted father who played with the kids often and coached his son's soccer team. I wondered whether he'd leave his kids. Then again, maybe they weren't his kids. Anything was possible. Until we found a body or signs that someone murdered him, he wasn't a priority. I had actual work to do.

***

Peyton Weldon shifted on his seat and then glanced over his shoulder to the backseat of his SUV. The rear tinted windows blocked most of the sunlight, leaving the rear seat—and his guest—shrouded in shadows. Dr. Hines didn't bother struggling against the restraints anymore. He knew the metal shackles would only cut into his skin.

"How you feeling, Doc?"

Hines said nothing, mostly because a ball gag kept him from being able to move his jaw. Peyton looked at the elementary school and then pulled out the doctor's cell phone to call 911. The dispatcher answered on the first ring.

"St. Augustine County Sheriff's Department," said a chipper voice. "What's your emergency?"

Peyton forced a tremble into his voice.

"I just drove past the elementary school on Fourth Street and saw a man with a black rifle walking toward the door. He had black hair, pale white skin, and he wore a black tactical vest. You need to send out officers now."

"Okay," said the woman, her voice taut. "Are you safe, and can you see the gunman still?"

"I'm still at the school. I think he saw me," he said, forcing his voice to break as he hit the down button on his window and reached for his pistol. He fired it at the ground outside. "Shit! He just shot at me!"

"Get to safety, sir," said the dispatcher. "I've got officers on the way."

"Thank you," said Peyton, his voice strained. He put the car in gear and accelerated hard. The engine roared, and the heavy SUV took off from the curb. Before parking two blocks away, he wiped the phone down and tossed it out the window. Then he looked at Dr. Hines before looking at his watch. Hines kicked and bucked and tried to scream, but few sounds came out. Peyton closed his window and pulled the magazine from his pistol.

"One kid dead," he said, pushing a round from the clip and then tossing it to the doctor. He did it again about ten seconds later. "That's a second kid."

He continued at ten-second intervals, flicking rounds at the doctor until his magazine ran dry. With each unspent round, the doctor flinched. Tears ran down his face.

"That's eight kids dead before the first police officer gets here," said Peyton, upon finishing his first magazine and reaching for a second from his pocket. He got through four more rounds before a Volvo station wagon screeched around a corner. An attractive blonde woman sat in the front seat, and she passed the SUV without a second glance. When the vehicle reached the school, its tires chirped as the driver skidded to a stop and jumped out, a pistol held in front of her.

Peyton looked at his watch.

"Two minutes and forty-four seconds," he said, looking back at the doctor. "That's a good response time. She must have been close. I wonder if she'll be that close when I do this for real and aim for your children."

Dr. Hines's face turned bright red as he struggled. This time, he kicked the door. Peyton shook his head and looked in the rearview mirror to make sure they were clear before pulling away from the curb.

"If you don't learn to cooperate, you'll have a rough couple of days," he said. Hines kicked the door again. Peyton shook his head and sighed. "Cheer up, buddy. You've got the power in this relationship. I don't want to hurt your family. I don't even want to hurt you. This is a job, and if you help me do it well, I'll leave before your kids ever meet me. If you don't, I'll be the last thing they ever see. Your choice, bud."

Chapter 26

As I pumped gas into my old Volvo, my phone rang. I didn't recognize the number, but it had a St. Louis area code. On another day, I might have let it go to voicemail, but I was working on a major case, components of which had happened in St. Louis. I slid my finger across the screen to answer and then held it to my ear.

"Joe Court," I said. "What's up?"

"This is Detective Court?"

It was a woman's voice, one I didn't recognize.

"Yeah. Who is this?"

"I'm Stacy Steinbrick with the Riverfront Times in St. Louis. How are you today?"

I closed my eyes and groaned under my breath.

"Your paper's probably great, but I'm not interested in subscribing."

"I'm not calling about that," she said. "As you know by now, there was a recent shooting in which several armed guards died at the Galleria. Are you working that case?"

I shook my head and wished I hadn't taken the call.

"I'm not, so if you want information, call the public information officer at the St. Louis County police headquarters. Sound good to you?"

"But you are working the shooting at Henderson Angus in St. Augustine. I hear the two are related."

She was right. The ladies who robbed the armored truck at the Galleria had sought medical care from Dr. Henderson at Henderson Angus, but we hadn't released that information to the media. She had a source. I looked down and then jumped as a gunshot echoed from somewhere nearby.

"Lose my number," I said. "I won't comment on an open case."

"What was that noise?" she asked. "It sounded like a gunshot."

I hung up and then called my dispatcher, my heart already beating faster. Before Trisha answered, an emergency message flashed across my screen. Muscles all over my body tensed, and a fluttery, almost nauseated feeling began growing in my gut.

Shots fired. Fourth and River Road. All officers respond.

If I had a police radio, its alarm would be screaming. Since I didn't, the gas station seemed eerily quiet. I shoved the nozzle back into its holder on the pump before finishing the transaction at the small touch screen. Within seconds of the message, I was in my car. The intersection of Fourth Street and River Road was only four or five blocks away, and I had driven past it half a dozen times in the past few days because it was on my path home. Nearly every time, I had seen kids playing on the playground or relaxing on the front lawn at a private elementary school.

My old Volvo wasn't built for speed, and the back end kicked out whenever I careened around a corner, but I didn't care. I sped toward the school and then slammed on my brakes. My tires chirped and skidded before biting into the concrete. The rear of my station wagon rose and then fell as its momentum waned.

The instant it stopped, I jumped out of the car, my pistol held in front of me. Then I grabbed my phone and dialed my dispatcher's number, my breath coming in quick spurts.

"Trisha, I'm at the school. Where's the shooter?"

"I don't know," she said. "Hold on. I'm patching you through to the emergency channel."

I waited a moment. Nothing seemed to happen, but then I heard someone's breath.

"Dispatch, I'm on my way," came Dave Skelton's voice through the speaker. "ETA three minutes."

"Understood, Dave," said Trisha. "Detective Court is on site and armed."

"What do you see?"

The voice sounded like Katie Martelle, but I couldn't tell on the radio.

"No movement," I said, already running toward the side of the school as beads of nervous sweat began running down my brow. "I'm wearing a white shirt and jeans. Take note when you get here. I'm approaching the east side. No sign of our suspect."

A siren shrieked somewhere in the distance. Then I heard two more. I rounded the east side of the building but still didn't see the shooter. I picked up my phone again and held it to my ear.

"Is the school locked down?" I asked.

"It is," said Trisha. A marked cruiser shot past me on the road. I waved as it screeched to a halt. Bob Reitz stepped out and then reached inside for a shotgun.

"What do you see?" he shouted.

"Nothing," I said. "Head east and around. I'll head west and meet you by the front entrance."

He nodded and started running. Another cruiser skidded to a halt on the corner of Third Street and River Road. Katie jumped out and sprinted toward me. I motioned her to follow. Bob reached the front entrance before we did. All of us were huffing and puffing.

"Could the shooter be inside?" asked Katie.

"We'll see," I said, looking to Bob. "You've got the shotgun, so you're taking point. Katie, you and I will follow. Sound good?"

They nodded. Bob had a radio on his shoulder, so he called Trisha and told her we were going in. She had the principal on the line and said he'd buzz us in. The three of us walked through silent hallways decorated with posters, drawings, paintings, and other projects. Kids should feel safe in school.

I hated knowing that children were hiding in classrooms around me. My throat felt tight, and my skin tingled all over.

No kids crowded the hallway, but I had heard the gunshot at the gas station. I kept expecting to turn a corner and find a child on the ground or a man with a gun. I felt almost sick.

The halls were empty, though, and we left about ten minutes after we arrived. By then, there were almost a dozen uniformed officers on the front lawn, preparing to go inside. Sheriff Kalil and George Delgado stood beside a black SUV on the street. Bob and Katie joined the other uniformed officers. They'd search the school room by room, but our shooter had disappeared.

I walked toward Delgado and the sheriff. My breath was more even than it had been, but my shoulders refused to relax. The feeling of intense wrongness pervaded the afternoon. Both men said hello to me.

"You can take a minute to catch your breath," said Kalil.

"I'm fine," I said. "I was the first officer to arrive. Bob arrived next. We ran around the building, but nobody saw anything. Then Bob, Katie, and I went inside. Again, though, we found nothing."

Delgado looked at the sheriff.

"Trisha said she heard a gunshot on the initial call," he said. "She's been a cop for a long time, so she knows what a gunshot sounds like."

"I heard it, too," I said. "I was getting gas at the BP station. Someone fired a gun, and it was close. This wasn't a crank call."

Kalil looked around. Aside from the school, houses stretched up and down the street. The BP station and a small strip mall were the closest businesses, but they were four blocks away. The sheriff considered me and then the uniformed officers.

"We need to knock on doors," he said. "We might have a domestic situation in a neighboring house."

"I agree," said Delgado. "To stay safe, everybody should partner up."

It was a fair idea.

"Did the caller describe our shooter?" I asked.

"He said the gunman has pale skin and black hair. Unfortunately, the caller hung up after the gunshot," said Kalil. "We've got his phone number, though, and Trisha's been trying to call him. He lives out on Pinehurst. I was thinking of going by his house to see if he made it home."

"If he lives on Pinehurst, he's rich," said Delgado. "You should send Joe. She might know him."

Kalil narrowed his eyes for a second. I straightened and clenched my jaw but said nothing.

"What does that mean?" asked the sheriff. I glanced at Delgado but tried to keep my face neutral.

"George is trying to make a joke. He thinks he's funny," I said, my lips flat. "Give me the address and I'll head out."

Kalil pulled out his cell phone.

"Caller was Nico Hines," he said, reading a message. "He lives at 14 Pinehurst Road. I can give you his phone number, too."

I straightened and drew in a sharp breath.

"Dr. Nico Hines?" I asked. The sheriff nodded. Even George went quiet.

"That's him," he said. "You recognize the name?"

"I do," I said. "George does, too."

Delgado's shoulders dropped for a second, but then he pulled them back up as he pressed his lips together.

"Dr. Hines is a dirtbag," said Delgado. "He used to be number three on our most-wanted list when I was sheriff. We've never been able to make a case against him, but he sells opioids to addicts at a pain management clinic. I've got a file on him half an inch thick."

"His wife, Kira Hines, reported him missing this morning," I said. "I've been looking for him all day, but I haven't had any luck. His wife is cheating on him with her personal trainer. I figured he found out and left town rather than divorce her."

The sheriff crossed his arms.

"He's obviously not left," he said. "Why would he be at the school?"

"Because he's got three kids," I said. "I talked to his neighbors earlier. Several remarked that he seemed like a good father. Maybe he wanted the school to evacuate so he could get the kids without his wife interfering."

The sheriff furrowed his brow.

"If he wanted the kids, why wouldn't he just pick them up?" he asked. "He could say they've got a dentist's appointment or something. Then he could drive off without his wife even knowing they were gone."

I sighed and closed my eyes.

"Maybe he's not on the pickup list," I said. "Or maybe he's having some kind of mental breakdown. I don't know."

"Mental breakdown or not, this was a shitty thing to do to a school," said the sheriff. He focused on me. "Find him."

"Will do," I said. The sheriff started toward our uniformed officers, but I spoke before he could get far. "Hey, boss." The sheriff turned and raised his eyebrows. "George mentioned his old most-wanted list. Vic Conroy used to be number one on that list, and now he's dead. Dr. Hines was number three, and now he's missing. Anybody else on that list dead?"

Delgado opened his eyes wide.

"Are you accusing me of something, Detective?"

"No," I said. "I'm asking a question."

"Just focus on the case ahead of you," said Kalil. "Keep the speculation to yourself. We don't need it."

"Sure," I said, forcing a smile to my face even as my annoyance built. "I'll see what I can do about tracking down the doctor's phone."

"You should have done that the moment his wife reported him missing," said Delgado. "If you had, maybe we wouldn't be here now."

I lowered my chin and narrowed my eyes.

"George, you're not the sheriff anymore," I said. "You don't get to second-guess my decisions."

"It's a good question. Why didn't you track Hines's phone down?" asked Kalil, crossing his arms. Before speaking, I clenched my jaw tight.

"I did my job, boss," I said. "I called his phone multiple times and left multiple messages, and I went by his house and office. I talked to his neighbors, his colleagues, and his employees. Nobody had seen anything. If I had suspected he was in danger or that he had committed a crime, I would have tracked his phone down, but he hadn't even been missing twenty-four hours. You would have done the same thing in my position."

Delgado opened his mouth to say something, but the sheriff interrupted him.

"Thank you for the explanation, Detective. Now you've got cause to take the next step," he said. "George, you're coming with me. We'll search the school room by room to make sure it's empty. You both clear on your assignments?"

Both Delgado and I nodded.

"Then get to it," he said. "Good luck."

I thanked him and walked back to my car, my face still warm. The sheriff was right. I had work to do. I might as well get to it.

Chapter 27

I drove back to my station and called Dr. Hines's cell phone from my office. As it had every other time I had called it, the phone went to voicemail, so I called his carrier's law enforcement line and told them I suspected him of making terroristic threats at an elementary school and needed his location data. They looked him up, but he had powered his phone down, so there was little we could do to find it. If he turned it on again, someone would call me.

After that, I pushed back from my desk and spun around as I thought. Dr. Hines was a dirtbag who sold drugs to anyone willing to pay him enough money. He had slipped through our attempts to prosecute him by claiming he provided his patients medical care in line with the standards of his profession. Our prosecutor could have fought him, but a prosecution would have required us to bring in medical experts to counteract his paid medical experts. The trial would have cost the county millions of dollars we didn't have, and even then we might lose.

Vic Conroy was a dirtbag, too. He also hurt people and brought an unsavory element into our town. With his death and his spouse's reluctance to continue his work, prostitution arrests would have been down across the region, and his former businesses would have stopped being cesspools of illegality. They might have even become assets to the area. Maybe I was paranoid, but all that made me wonder.

I stopped spinning and focused on my computer. St. Augustine County had a high per-capita murder rate, but because our population was so low, we didn't get too many murders in an average year. I called up every homicide and missing-person report in the past twelve months and started reading.

And that was when the fine hairs on the back of my neck started standing on end. In the past twelve months, three of St. Augustine's most unsavory residents had died or vanished. Dale Wixson murdered Vic Conroy, Dr. Nico Hines disappeared while at work, and Richard Clarke went missing while hiking on his own property.

Richard Clarke was the interesting figure in that bunch. He didn't sell drugs or pimp out young women; instead, he ran a church that promoted white supremacist ideology. He and his congregants held up signs at our Spring Fair and protested new construction in town. They were vile human beings, but they didn't break the law. In fact, Clarke had even run for Congress on a pro-segregation platform about twenty years ago and had won far more votes than I would have thought possible. Clarke didn't need to break the law; he had enough support to change the law to fit his worldview.

According to the case notes, George Delgado had worked Clarke's case but didn't get far with it. Clarke's family, friends, and church refused to cooperate, and Delgado had little interest in finding an old racist. Without a body on the ground or a sign that he had been abducted or hurt—or even a compliant family—I couldn't blame him. We couldn't investigate a crime without a minimal level of cooperation, and in Richard Clarke's case, we didn't even know whether we had a crime.

I pushed back from my desk and left my office. Trisha was still at the front desk. She smiled when she saw me.

"Hey, Joe," she said. "Have you found Nico Hines yet?"

"No. His phone's off, and he's not answering his messages," I said. "He'll turn up. Let me ask you something: have you noticed that St. Augustine's bad guys seem to be dropping like flies in the past year?"

For a second, she didn't react. Then she furrowed her brow.

"What do you mean?"

"Our bad guys. They're dying or disappearing," I said. "Dale Wixson murdered Vic Conroy, and Dr. Hines disappeared. I also found out Richard Clarke went missing a couple of months back."

She hesitated.

"You may be looking too much into this," said Trisha. "Wixson murdered Vic Conroy, but the case was closed.

Marcus did a good job on it. And as for Dr. Hines... he's still out there. You haven't found a body yet, have you?"

"No, but he's gone all the same," I said, shaking my head and considering how I wanted to say this. "I've worked in St. Augustine for seven years now, and in those seven years, we closed some big cases. Despite everything we did and everything we knew about them, Conroy and Hines always slipped away, but now they're both out of the picture. So is Richard Clarke. He may not have broken the law, but he hurt people. With his disappearance, three of the biggest problem children in the area have disappeared in less than a year."

Again, Trisha paused. Then she drew in a breath and leaned forward.

"Be careful of what you're saying, Joe," she said, her voice low as the smile slid from her face. "You left this place with a cloud over your head, and our new sheriff welcomed you back into the fold, anyway. With good reason, you don't like or trust some of our colleagues. I get that, but don't you think it's time to bury the hatchet instead of trying to dig it in deeper?"

I straightened and tightened my jaw for a moment before forcing my lips to curl into a tight smile.

"Okay. Message received."

I wanted to argue that I wasn't overreacting or speaking ill of our colleagues, but it wouldn't have gotten me anywhere. However I looked at it, we had genuine cause for concern.

If one bad guy had gone missing, I wouldn't have thought anything of it. Three, though, was a pattern, and I intended to prove it.

My jaw was set as I left the building and walked to my car. Richard Clarke's Church of the White Steeple owned a two-hundred-acre piece of rural Missouri. It was hillier than my property but just as pretty. Unfortunately, the church had ringed its land with corrugated metal barriers and barbed wire like some kind of trashy fortress.

I drove for half an hour until I reached their driveway. As was custom at the church, I parked outside their gate and honked my horn three times and waited. Five minutes later, a young blonde woman on a four-wheeler drove out and asked what I wanted. I flashed my badge at her and said I needed to talk to Michael Clarke—Richard's son. She seemed wary, but she called in my request on her radio and then told me he'd be out shortly. I thanked her and sat on the hood of my car to wait. Five minutes later, a dusty white minivan came down the gravel road and stopped on the other side of the gate. Michael Clarke—the driver—rolled down his window and talked to the girl before stepping out and looking to me. The girl drove away on the four-wheeler.

"Mr. Clarke," I said. "I'm Detective Joe Court. We met about a year ago."

"I remember," he said. "My dad took a real shine to you. He always thought it was a shame you weren't willing to get pregnant for the cause."

I forced myself to smile even as I shuddered inside.

"Yeah, I remember. He thought I'd make beautiful Aryan babies."

"You still can," said Michael. "There's always time, and I bet I could find you a willing husband right here on the property. We've got a lot of fine young men available."

"Some other time," I said. "I'm here to talk about your dad. You have any idea where he is?"

The smile left Michael's face. He crossed his arms.

"My father's dead. I told you people that months ago, but nobody did anything. We can't even bury him because we don't know where his body is. How can a man resurrect when Christ returns if he has no body?"

I couldn't answer his theological question, but I took a notepad from my pocket.

"I can't change the past, but I can help you out now," I said. "Why do you think your father's dead if you don't have a body?"

"We have blood," said Michael. "Or at least we had blood. That was months ago. It's rained since then."

Delgado's reports hadn't mentioned that. I leaned forward slightly.

"Okay," I said. "Tell me about the blood."

"It was in the woods," said Michael. "There wasn't a lot, but it was on some trees and grass. If you ask me, I think somebody attacked him in the woods and then hid the body."

"Did you show the police the blood?"

Michael drew in a breath through his nose. His face was growing redder.

"I tried to," he said. "Your detective and two uniformed officers walked onto the property, looked around, and said they weren't comfortable. They were worried for their safety, but they were as safe as a babe in its mother's arms."

I shook my head.

"They felt threatened for a reason. How many people were here?"

Michael's eyes shifted up and to his left, and he cocked his head to the side.

"Twenty to thirty, maybe," he said. "Our secretary has the exact count and a registry with everyone's name and contact information. Your detective didn't even ask for it."

I forced a smile to my face.

"How many of them were armed?"

Michael snickered and lowered his chin.

"Honey, do you have any idea what kind of world we live in?" he asked. "We are in a fight between civilization and barbarism. We won't win that fight if we're unarmed."

"So everyone had a gun?"

He sighed.

"That's a fair assumption."

I saw why Delgado hadn't wanted to pursue the case.

"I'm here now, and I'm talking to you," I said. "Who do you think killed your father?"

"I haven't got the foggiest idea," he said. "And I'm not interested in helping you. Our community has moved on. I love my dad, but I've made peace with his death, and I will not let you drag his name through the mud."

I held up a hand with my palm toward him in a stop motion.

"No one will drag his name through the mud. If your father is dead, I'll do my best to find out what happened to him. That's my job."

"I don't care," said Michael. "Now get off our property. If you come back, you'd better have a warrant."

I stepped back.

"I'm sorry about your father, and I'm sorry you feel my department didn't handle his disappearance well," I said. "These cases are never easy, and the remoteness of your church makes it harder still. I can't guarantee that I'll find out what happened to your father, but if you cooperate, I promise to do my best. Please let me do my job."

He looked at the ground and spit before shaking his head.

"Your department has had its chance. We're done here. Now get off my property. After our founder's death, my people have become trigger happy when they see me in distress. I'd hate for you to have an accident, especially if it's preventable."

I let my eyes dart to the surrounding woods, wondering how many congregants of that church had rifles pointed at me at that moment. Then I held up my hands to show him I wasn't a threat before backing up toward my Volvo's door.

"If you change your mind, you know where to reach me."

"I do," said Michael. "I won't change my mind, though. Thanks for coming by, Detective."

I got in my car, and backed onto the road. Only when the gate was a distant spot behind me did I breathe easier. I didn't know what had happened to Richard Clarke, but this wasn't right. My county had a problem, and I intended to find out how big it was before more people died or disappeared.

Chapter 28

After leaving the Clarke's property, I drove back to my station and found a message from George Delgado on my office voicemail. A uniformed officer had found Nico Hines's phone on the sidewalk half a block from the elementary school. The phone was locked, so he couldn't open it without Hines's fingerprint, but at least we knew where it was now.

As I often did when I wanted to think, I pushed back from my desk and leaned back in my chair. The situation made little sense. A lot of suspects threw out their cell phones so we couldn't track them, but if Hines didn't want us tracking him, why had he called the school on his own phone? He could have gone to a convenience store, purchased a burner phone for cash, and then made the same call anonymously. He could have disappeared.

By calling us on his own phone, though, he had tied himself to a crime—a felony in this case—and he got nothing out of it. His kids were out of his reach, his wife was still cheating on him, and now he had lost an expensive phone. He was too smart for that. We were missing something important.

I wrote some notes and let my mind drift. Dr. Hines had hurt children at an elementary school with his phone call, but they weren't my only school-age victims. Makayla Simpson was, too, and I hadn't checked on her case for a while. I called her file up on my computer. Detective Delgado and Shaun Deveraux, our prosecutor, had successfully petitioned the court for a search warrant for Sean Kirby's cell phone, which allowed us to get the young felon's call history and text messages.

Delgado believed that Makayla was a drug dealer who had been hurt by a rival, and Sean Kirby's text messages certainly pointed in that direction. The messages led Delgado to Tyvos Sizer and Nick Moore, two gangbangers who worked for a major drug organization in St. Louis. The three of them had planned the entire assault over text message. Delgado had sworn out arrest warrants against them both, so hopefully the police in St. Louis would catch them before they hurt anybody else.

After reading through Delgado's reports, I pushed back from my desk and crossed my arms. Delgado had ID'd the bad guys, but I still had to wonder why it had come to this and why Makayla still refused to cooperate. With the evidence we had against them, Tyvos, Nick, and Sean would spend at least the next seven years in prison. By the time they got out, she'd be an adult with a life of her own. She could change her name and disappear if she wanted. They would have ceased to be a threat to her.

Moreover, she didn't have to worry about the drugs in her locker, either, because the prosecutor didn't think the vice principal's search would hold up in court. Despite all that, she refused to talk to us. There was something more here, and until we had the whole story, I was worried.

I worried even more for St. Augustine and my department. Someone was knocking off bad guys in town. Richard Clarke had embarrassed the entire county with his racist signs and protests at the Spring Fair, Vic Conroy had turned a corner of the county into a cesspool of peddled flesh, and Dr. Hines had turned hundreds—if not thousands—of men and women into drug addicts. All three men were now gone, and all of their cases had serious open questions. Despite that, the sheriff wasn't interested in looking into them.

After thinking in my office for an hour and getting nowhere, I shut down my computer, got in my car, and drove home. When I reached the house, Roy barked at me from the dog run in the back. Usually, he lightened my mood, but today his powers had little effect. We went for a walk, and then we went inside for dinner. I slept fitfully that night and woke up at a little after six the next morning feeling more tired than I had the night before.

I got into work right on time to sit through the morning briefing. Unfortunately, I didn't have a whole lot to do. The FBI had taken over the shooting at Henderson Angus, Delgado was still working Makayla's assault, and nobody wanted to hear about my suspicions surrounding Vic Conroy, Richard Clarke, or Nico Hines.

At twenty after eight, I headed to my office and sat down to think. My boss hadn't given me a new case, but I wanted to do something, so I read through the emails, reports, and other communications between Special Agent Costa and his team. They were still looking for their four blonde Jane Does, but they were focusing on the forensics and technical details. A little old-fashioned grunt work might do them some good.

St. Augustine was about an hour south of St. Louis, but we still shared information with the city and county police departments where possible. I called up the appropriate database and searched for incident reports from the past week involving blonde women. Unsurprisingly for an area with a million residents, I got a lot of hits, so I narrowed my search to include complaints of home invasions, robberies, and reports of squatters. That narrowed things considerably.

After reading reports for an hour, I had a list of nine locations our perps could have hidden in. All of them were long shots, but Sheriff Kalil hadn't given me another assignment. I got in my car and drove north on the interstate to the city and then hit surface roads for the next thirty minutes to the first address on my list. It was a shuttered bodega on Nineteenth Street. Thick wrought-iron bars and plywood covered the windows. Weeds popped through cracks on the sidewalk. A caller had said a blonde woman with tanned skin had tried to break in two days ago, but I couldn't see any signs of habitation, so I moved on.

For the next two hours, I checked out locations on the northeast side of town before moving west to more prosperous areas. The first three spots were empty buildings, but the fourth and fifth had people living inside. They seemed sober, the homes they inhabited were abandoned, and they didn't attack me. I left them alone. Removing them would be a civil matter.

My sixth location was a small commercial warehouse building near the airport. According to my notes, a realtor had called the county police after the alarm malfunctioned. A pair of uniformed officers had then walked around the building but found it closed tight. Two guys who worked at the plumbing supply warehouse down the street, though, had reported seeing two unfamiliar blonde women walking alongside the road within the past twenty-four hours. It was worth following up on.

I parked in front of the building and checked to make sure my badge was visible on the lanyard around my neck before getting out of my car. The air was cold, but not cold enough for my breath to turn to frost. The street out front—wide enough to accommodate three semitrailers—was empty. No one had parked in front of or beside the warehouse, and from the street, it looked closed tight. Had the location been better, it could have been a kitchen designer's showroom. In the flight path of every plane going to the airport, though, it was loud and looked forlorn.

I tried pulling open the frosted glass front door, but it didn't budge, and I couldn't see anything through it. Nothing around me moved, so I walked down the side of the building and then stopped when I reached the rear parking lot. A maroon Honda Odyssey minivan was parked by the rear door. Someone had removed the front license plate, but it looked like the one stolen from the parking lot of Vic Conroy's old truck stop.

I looked toward the warehouse. The back of the building had a steel security door with a deadbolt and a loading dock with a white rolling door. I walked toward the minivan and found blood spatter on the back door. Adrenaline began flowing through me. My heart started beating faster, and my breath became shallow. I ducked behind the minivan, putting it between me and the warehouse, as I pulled out my cell phone to call for help.

Then I heard the gunshot.

I dialed 911 as I ripped my pistol from its holster. The dispatcher picked up before the phone rang a single time.

"911. What's your emergency?"

"This is Detective Joe Court of the St. Augustine County Sheriff's Department. I'm at the Hanley Industrial Court in Brentwood. I have multiple armed suspects and shots fired. These are the ladies who robbed the armored car at the Galleria. My Volvo station wagon is in front of the building.

Send me everybody you've got, and let them know there's an armed law enforcement officer on site. Also, call Special Agent Bryan Costa of the FBI. And do it now."

I waited for the dispatcher to respond.

"What department are you with?"

"St. Augustine County," I said. "I'm working a case with the FBI. Send me some help."

The instant the words left my lips, the warehouse's rear door opened, and a blonde woman with a tactical rifle stepped out and looked left and right. I dropped my phone and raised my pistol.

"Police officer!" I shouted. "Drop your weapon!"

She dropped to a knee and lined up a shot.

"Shit," I said, squeezing my trigger twice. She was fifty yards away, and I didn't expect to hit her, but I needed to buy some time to get to cover. She didn't even flinch. I dove to the ground as her rifle opened up. Round after round slammed into the minivan above me as I crawled toward its rear. The glass broke, and then the car dipped as a tire burst. The sound was deafening. I crawled backwards onto the grass behind the building and rolled into a shallow drainage ditch. My heart pounded.

Then the gunfire stopped.

I looked up and saw a woman running. Then another woman with blond hair stepped into the doorframe. My hands trembled, and the muscles in my legs tingled, screaming at me to run and get the hell out of there. I couldn't leave, though. They had Lily Henderson and Cassie Prescott. I refused to abandon them.

I shimmied forward across the grass and crept toward the parking lot, trying to avoid drawing attention to myself. The women stepped back, leaving the doorway dark. These ladies had me outgunned, but if I could reach my phone, I could at least call this in. As I reached the edge of the parking lot, a car honked in front of the building, and then it sounded as if a door had opened. I waited a moment, but nobody came out of the rear of the warehouse, so I pushed up and ran, grabbing my phone on the way to the warehouse's rear door.

My heart thudded into my chest as I pressed my back to the stucco exterior near the rear door. The 911 dispatcher had ended our call. Somewhere in the distance, though, I heard sirens.

Then I heard a moan inside the building. I peeked around the corner. A pistol barked, and a round buzzed past me as I scrambled back to the relative safety of the building's exterior.

"If you follow us, Cassie will die," shouted a voice from inside. "We'll let Lily go as soon as we can."

"Let her go now," I shouted. "Let them both go. I've got officers on the way. I can hear their sirens already."

Instead of answering, the woman inside fired her pistol again. Someone gasped and cried out in pain. Without thinking, I vaulted around the corner, my pistol held in front of me. The interior looked dark, but I swept the room with my weapon, anyway, ready to fire at anything that moved.

I had stepped into an office space with big windows overlooking an empty warehouse. A blonde woman sprinted toward the front door. I couldn't chase her, though, because Cassie Prescott sat duct-taped to a black office chair in the middle of the floor. Her face was pale, and her eyes were closing. She looked sick. Dark blood glistened on her legs and abdomen from separate gunshot wounds. Without treatment, each would probably be fatal.

"Shit," I said, running toward her and kneeling. There was a plastic canvas sack with a red cross on its exterior beside her. It was a trauma kit, the kind paramedics might carry. I ripped open a green vacuum-sealed package of QuikClot Combat Gauze and pressed it hard against Cassie's leg. Then I grabbed a second package, tore it open, and pressed it to her abdomen. The gauze soaked up her blood like a sponge, so I grabbed more gauze and held that. Her breath was shallow.

As I pressed against the wound on her thigh, I grabbed my phone and called 911 again. The sirens were closer, but I needed help now. Once the dispatcher answered, I gave her my location and told her I needed an ambulance for a victim with multiple gunshot wounds. Then I dropped my phone and focused on Cassie again.

My entire body trembled, and I felt sick to my stomach. These ladies knew what they were doing. If they had killed Cassie, I would have chased them. Instead, they wound-ed her enough that she'd die without help and then left a trauma kit beside her so I could try to save her life. I had always tried to leave my feelings out of my work. I had tried to be dispassionate and cool, to observe the things around me without allowing them to affect me. But now a young woman was bleeding in my arms. My objectivity disappeared. They had made this personal.

Chapter 29

Peyton didn't know what the men and women on his list had done, but that mattered little. A client gave him a name and occasionally a method, and Peyton provided a quote for a bespoke service. He had murdered Richard Clarke by shooting him in the head from a distance and then hiding the body—as per the contract. He had paid a destitute drug user named Dale Wixson five thousand dollars cash to shoot Vic Conroy, and then he had killed Dale. Dr. Nico Hines's death had to look like a suicide.

He had three names left on his list. Once he finished, he could finally leave this shit hole town and county for good. This had been a big job, and his client had paid him well, but if he ever had to step foot in rural Missouri again, it'd be too soon. He missed home. Prior to this job, he had never thought he could miss Seattle's gloom, but he did. The weather here was too sunny, and the drivers here were reckless enough that he risked his life every time he sat behind the wheel of his car. Soon he'd go home.

He parallel parked on the street about two blocks from his target's office in downtown St. Augustine. This part of town had older two- and three-story brick buildings, all of which were connected like row houses in a major city. The first floors held fashionable boutiques, candy shops, and specialty gift stores, while the upper stories held apartments and condos. The restaurants nearby cost more than most of those in downtown Seattle, and the bars and pubs did a brisk business even on weeknights.

The town's prosperous tourist trade had surprised and impressed Peyton upon his arrival, but the novelty had worn off when he learned he had to wait in line fifteen or twenty minutes for a single-person table on a Thursday evening for dinner at most of the bars.

Still, the town's streets were clean; the service people were polite; and the parks, trails, lakes, and other outdoor areas were expansive and cheap to visit. Something here was wrong, though. For one thing, St. Augustine had more money than it ought to. It was a tiny town on the Mississippi River. It shouldn't have had its own amphitheater or arts district. For another, he hadn't found a single panhandler or drug dealer. Tourists loved drugs, and panhandlers loved tourists. Even if the police arrested every vagabond they saw, they wouldn't get everybody. And yet it seemed they had. That unnerved him.

His target today was Arthur Murdoch, an older man who owned a significant portion of the waterfront south of downtown St. Augustine. Like all of his targets, Peyton had studied Arthur for the past few weeks. Arthur, from all

Peyton had learned, was a conscientious, kind, and understanding landlord who provided decent, affordable housing for many of St. Augustine's blue-collar workers.

He and his extended family lived on a two-hundred-acre compound overlooking the Mississippi River, but that was the only piece of luxury property he owned. Still, none of the porches or roofs on his rental homes sagged, none of the commercial buildings he owned and managed had water stains or other signs of distress, and he had turned the only vacant lots he owned into community gardens. Murdoch made a tidy profit on his properties, but he had only evicted half a dozen tenants in the past five years. The old man may not have been a saint, but he exemplified the compassionate business ideals espoused and venerated by past generations of affluent men and women.

It was no wonder someone wanted him dead.

Peyton's client hadn't restricted the methods he could use to kill Murdoch, but he didn't want to get caught or kill those he didn't have to if he could help it. He had considered sneaking onto the businessman's family compound and shooting him with a rifle from five or six hundred yards—just as he had done to Richard Clarke—but a murder like that would draw attention he didn't need. Nobody cared about a racist asshole who'd created a church to dodge taxes, but a landlord who gave his tenants breaks on the rent when they lost their jobs mattered to an awful lot of people.

This murder had no room for mistakes, and it required a person to blame. As it happened, the perfect patsy was number five on Peyton's list.

Murdoch worked out of a second-story office above a place called Discount Smokes. The store carried a few cigars and half a dozen different pipe tobaccos, but mostly it sold cigarettes by the carton.

Murdoch wouldn't be in his office today, though. He was busy relighting the pilot light on a water heater in an apartment complex on the edge of town. Peyton had called in the complaint half an hour ago, pretending to be the son of one of the residents, and Murdoch had left to fix the problem. He was a good man. He didn't play games and pretend to fix things when he hadn't, and he didn't mistreat those who worked for him or those who lived or worked in his buildings. If a resident needed help, Murdoch did everything he could to help. And if he couldn't help, he found someone who could.

When he reached the smoke shop, Peyton walked down the alley that ran alongside it, stepping across what seemed like several hundred cigarette butts, before emerging in a small rear parking lot, where he found three doors. One led to the smoke shop, a second led to a storage closet, and a third had steps that led to the offices above. He picked the deadbolt on the correct door and walked up the steps to his target's office.

The room was a mess. It had brick walls painted white and three industrial metal desks but only one chair. Since it had no windows, the only light came from a rectangular fluorescent light on the ceiling. Murdoch had attached brown pegboard to two of the walls and inserted hooks in every hole. On those hooks hung hundreds of keys representing the doors of dozens of small apartment and commercial buildings.

Peyton ignored all that and reached into his pocket for Ziploc bags containing the evidence he needed to incriminate his fifth target. He stayed two minutes in the office, but those two minutes were the culmination of several weeks of surveillance. By the time he left, he was one step closer to going home.

Now he had to get an alcoholic drunk. That part, at least, was easy.

***

Nadine gripped the steering wheel tight. Her gut churned, and a worried frown refused to disappear from her face. On the middle seat, Lily cried, but neither Robin nor Ursa tried to comfort her. They were too busy focusing on Wendy, who lay in the back. She had torn open her wound and was bleeding. Worse, her temperature had risen again. Everything was falling apart, and Nadine was ready to break.

She looked in the rearview mirror.

"Lily, honey," she said, trying to smile. "Everything will be okay. They're taking Cassie to the hospital. I need you to calm down."

Her crying became louder.

"Let's take some big balloon breaths," said Nadine, remembering something she had seen Cassie do with her. "Breathe in through your nose and feel your belly grow like a balloon. Then let it out and feel your belly shrink."

Lily screamed harder still.

"Just shut up, Nadine," said Robin. "It's not working."

Nadine closed her mouth and listened to the kid cry. Her throat felt tight, and her skin felt hot. It shouldn't have ended like this.

"I can't stop the bleeding," said Ursa from the green SUV's rear seat. They had stolen the vehicle from a used-car lot in the city and then a license plate from a matching car in the parking lot of a mall in west St. Louis County. The car had almost three hundred thousand miles on it, but the engine felt strong and the brakes worked. That was all she could ask for, given the circumstances.

Robin closed her eyes and brought her hands to her forehead.

"I don't know what to do."

Nadine looked in the rearview mirror and considered her friends.

"She needs a doctor," she said. "We can't help her anymore."

"We tried that route, Nadine," said Ursa. "We couldn't find one."

"I know," said Nadine. She gritted her teeth and then sighed. "She needs to go to a hospital."

Aside from Lily's crying, the car went silent. Robin rubbed the little girl's back but said nothing.

"If she goes to the hospital, the police will arrest her," said Ursa. "They'll charge her with murder. We've already talked about this."

"But she'll live. We owe her that."

Robin looked back at her sister.

"She said she'd rather die than go to prison."

"Then she can kill herself in prison if she wants. That's her choice," said Nadine. "I won't let my friend die if I can help it."

The other ladies said nothing until Nadine pulled onto I-70. Finally, though, Robin drew in a breath. She had tears in her eyes, but it looked as if she were trying to hold them in.

"I don't want my sister to die."

The weight left Nadine's shoulders. Even Wendy seemed to relax some.

"Good," said Nadine. "We'll put her somewhere public and call the police. They'll get an ambulance."

Both Ursa and Robin nodded. Nadine drove for a few minutes and then pulled off the interstate and drove to St. Louis Community College. The school's parking lots were full, but the parking lot outside the Baptist church and community park across the street were empty. Lily had stopped crying by then, but Robin kept rubbing her back as Ursa and Nadine carried Wendy to a picnic table on the church's lawn. Then Nadine called 911 on her burner phone.

"My name is Gail Parkwood," she said, giving the name on her fake ID when she was in high school. "I'm at St. Louis Community College, and I just saw something weird. Three women carried another woman from the back of a white paneled van and put her on top of a picnic table. They're at a little park across the street. It's by a church."

The dispatcher seemed incredulous and asked her to repeat what she'd said. Nadine elaborated by saying all the women were blonde and young. That seemed to get her attention. She said she'd route officers and an ambulance there immediately. Nadine thanked her and hung up before the dispatcher could ask for additional contact details.

They left Wendy at the park and drove about a block and a half to an expansive parking lot outside an office building to wait. Within five minutes, the first police officer arrived. It was a single patrol car, but he saw Wendy and then ran back to his cruiser for something, probably a first-aid kit. He stayed at Wendy's side until the paramedics arrived a few minutes later. They put her on a back brace, carried her into their ambulance, and then drove off with their lights and siren blaring. Robin cried.

"She'll live," said Ursa, squeezing her friend's shoulder. "It'll be okay."

Robin looked at Lily.

"Lily's breath smells sweet," she said, rubbing tears out of her eyes. "Cassie warned us about that. We should have left her with Wendy."

Nadine looked in the rearview mirror and shook her head. Her gut churned, and her breath seemed to catch in her chest every time she spoke, but she forced herself to sound calm.

"We still need her," she said. "As long as we've got her, the police will hesitate before coming after us for fear of her getting caught in the crossfire. We've got one more job to do, and then we're done. We'll send her home after that. She'll be fine. Understand?"

The other woman sat straighter and nodded.

"Good," said Nadine. "One more job, and then we disappear. First, though, we need somewhere quiet to lie low for a while. Robin, start looking for homes for sale. It's preferable if they're rural, and it's better if the pictures don't have furniture. That means the homeowner's already moved out. Ursa, call your friend with the armored-car company. With Wendy out, we'll need some backup. Offer her fifty grand cash for her help. We're going to finish this last job, and then we'll retire."

Both ladies got to work on their cell phones. Nadine watched them and knew this was likely all in vain. After what they had done, they were all going to end up dead on a slab sooner rather than later. It'd be worth it if she could get her husband her share of the proceeds. One day, Nadine hoped Charlie would understand why she had done what she had. He deserved a better life than she could give him on her salary. If her death meant he got the care he deserved, that was the price she'd pay. He was worth it.

Chapter 30

A pair of uniformed police officers arrived at the warehouse within moments of my call, but the paramedics took a couple more minutes. They took over for me, and I stepped back. I had blood all over my clothes and on my hands and face, so one of the uniformed officers got bottles of water, paper towels, and wet wipes out of his car. The wipes, towels, and water couldn't wash all the blood, but they were better than nothing. Cassie was alive as the paramedics took off, but her breath was shallow and rapid, and her face was pale. St. Louis had excellent hospitals, but their doctors weren't miracle workers. I hoped they'd be good enough.

A pair of county detectives came next. I introduced myself, told them what had happened, and asked them to call Special Agent Bryan Costa with the FBI and my boss. By the time Costa arrived, I was sitting in the back of a police cruiser, waiting for word about Cassie, while county officers worked the scene.

"You okay, Joe?"

I glanced at Costa and shrugged.

"Yeah, I'm fine," I said. "I didn't expect to find anybody when I came out here. I was just trying to cover all our bases."

Costa straightened and looked toward the warehouse.

"This was better than covering our bases," he said. "It was good police work. We should have done it ourselves. I plan to write a letter of commendation to Sheriff Kalil on your behalf."

I smiled but couldn't put much enthusiasm behind it. "Thanks."

He nodded but said nothing. I laced my fingers together and leaned forward.

"Any word on Cassie?"

"She's alive because of you," he said. "Last I heard, they were prepping her for emergency surgery. Surgery is always tricky, but she's young and strong, and they got to her within minutes of her being shot."

The knot in my belly loosened.

"I'm glad," I said before sighing. "They took Lily. I couldn't stop them. They shot Cassie in front of me so I'd be forced to help her. Then they ran. It was cold-blooded."

"It is," said Costa. "We've got them on the run, though. The St. Louis County dispatcher got a call about fifteen minutes ago about a blonde woman who was dumped on a picnic table near the St. Louis Community College. We haven't ID'd her yet, but she sounds like one of our perps."

"She dead?" I asked, raising my eyebrows.

"Close," said Costa. "Paramedics said she had been shot and looked sick. Her temperature was elevated, and her breathing was irregular and weak. They got her to the hospital quickly, but you never know what'll happen. I was on my way over. You want to go?"

I looked down.

"I'm covered in blood," I said.

"Stick around, then. I'll be right back."

I didn't have anywhere else to go, so I agreed. He left and came back about twenty-five minutes later with a plastic bag from Walmart.

"I didn't know your size, so I got you mediums," he said, looking into his bag. "Here's a shirt, pants, and socks. I assumed your shoes were okay. Before you look at anything, realize that I know nothing about women's fashion."

I smiled and took the bag and looked inside.

"You're not wrong about your fashion knowledge," I said, "but this is great. Thank you."

"My SUV has tinted windows if you want to change. Just put your blood-stained clothes in the bag."

I thanked him again and then changed into the baggy gray sweatshirt and black pants he had bought for me. The clean clothes made me feel better. Afterwards, I gave my blood-stained clothes to a forensic technician with the county police, and Agent Costa and I drove to Mercy Hospital on Ballas Road in western St. Louis County. There, we sat in the ER's lobby and waited for news. About two hours after we arrived, a physician came out and took us aside. He had a grim, tired expression on his face. Before he even opened his mouth, I knew somebody was dead.

"Who'd you work on?" I asked. "Cassie Prescott or a Jane Doe?"

"Your Jane Doe," he said. "Somebody else must have Cassie."

I exhaled a slow breath and closed my eyes. Agent Costa seemed to breathe easier, too.

"What happened to the Jane Doe?" asked Costa.

"My team did what we could, but she was in very poor shape upon arrival," he said. "The patient presented with a penetrating wound to the lower left abdomen and sepsis. Her oxygen levels were extremely low, and there were signs that her organs were shutting down. We did everything we could, but she was too far gone. If we had gotten to her yesterday or the day before, we might have saved her, but she died on the table. I'm sorry."

I sighed and looked down, having expected that.

"Before you send her to the morgue," said Costa, "can you do me a favor and take a picture of her face with my cell phone?"

The surgeon cocked his head.

"Excuse me?"

"She's a suspect in multiple homicides," he said. "A picture would help us ID her."

The doctor hesitated.

"I guess I can do that," he said. He took Agent Costa's phone and then returned about ten minutes later after taking several photos. We thanked him for his time and work. I sat down to wait for news about Cassie Prescott, while Costa sent the pictures to his technical team. Half an hour later, he went to get coffee and came back with his phone to his ear. I waited until he finished his call before speaking.

"They out of coffee?"

His lips curled into a tight smile as he shook his head.

"I didn't get that far," he said. "One of my techs called. They've identified our Jane Doe as Wendy Brady. She's thirty-four, and she lives in Belleville, Illinois. It's just across the river, so she's a local. She's never married, but her sister, Robin, lives with her children down the street from her."

I crossed my arms.

"Is her sister a blonde?"

"Not naturally," said Costa. "But neither is Wendy. We're still early, but I've got six agents digging into her life right now. We'll search her home as soon as we can and show her picture to Cassie when she's out of surgery."

I looked toward the sliding automatic doors that led into the ER.

"Assuming she survives," I said.

"Yeah," said Costa. "Like I said earlier, though, Cassie's young and fit, and paramedics got to her right after she was shot. She's got a good chance."

I didn't know whether I shared his optimism, but I still appreciated his take on the situation. As we waited, he got updates from his agents about things going on in the field, but little of it affected me or my work.

Unfortunately, Costa's search team found little of interest anywhere in Wendy's house. She didn't even have weapons. They did find several boxes of platinum blonde hair dye beneath the sink in the bathroom, though. A forensics team would comb through everything, but, aside from the hair care products, it looked like the search was a bust.

Shortly after we got calls about the search at Wendy's home, Julie Prescott—Cassie's sister—and their parents came into the ER. All three looked flustered, and they begged the front desk nurse for details about their loved one, but she didn't have any to give.

As the sun went down, I stepped outside the building and called Preston Cain, a friend and former colleague, from a spot beneath the covered awning out front. It was a pretty evening.

"Hey, dude," I said. "It's Joe. I'm stuck on a case in St. Louis. You mind swinging by my house and feeding Roy?"

"Sure, that's no problem," he said. "Shelby made chili for dinner. I can put a bowl in your fridge while I'm at your house."

I smiled.

"I wish I had more friends like you guys."

He laughed.

"She and I are pretty special," he said, then paused. "You doing okay? You sound tired."

"I've had better days," I said before tilting my head to the side. "I've had worse ones, too, though. I'm in the ER at Mercy Hospital in St. Louis with an FBI agent. We're hoping to talk to a woman when she comes out of surgery."

Preston whistled.

"You live a far more exciting life than I do, Joe."

"Excitement's overrated," I said. "I'd settle for simple."

"One day, I hope you get it."

I smiled and thanked him. We didn't talk long, but it felt good to talk to a friend. He said he'd tell Shelby hello for me, and I thanked him and hung up. Afterwards, I walked back inside and found a pair of doctors talking to the Prescott family. Cassie's mom had her hands to her face. Tears fell down her cheeks. Her father stood beside her. Julie Prescott smiled when she saw me.

"She's alive!"

I closed my eyes and exhaled a slow breath. Religion had never been a big part of my life, but I thanked God—or whoever might have been listening—and crashed onto a nearby chair.

Agent Costa and I waited another ten minutes before the doctor came to us with the news. Cassie was weak, but she had already asked to see us. We'd have five minutes with her once they got her into a regular room, but he warned us she was groggy and needed her rest. We said we understood.

An hour later, a nurse technician led us to Cassie's room. An oxygen tube snaked across her face and beneath her nose, while a monitor beside her bed showed her heart rate. It looked strong and regular.

Before letting us say a word, the nurse technician asked Cassie whether she felt able to talk to us. She nodded, so we stepped forward. The tech stepped back but didn't leave the room.

"Hey," I said. "I'm Joe. The old man beside me is Bryan. How are you feeling?"

"Tired," said Cassie. "They said you saved my life."

"I was just doing my job," I said. "Bryan's got a picture he needs to show you. Do you mind looking at it?"

She said no, so he flipped through the pictures on his phone until he found the one of Wendy Brady. Immediately, she closed her eyes.

"That's her," she said. "They wanted me to operate on her and take a bullet out of her abdomen, but I couldn't. I cleaned up her wound, though."

Costa flicked a finger across his phone again to a new picture, this one of Robin Brady, Wendy's sister.

"Her name is Robin," she said. "There was another woman named Ursa and a fourth woman named Nadine. They all had blond hair."

Costa thanked her before excusing himself from the room. I focused on Cassie.

273

"You did great," I said. "We'll talk later, but we don't want to stress you out now. And I'm sure your family would like to see you."

I started to go, but she reached for my hand.

"Did you get Lily?"

I forced myself to smile.

"Don't worry about Lily," I said. "Focus on getting well."

"She's sick," said Cassie. "She needs insulin. When I last saw her, I could smell ketones on her breath. And last night, she felt nauseated. Lily will die unless you get her. You don't have much time."

The weight that had lifted earlier began pushing down on me again, but I kept the smile on my face.

"You just had major surgery. Relax and get better. You did everything right. Now it's our turn to work."

She wanted to say something else, but I had already started leaving. The nurse technician stepped in to check her pulse and calm her down. My heart beat faster than I wanted, and a knot grew in my stomach. I found Bryan in the lobby, still on the phone. Once he saw me, he hung up.

"I'm sending Robin Brady's picture to every law enforcement official I can," he said. "If she shows her face in public again, we'll pick her up."

"We need to do better than hope she shows up," I said. "We need to anticipate where Robin and her friends are going and be there before they arrive. Lily Henderson is sick. We need to find her now."

Costa looked down.

"And where do you anticipate Robin and her friends will be?" he asked.

"No clue."

Chapter 31

Costa and I drove back to the warehouse where Robin, Wendy, and the others had stayed, but we learned little new. Prior to the ladies breaking in, the building had been empty for over a year, and it didn't have surveillance cameras. Moreover, the area had so many trucks and cars going to other businesses that no one noticed four women and their minivan at an empty warehouse.

I drove home at about eleven that night and found Roy sleeping on the end of my bed and a bowl of chili in my fridge. The food was delicious, so I texted both Shelby and Preston to thank them and then went to sleep. The dog didn't even raise his head.

Roy woke me up early the next morning, so I fed him and let him outside before going back to bed. Unfortunately, the butthead then started barking and wouldn't stop, so I didn't get back to sleep. Instead, I changed, put on some coffee, and went for a jog in the woods. Roy followed for a couple hundred yards, but then he turned around. I kept going. My mind stayed on Lily. Then, my mind shifted to another little girl I knew named Cora. She lived in North Carolina, and I had been her nanny for a summer. She and her mother were wonderful friends, and I missed them both.

Had Cora been missing, I never would have come home last night. I would have driven around town, looking for her, even though I would have known how hopeless that was. I shouldn't have stopped looking for Lily. She didn't have time for my dawdling. Until we found her, sleep was an expense I couldn't afford.

I jogged home, showered, and then went into work. Almost a dozen people had left me messages, but I had to prioritize who I responded to, starting with Agent Costa. He answered on the second ring and sounded groggy.

"Bryan, it's Joe Court," I said. "I'm returning your call. You got a minute?"

He cleared his throat.

"Yeah," he said. He paused and then cleared his throat again. "I was taking a nap."

"Sorry to wake you up."

"It was time," he said, sighing. "We've made some progress overnight. We've ID'd the other names Cassie gave us in the hospital. Ursa is Ursa Bauer. She's a thirty-eight-year-old former officer in the Air Force. She was honorably discharged in 2009. Nadine is Nadine Kaiser. She's thirty-three, married and lives in Belleville, Illinois.

"Wendy, Nadine, Ursa, and Robin all spent time in the military. We're trying to get their service files now. We're also running full background checks on them. In the next few hours, we should have a much clearer picture of who we're dealing with and what resources they might have."

Their ability to shoot and stay calm in a firefight made sense now. These ladies were far more dangerous than we'd realized.

"Okay," I said. "Send me everything you've got, and I'll look over it and give you my opinion."

"Will do," he said. "In the meantime, good luck."

I thanked him and hung up. Costa had a superb team with resources far beyond those of my station, but I liked to do my own research where possible. I wrote down the names he had given me and then started looking them up one by one. Wendy Brady, our deceased perp, was active on Instagram and posted frequent pictures of her backyard garden and various projects around the house. She had never married, but a man named Drew Weiler frequently commented on her pictures and remarked that he wished he were there with her.

Drew sounded like a boyfriend, so I looked him up next. By the looks of things, he was an active-duty Air Force officer, and he was stationed at Osan Air Base in South Korea. I doubted he was helping her, but I wrote his name and unit down anyway in case we had to contact him.

After Wendy, I looked up Robin Brady. She had three kids and a house in a middle-class neighborhood near her sister. She frequently posted pictures from her time in the Air Force, but she never mentioned her children's father, and few men commented on her pictures. I considered searching for her children's birth certificates to see whether they had the same father, but I didn't think it was necessary yet. Besides, Costa's background check would tell me everything I needed to know.

I searched for Nadine Kaiser next and found that she had a blog. I read about a dozen entries and then stopped because I felt too much like a voyeur. Nadine was open about her life and treated her blog almost like an intimate diary. She was married to a man named Charlie and loved him dearly. She called him her hero and her Prince Charming.

Unfortunately, Charlie had sustained a traumatic brain injury in the Army, and finding adequate care for him was a struggle. I felt sorry for her. She and her husband both had sacrificed for their country, and, because of that sacrifice, none of their dreams had come true. That didn't excuse her actions, but it mitigated things a bit. I'd still send her to prison for the rest of her life, but in the back of my mind, I'd wonder what she could have done had her husband not sustained the injury he had.

Last, I searched for Ursa Bauer and found almost nothing. She commented on Nadine's blog and on the Brady sisters' posts on Instagram, but she never posted anything herself. Hopefully Agent Costa would have more luck learning about her than I did.

After that, I turned to my email and the reports from Costa's team. Everything he sent taught me something new, but

I didn't know how much of it would help me find anybody. He did, however, send me credit reports. Nadine, Robin, and Wendy had mortgages, while Ursa lived in an apartment. All of them had credit card debt, but nobody owed more than ten thousand dollars. They looked financially stable, but none were wealthy, and none had the savings to survive an extended economic downturn. By the looks of things, the ladies—like most Americans—lived paycheck to paycheck.

I started to close Wendy's credit report when I noticed something unusual: an assisted-living center in St. Louis had run a credit check on her eleven months ago. Robin's credit report had a similar check. After those credit checks, the facility began withdrawing nine hundred dollars a month from each woman's bank account.

I grabbed my phone and called the facility's main number. A chipper woman answered within moments, so I introduced myself and asked to speak to a manager. She transferred my call to Dr. Ava Kravitz, to whom I introduced myself again. She paused and drew in a breath.

"Okay, Detective," she said. "What can I do for you?"

"I'm working a case involving Wendy and Robin Brady. They each send your facility nine hundred dollars a month. I'm calling to ask why."

She paused, and then I heard typing. A moment later, she drew in a breath.

"Wendy and Robin are both listed as the next-of-kin of one of our residents. They've never missed a payment."

I leaned forward and grabbed a pen from my desk.

"And who's the resident?"

"I'm not comfortable giving out that kind of information."

"That's fine," I said, "but if you don't talk to me, an FBI agent will show up in your office with a warrant. Would you prefer that?"

Dr. Kravitz, again, paused.

"What's going on, Detective?"

"This is an active investigation, so I'm limited in what I can tell you," I said. "That said, Wendy is dead, and her sister is wanted for multiple homicides. Clearly, both ladies cared about one of your residents. If possible, I'd like to talk to that resident and make sure he or she is safe and to ask whether Wendy or Robin have been in touch."

Dr. Kravitz sighed.

"Damn," she said. "This will break Corey's heart."

"Is Corey their father?"

"No," said Kravitz, sighing again. "Corey is Wendy and Robin's brother. He's one of our long-term residents."

"Can I meet him?"

She drew in a breath.

"Corey has Down syndrome," she said. "He shuts down when faced with stressful situations, and losing his sister will be the most stressful thing he'll have experienced since his father's death. We need to handle this very delicately."

I tried not to grimace, but that wasn't what I had hoped to hear.

"Okay, I understand," I said, drawing in a breath. "What can you tell me about his sisters? Do they visit? Do they help Corey? Are they polite?"

"They're wonderful," she said. "Most of our residents live independently in our apartments, but we share meals in a central cafeteria. We provide cleaning services, career advice, and an on-site counselor, who's available twenty-four hours a day. We also provide any sort of emergency services our residents might need.

"Corey thrives here. He works in a grocery store on weekdays and volunteers in a food pantry every other weekend. He's a lovely man, and his sisters dote on him. They visit once or twice a month, and they help pay his bills. He loves his nieces and nephews and talks about them every chance he gets. I wish all of our residents had families as devoted as Corey does. This will break his heart."

I said nothing as my mind processed her statement. Then I blinked.

"Have you seen them lately?"

"I haven't," she said, already typing. I waited a moment. "It looks like Robin last signed in four weeks ago. She ate dinner with him and then left."

Four weeks ago, they were robbing armored cars. Corey meant a lot to his sisters if they still visited him in the midst of that. I wondered whether Robin would come back for him before she disappeared.

"Thank you for the information," I said. "We're still looking for Robin. If she calls, or if she comes to the facility, please don't let her know that we've been in contact, and please call the police."

"I will," she said. She wished me luck before hanging up. I typed some notes and sent them to Agent Costa to let him know what I had found and to suggest that he might want to keep the brother under surveillance in case our perps showed up. Then I spun around in my chair. I was getting a better picture of these ladies, and, like most of the people I arrested, they weren't all bad. Part of me even admired their willingness to do anything to protect their families. If my biological mother had possessed half their drive, my life would have turned out much differently.

Their intentions changed nothing, though. They had tied Cassie Prescott to a chair and shot her twice, they had abducted a little girl with serious medical needs, they had murdered Lily's family, and they had shot and killed over a dozen guards during their armed robberies. If anything, knowing who they were sharpened my resolve because it told me how dangerous they were. Unfortunately, it didn't put me any closer to finding anyone.

Hopefully Bryan was having better luck than I was, doing whatever he was doing.

Chapter 32

Despite the chilly air, sweat slid down Peyton's forehead and into his eyes. Dirt clung to the hair on his forearms and his white T-shirt, and his hands ached inside his work gloves. He wouldn't have blisters, but the arthritis in his fingers had begun acting up.

He looked to his left at the disheveled man beside him. Zach Brugler was forty and bald. He had big hands but slender shoulders and a thin face with a scraggly red beard. His mother might have found him handsome, but then again, she had been drunk most of his childhood. She probably didn't even remember she had him.

"Something wrong, chief?" he asked. Brugler had called him chief almost from the moment they met outside a bar in downtown St. Augustine. At first, he had hurled the name at him so it was almost an accusation, but over a course of a week, Brugler's tone had softened, and chief became a title of respect. It probably came from Brugler's time in the Navy. He only mentioned his previous career when he got drunk, but it had meant a lot to him.

Both men stood chest deep in a hole in the ground with shovels in hand. On television and in movies, graves were always dug to six feet, but in reality, they didn't have to be anywhere near that depth. When digging a grave, you wanted to dig deep enough that no one was likely to disturb the site if they happened to dig in the area, and you wanted enough soil atop the body to contain the smell. Four to five feet was just fine.

He looked at Brugler.

"We're good," he said, pressing his shovel's tip into the soil so it stood. Then he wiped soil from his forehead with the back of his hand. Brugler grinned.

"Did I do okay, boss?"

"You did," said Peyton. Brugler grinned and then leaned against the earthen wall of the hole they had dug.

"You care if I smoke?"

"Not at all," said Peyton, positioning his shovel across the top of the grave so he could use it to pull himself up and out. Peyton didn't know St. Augustine County well, but Brugler had assured him very few people visited this part of the county. A motel chain had once owned the land, but, as best Peyton could tell, the company had done nothing with it. He didn't know who owned the property now, but he hadn't found a single human footprint anywhere near their current spot.

Peyton reached down and pulled Brugler up. Brugler then sat at the edge of the grave, near a pile of dirt, lit a cigarette, and then leaned back.

"What's the hole for, anyway?"

Peyton considered him. When his client had approached him with this job six months ago, Peyton had known nothing at all about his targets. The job had come in via email. It was a simple note with six names and six dollar figures. The original offer was always low, but that didn't matter as long as the potential client included numbers. It showed they were serious and that they had thought about what they wanted done.

Peyton then wrote back and asked for ten thousand dollars so he could research the targets and determine a reasonable fee. The client agreed, so Peyton had then flown into town and posed as a tourist for a week. He scouted his targets' homes and places of business and considered the feasibility of his client's wishes.

Because of the restrictions on his method of death, Dr. Hines had seemed like the hardest. His death cost a hundred grand. Arthur Murdoch cost seventy-five grand, mostly because Peyton had liked the old man. Richard Clarke, the racist minister, cost five grand, but Peyton would have killed him for free. Vic Conroy had cost seventy-five because Peyton had to convince a third party to kill him on camera. Dale Wixson was ten grand.

Brugler was an enigma. The original email from the client had suggested a price of one grand. Peyton couldn't do a job for such a small amount, but he had found little reason to charge more. Moreover, he had found no reason why anyone would want him dead. Brugler lived alone in a tiny house with a garden out back. On warm days, he helped his neighbors pull weeds or mow their lawn, and they gave him enough money to buy those goods he couldn't build, grow, or acquire on his own. He was a drunk, but he was a conscientious drunk who drank himself into a stupor and then passed out.

Peyton glanced at him and sighed.

"Hole's for my dog," he said. "He died. I didn't want to bury him on my own."

Brugler lowered his voice.

"I'm sorry, man," he said. "Dogs are special. I had a Rottweiler growing up. We called him Hot Dog. He was my best friend."

"Tell me about him," said Peyton.

Brugler rambled for almost ten minutes straight, barely taking a breath. Peyton didn't want to kill him, but this was a job. He walked to the truck for a bottle of vodka, twisted off the top, and pretended to sip from the bottle before passing it to Brugler. He took a gulp and then exhaled.

"That's good," said Brugler before pausing. "I hate to ask, but I've got to get paid, boss."

"Sure," said Peyton, reaching into his pocket. He pulled out a wad of bills and peeled three twenties from the stack. Then he paused and took another. He handed all four to Brugler. Brugler shook his head and tried to refuse.

"I don't need extra," he said. "I'll just take the fifty we agreed on."

"You earned it," said Peyton. "After the past few days I've had, it was nice to spend the morning with someone normal."

"I hear you there," said Brugler, slipping the money into his pants pocket. "What was his name?"

"Huh?" asked Peyton, narrowing his eyes.

"Your dog, man," he said. "What was your dog's name?"

"Ace," he said, thinking quickly. "He was a golden retriever. He was a good dog."

"Ace is a good name."

Peyton agreed and stayed still for another few moments for Brugler to drink more vodka. Then he took the bottle and helped his target stand.

"You can have the rest of the bottle when we're done," he said. "Then we'll both get drunk."

"For Ace," said Brugler.

"Yeah, for Ace," he said.

They walked back to his SUV and drove toward St. Augustine where, ostensibly, Peyton planned to pick up his dog. In actuality, he had a task to perform. He drove to the south side waterfront and then turned toward a two-story brick apartment building with black wrought-iron railings on the outside like a cheap motel. Arthur Murdoch was inside one of those rooms at that moment, waiting for a new tenant to sign his lease. He had no idea of what lay ahead of him.

After parking, Peyton reached for the vodka on his backseat and pretended to take a long draw before handing the bottle to Brugler. He took a long pull, downing at least another two shots. If Peyton had to guess, he'd say the man had ingested about seven shots in fifteen minutes. Even with his tolerance, that much liquor in that short a time should inebriate him. The massive dose of ketamine he put inside the bottle wouldn't hurt, either.

They exited the car simultaneously. Brugler stumbled and had to reach toward the door to steady himself.

"You all right, buddy?" asked Peyton, already knowing the answer.

"Yeah," said Brugler. "I just got a little light-headed. Probably all the exercise."

"Probably," said Peyton. "Come on. Ace is upstairs."

Peyton led Brugler up the wrought-iron staircase to a furnished one-bedroom efficiency apartment at the end of the building. Arthur Murdoch must have heard them coming because he stepped out while they were still about twenty feet away. He smiled at them both. Brugler waved but then had to reach for the railing to avoid falling. Murdoch raised his eyebrows and looked at Peyton.

"Your friend all right?"

"He's had a rough day," said Peyton, walking forward and lowering his voice. Brugler followed slowly behind. "We've been burying his dog. He had a few drinks. He's not usually like this."

"I hope not," said Murdoch. He considered them both and then swept his arm toward the apartment. "Come on in, gentlemen. You'll be very happy here. This is a clean one-bedroom, perfect for a man getting back on his feet. My maintenance team just replaced the weather-stripping on the doors and windows, so your heating and cooling bills should be low. The washer and dryer are downstairs. You have to pay to use them, but I try to only charge for the water and wear and tear on the machines."

Peyton followed Murdoch into the apartment. Brugler came a few steps afterwards. The apartment's bedroom doubled as its living room, but it had a balcony overlooking a small stream out back. The kitchen had enough counter space to cut some vegetables, but it would have been tight for major meal prep. Still, it was clean, safe, and warm. Many people down on their luck would have been happy there—especially for three hundred bucks a month.

"Bathroom's to the right," said Murdoch. "This apartment doesn't have a front hall closet, so you'll want to get a coat rack. It's wired for cable, but that's not included in the rent. If you'd like, I can get you the number of the local cable company. A basic package is about thirty bucks a month."

Brugler walked to the double bed in the living room.

"Put some pillows on this, and it'll look like a sofa," he said. "For guests."

"A lot of our residents do that," said Murdoch, before reaching into his pocket for a folded piece of paper. He unfolded it on the kitchen countertop near Peyton. "Sign at the X, and this place is yours."

Peyton reached into his pocket for a pen and then furrowed his brow.

"Where, exactly, do I sign?" he asked. "I don't read a lot of contracts."

"That's all right," said Murdoch. He looked over the contract and pointed to a solid line at the bottom. With the old man's attention focused on the paper, Peyton reached up, grabbed him by the scruff of his neck, and shoved his head forward as hard as he could against the kitchen's upper cabinets. Murdoch's head bounced like a basketball, and he fell straight down.

Brugler ran over, his eyes wide.

"What the hell just happened?"

"He fell," said Peyton. "Check his neck for a pulse. I'll call 911."

Brugler practically jumped down. Peyton pulled a syringe from his pocket and stabbed the alcoholic in the neck and depressed the plunger. Brugler shot to his feet and ripped the syringe out, his brow furrowed and a confused expression on his face. Then, the drugs started hitting him. He stumbled and blinked, his eyes already going cloudy as ketamine began working through his system. He fell to a knee and brought a hand to his face as he fell forward. His eyes closed.

Peyton knelt and felt Murdoch's throat. He was alive, but barely. He'd have to take care of that, but first, he dragged his unconscious body to Brugler and then forced his hand to scratch at Brugler's neck. It left marks, but more than that, it'd get Brugler's skin cells beneath his fingernails. Then he picked Brugler up and slammed his forehead against the kitchen counter with a thud that rattled the silverware inside the drawers. As Brugler dropped, he left a smear of blood on the beige counter.

Peyton grabbed the drunk's hand and used it to open a drawer with silverware. Then he reached into his pocket for his work gloves and grabbed a steak knife.

"Sorry, Mr. Murdoch," he said, standing over the older man's slumped body. "This isn't personal."

He stabbed him through the rib cage and felt the tip of the knife enter his heart. Then he flicked the tip, opening him up. Blood poured out. Peyton didn't enjoy killing him, but he could at least make sure the older man didn't hurt.

Brugler lay on the ground, unmoving, as the old man's blood began pooling around them both. Peyton reached down and tried picking him up, but the blow to the counter must have been harder than he expected because Brugler was already dead. Peyton put his hands on his hips and considered.

"Well, shit."

He had planned to kill Brugler elsewhere and dump his body in the grave in the woods, but he could just as well use the scene he had. He picked up Brugler's foot and then dragged it through the blood as if he had slipped. Then he positioned Brugler's body so he lay on the ground near the countertop with his blood on it. He also grabbed the knife from Murdoch's chest and put it in Brugler's hand. Afterwards, Peyton stepped back.

Both bodies were in the kitchen. When the police came through, they'd find scratch marks on Brugler's neck and then find his skin cells beneath Murdoch's fingernails. They'd then match the knife wound in Murdoch's side to the knife in Brugler's hand. When they searched Murdoch's office, they'd find Brugler's hairs, which Peyton had planted yesterday, inside the center drawer of Mr. Murdoch's desk.

This should work just fine. As he left the apartment, he pulled the door shut behind him and made sure no one looked at him as he walked to his car. As he drove away, he sighed.

"One more job."

He hoped it went better than this one.

Chapter 33

I was reading forensic reports about the house on Grantwood Lane when my desk phone rang, startling me so badly I almost jumped. Then, I answered and waited as the line beeped.

"Hey," I said. "This is Joe Court."

"Joe, it's Marcus. I'm at a crime scene. You busy?"

I leaned back and shrugged.

"I've got a minute," I said. "How did you learn my number?"

"I don't know your number," he said. "I just called the main line and told the computer who I wanted to talk to."

I leaned forward.

"We can do that now?"

"Yeah. Cool, isn't it?"

I drew in a breath and shook my head.

"I don't even recognize this place anymore," I said. "You remember when Travis Kosen was sheriff and his windows leaked so much it rained inside his office?"

Marcus laughed a little.

"I do," he said. "That was a long time ago."

I smiled.

"Tell me about your crime scene."

"It's a double homicide at the King's Court apartment complex on Second Street near the river," he said. "I'd like a second opinion."

I didn't know that apartment complex, but I knew the area he described. I pushed back from my desk and grabbed the navy blazer I had hung behind my chair.

"Give me ten minutes," I said. "I'm on my way."

He thanked me, and I hurried out of my office. The scene wasn't far, so I drove over and parked on the street near a minivan from our forensics lab. The rear door was open, and Dr. Darlene McEvoy was looking through a box of supplies. She straightened when she saw me.

"Afternoon, Joe," she said. "The boss call you in for this one, too?"

"Nah, Marcus wanted a second opinion."

She smiled.

"He's a good cop. I wish he didn't second-guess himself so often."

"Confidence comes in time," I said, tilting my head to the side. "He'll get there. Have you been inside yet?"

"Yep, but I don't want to color your opinion with my own. The coroner's handling a funeral today, so he's running a little behind. I'm told he'll be here in a few hours."

I shook my head and swore under my breath. Dr. McEvoy smiled.

"At least Mr. Rivers doesn't get sick at the sight of dead bodies," she said. "When I started working here, the county coroner was a former dispatcher. He didn't even have a mortician's training. Rivers is, believe it or not, a step up."

"But he's a huge step down from Dr. Sheridan."

"Most forensic pathologists would be a step down from Dr. Sheridan," she said. "We'll do our best with what we've got."

She was right, so I wished her luck. She said likewise to me. The apartment building was L-shaped and had two stories. It looked like a cheap, roadside motel complete with an in-ground pool in the parking lot. I took the stairs to the second floor and walked toward an apartment on the end. The door was open, and Carrie Bowen, a uniformed officer, stood outside with a log sheet. As I signed in, Marcus walked through the door and nodded hello.

"Thanks for coming by," he said. "Watch your step. The scene is just inside."

"Sure thing," I said, sticking my hands in my pockets so I wouldn't touch anything. The apartment looked like a single room and was, maybe, fifteen feet wide by twenty-five feet long. A glass sliding door led to a patio out back, while an open door on the right led to a bathroom. A pair of bodies lay on the linoleum floor in the kitchen to the left of the front door.

"Place look like this when you got here?" I asked, looking to Marcus.

"Yep. Carrie got the call. A resident in the apartment beneath us called the police when he heard what sounded like a struggle in the vacant apartment above him. Carrie came out, found the door ajar, and looked into the apartment and found a pair of bodies. She checked them out to make sure they were dead and then called for help."

I looked toward the door. Officer Bowen stood outside, pretending as if she weren't listening to us.

"Good work, Carrie," I said. She looked at me and smiled.

"Just doing my job."

Which I appreciated. Our officers did a good job on most cases, but even minor mistakes could multiply in complex investigations. I looked at Marcus.

"So you want my opinion?" I asked. He nodded, so I looked at the two bodies on the ground. "Looks like a fight between a landlord and a potential tenant. There's a lease on the counter, but it's not signed yet. The older victim has a wound to his face that looks consistent with blunt-force trauma. My guess is that he was shoved and hit his face against the upper cabinets. There's a blood spot that you can see."

I pointed toward it, and Marcus nodded.

"The younger victim has light scrapes on his neck. They could be scratches from fingernails, so you need to look at the older victim's hands. While the older man attacked him, the younger man reached into the cabinet for a knife, which he used to attack the older man. He stabbed him in the chest. If the blade was long enough, it could have penetrated the heart. That would explain the quantity of blood on the ground. The younger man, in his haste to escape, slipped on the blood and hit his head on the counter. That killed him. So we've got one count of murder and one count of death by rotten luck."

Marcus smiled.

"I had similar thoughts, but I wanted to run it by you first. It feels a little far-fetched, like something out of a mediocre crime novel."

"Some days, I feel like every case I work is but one event in a long series of mediocre crime novels," I said. "We'll get a tox screen on both victims. It smells like booze in here. They may not have been sober. You ID'd them yet?"

Marcus pulled a notepad from his pocket.

"Older man is Arthur Murdoch," he said. "He owns this building and a number of others around town. The younger man is unknown. He's got a wallet in his back pocket, but I wanted to wait for the coroner to get here before checking it."

I pulled a pair of gloves from my pockets and snapped them on before kneeling beside him.

"The coroner will be busy for the next several hours," I said, reaching into the victim's back pocket for his wallet. "I won't tell if you won't."

"Your secret is safe," he said. "Cross my heart."

The victim had eighty dollars cash and an expired two-for-one coupon to a local deli but no credit cards. I pulled out his license.

"Zach Brugler. He's thirty-eight, and it looks like he's an organ donor. Now that I'm a little closer to him, I can smell the alcohol on him. He's got a lot of dirt on his hands and clothes, and he smells like sweat. Maybe he's a landscaper or gardener."

Marcus squinted.

"That name is familiar, but I don't know why," said Marcus. He paused. "He live here?"

I looked at the ID and shook my head.

"He lives on Loganwood Drive," I said. Then I paused. "That's, what, four blocks from here?"

"About that."

I drew in a breath to think and then furrowed my brow.

"If he had a house, why would he sign a lease for an apartment here?"

Marcus raised his eyebrows and looked at the paperwork on the nearby counter.

"He didn't," he said. "Lease is blank."

I looked toward the front door.

"Hey, Carrie!" I shouted. She stuck her head in the door and raised her eyebrows. "Do me a favor. Go to your cruiser and look up Zach Brugler. If he's got a car or truck, see if you can locate it. Then check to see if he's got a criminal record."

She said she was on it. Marcus crossed his arms as I stood.

"What are you thinking?"

"I'm thinking this case is more complicated than it appears," I said. "Now come on. We'll walk to our victim's house and see what we've got."

Chapter 34

As Marcus and I walked to Brugler's house, Officer Carrie Bowen called to say that Brugler had a few speeding tickets but that he had never been arrested. He also owned a 2001 gray Ford F-150 pickup, but she couldn't find it anywhere near the apartment complex. I thanked her and hung up and looked at Marcus.

"If he didn't drive, how'd he get here?" I asked. "We don't have a bus system, and I doubt an Uber or Lyft driver would let him in the car smelling like he did and covered in dirt."

Marcus considered it and then shrugged.

"He only lives a few blocks away. He could have walked."

"That's possible," I said. "Let's check out his house, then."

He agreed. Carrie Bowen took custody of the scene. Marcus and I walked four blocks to a little bungalow with beige siding and a big front porch. A folding chair with ripped fabric slats leaned against the house beside the front door, and the yard had big patches of brown where there should have been grass or weeds.

Since Brugler was dead, we didn't need a warrant to search the building. At the same time, we didn't want to surprise anyone inside, so we pounded on the front door and waited. No one called out to us, so we walked around the building to make sure it was secure. Two windows had plywood sheets instead of glass, and a third window had aluminum foil over the windowpane. People who worked nights sometimes did that to block out the sun. I wondered where—or whether—Brugler worked. We'd have to talk to the neighbors.

Once we were sure the building was secure, we walked to the front again, and I picked the lock. The front room had beige walls, white painted woodwork, and pink, stained carpet. A musty smell wafted throughout the building, so we left the front door open for ventilation. The front room had two white, plastic lawn chairs and a small TV on a red milk crate. Beside the lawn chairs were empty bottles of vodka.

"Chopin vodka," said Marcus, slipping a pair of blue nitrile gloves over his hands. He picked up a vodka bottle.

"Let's clear the house. We'll circle back in a minute."

Marcus put the bottle down, and we searched the house room by room to ensure we were alone. The house had two beds but little other furniture. The fridge held some beer, cold cuts, half a loaf of white bread, and a jar of mayonnaise, but I couldn't find other food in the house. Brugler spent the bulk of his money, evidently, on booze and cigarettes.

After finding very little of interest elsewhere, Marcus and I returned to the front room. Brugler had three empty bottles of vodka on the ground beside the TV. I picked one up.

"Mr. Brugler likes to drink," said Marcus.

"He does," I said, thinking. "We found eighty bucks on him. Where'd he get the money?"

"Like you said, he was covered in dirt," said Marcus. "Maybe he was working. He's got a sizable garden in the backyard. Maybe he sold some vegetables."

It was cold to grow vegetables, but it was a good thought.

"You ever buy vodka?"

"I'm more of a beer man," said Marcus. "My wife likes red wine."

"Chopin costs about thirty bucks a bottle," I said. "I buy Stoli. It's much cheaper, but it's good."

Marcus nodded and crossed his arms.

"And you think it's odd that Mr. Brugler purchased a thirty-dollar bottle of vodka when he could have bought a cheaper one that's still good."

I glanced at him.

"I think it's odd that he didn't buy rubbing alcohol and try to drink that," I said. "This guy doesn't have thirty bucks to waste. That vodka cost more than his furniture. You smelled him in the apartment. Brugler's not a connoisseur. He's a drunk. Why would a drunk spend thirty bucks on a bottle of liquor when he could have spent seven or eight on the cheapest bottle in the store and accomplished the same thing?"

Marcus shook his head.

"I don't know."

"This case is weird," I said, putting the bottle down and resting my hands on my hips. "License bureau says he's got a truck, but it's not in the driveway, and it wasn't at the hotel. He's getting around somehow, though. Liquor stores in this neighborhood don't sell Chopin."

Marcus's lips curled upward, and he furrowed his brow, almost disbelievingly.

"You know that for a fact?"

I closed my eyes and sighed.

"Sadly, yes."

He considered me.

"Okay. Which liquor stores sell it?"

"A few across the county," I said. "It's the vodka I buy when I want to celebrate something."

Marcus drew in a breath.

"Then let's go visit those stores and find out who else has been buying it lately."

***

Peyton Weldon sighed and stepped into the rental house, hopefully for the last time. Before going down to the basement, he checked his iPad and flipped through the cameras at Dr. Hines's home. Kira Hines had taken advantage of her husband's absence by spending the day with her lover in her bedroom. The kids had been at school. He didn't know where everyone was now, but they weren't home. He could use that.

He took the stairs down to the basement. Dr. Nico Hines sat on a dining room chair beside the water heater in the home's unfinished mechanical room. Duct tape secured his arms and legs, while a ball gag kept him from screaming. When he saw Peyton, he lowered his head and cried. Peyton didn't care to see a grown man cry, but it showed how close Hines was to breaking. Now, he just needed another push.

"I'll be right back," said Peyton.

Hines didn't even bother fighting. Peyton hurried upstairs to get his iPad and then searched through the footage his cameras had shot from Kira's bedroom that morning. Dr. Hines loved his wife. He likely had an inkling she was having an affair, but this would still hurt. When he reached the basement again, he knelt in front of Dr. Hines and lowered his voice.

"Hey, buddy," he said. "I've got something to show you, but you won't like it."

Peyton hit the play button and held the iPad toward the doctor. At first, he seemed confused. Then, his eyes opened wide, and his chest began trembling as his wife began undressing her boyfriend. Hines closed his eyes and shook his head as if he didn't want to watch. Peyton softened his voice.

"She's kissing his neck," he said. "She seems happy."

Hines stamped his feet, his face growing red. He kept his eyes shut.

"Your wife is a beautiful woman," said Peyton. "And her lover seems to realize that. Now, she's kissing his chest."

Hines shook his head even harder.

"Now she's on her knees. You can guess why," said Peyton. "She is really going to town, too. Hard to believe she kissed your kids goodnight with that filthy mouth of hers."

Dr. Hines opened his eyes. Tears slipped down his cheek.

"You want to watch the rest?" asked Peyton. "It goes on for a few hours. Your wife is enthusiastic the whole time."

Hines cried harder. Peyton paused the video and left the mechanical room. He found a folding step stool in the kitchen, which he then used as a stand for his iPad. He set it in the mechanical room so Hines could watch. Then he went upstairs to find a pen and paper. He let Dr. Hines watch his wife for about twenty minutes before going back down. By then, Kira's lover lay between her legs. They were having a great time.

"They go at it like newlyweds, don't they?" asked Peyton. "Hard to believe she's been balling other guys behind your back all these years. You supported her, you bought her cars, diamonds, and a house. That has to hurt." He paused as if he had just thought of something. "Did you ever give your kids a paternity test?"

Dr. Hines clenched his jaw tightly around the ball gag and exhaled through his nose. Now, he had gotten through the shocked phase and entered the angry one. Peyton could use that.

"It hurts, I know," said Peyton. "My ex-wife did this to me, too. You know what made it better?"

Hines flicked his eyes toward Peyton.

"Telling everybody what a slut she was," said Peyton. "I wrote down everything she did. I was a devoted husband, and I worked my ass off for my family. She ruined everything, and I told the world. It all came out during the divorce. The judge even read my letter aloud in front of her. Her parents were in the gallery. Even they knew she was the problem, not me. I got the kids, I got the house, and I got the bank account. You want to get back at Kira, write down everything you see and everything you've done to support her. Would you like to do that?"

He nodded, so Peyton produced the pen and paper. He even gave Dr. Hines a hardback book on which to write. After cutting the duct tape on his forearms to free his hands, the doctor started writing. He didn't write long, but the note would work just fine. Peyton picked up the iPad, the book, and the letter and pen.

"I'll take care of this," he said. "The world will know what Kira did to you."

Hines drew in a breath through his nose. Peyton taped the doctor's arms to the chair again so he couldn't escape and then left the room. He put the letter on the kitchen table before getting a syringe and an ampoule of ketamine from his bag. Ketamine was the perfect drug. It worked quickly and effectively, and it wouldn't show up on a standard toxicology screen. He filled a syringe with two milliliters, a very strong dose.

Before going to the basement again, he pulled out his cell phone and booked a flight home. After that, he started gathering every document and ID he had with the name Peyton Weldon on it. He'd burn those in the backyard. Then he texted his client to let him know he was finishing the job. After that, he removed the SIM card from his phone and crushed that beneath the heel of his shoe before doing the same to his cell phone.

Finally, he removed his actual ID from a hidden compartment in his suitcase and became another man. Before going to the basement to drug Dr. Hines, he pulled out his actual battered cell phone and called his house in Seattle. His six-year-old daughter answered.

"Hey, sweetheart," he said in the singsong voice he reserved only for her. "Daddy's got one more assignment, but I think I'll finish earlier than I expected. Go tell mommy I'll be home late tonight."

Chapter 35

Marcus and I got lucky at the fourth liquor store we visited. The store had sold its only four bottles of Chopin vodka in a cash transaction a week ago. By itself, that wouldn't have been interesting, but their surveillance system caught the transaction on video. The shopper kept his eyes on the shelves and on the ground, so we didn't get a good picture of him, but his companion—Zach Brugler—looked directly at the camera and waved. A camera outside even got a clear shot of their black SUV's license plate. It was registered to a rental car company in St. Louis.

I called the rental car company from Marcus's cruiser in the parking lot.

"Hey," I said. "This is Detective Mary Joe Court with the St. Augustine County Sheriff's Department. You rented a vehicle to a man involved in a double homicide in St. Augustine. I need his name and other contact information."

I read the manager the license plate. She paused.

"That vehicle was rented to Doug McConnell of Baker City, Oregon, six days ago on a one-week rental. It's still out."

I wrote the name down.

"What else can you tell me about him?"

"Nothing without a warrant," she said. "I'm sorry, but that's company policy."

I gritted my teeth.

"Sure. Thanks."

I hung up before she could respond and turned to Marcus.

"Our suspect is Doug McConnell. He's from Baker City, Oregon, and he rented his car for seven days. He's got one day left, so he might be in town still."

"I'll call this in," said Marcus, already taking out his phone. I swung his cruiser's laptop toward me and looked McConnell up. Nearly every state in the country shared its driver's license information with each other, so we should have had a listing for McConnell, but I couldn't find him anywhere in Oregon. Then I looked up Baker City to see whether I could find the local police department's number, but I found nothing.

"We've got a problem, dude," I said. Marcus put his hand over the bottom of his phone and raised his eyebrows. "Neither Doug McConnell nor Baker City, Oregon, exists."

"You sure you typed the names right?"

"Yep."

Marcus told the person to whom he was speaking on the phone that he'd call her back. Then he focused on me.

"So, either the clerk at the rental car company is lying to us, or our suspect gave them fake information that was good enough to slip past their fraud detection programs."

"That's what it looks like," I said. "Unfortunately, we have nothing that ties him to our murders. All we know is that he and Zach Brugler purchased liquor together."

Marcus considered.

"He used a fraudulent ID to rent a car," he said. "Is that considered motor vehicle theft?"

"Maybe, but we'd have to talk to the prosecutors," I said. "And it wouldn't be a crime in St. Augustine. He committed that crime at the rental car's desk in St. Louis. We don't have jurisdiction to investigate, and as far as I know, the rental car company hasn't filed a complaint."

Marcus raised his eyebrows.

"So we've got nothing, huh?"

"We've got a crime scene with two bodies," I said. "If we can tie Mr. McConnell to that, we've got a lot."

Marcus agreed, and we drove back to the apartment building, where we spent the next several hours talking to neighbors. Everybody recognized Mr. Murdoch, but nobody recognized Brugler. At a little after six, I left Marcus at the apartment and drove back to the station, where I started writing reports.

Then my phone rang. It was Kira Hines, wife of Dr. Nico Hines. I paused before answering.

"Mrs. Hines," I said. "I'm sorry, but I don't have an update on your husband."

"He's dead," she said.

"Okay," I said. "Why do you think that?"

"Because he's hanging from a tree in our yard. He killed himself."

I opened my mouth but caught myself before I could gasp.

"Okay," I said. "Is there anybody with you?"

She paused. Her voice cracked.

"No," she said. "My kids are at a friend's house."

I stood up.

"I'm on my way," I said. "I'm sending paramedics and some uniformed officers, too. We'll be there shortly."

I hung up before she could say anything else and then ran out of my office. It took only a moment to reach the front desk. Trisha had gone home for the day, but Jason Zuckerburg smiled at me.

"Jason, I need EMS service and uniforms at the home of Dr. Nico Hines," I said. "He was a missing person, but his wife just found his body. They live on Pinehurst."

Jason didn't skip a beat before pulling out his keyboard and typing. Within seconds, he was on the radio, routing a pair of uniformed officers. He knew what he was doing, so I didn't need to stay and supervise. Instead, I ran to my car and drove until I reached the Hines's home on Pinehurst. It was a beautiful neighborhood with mature trees and enormous brick and stone homes. I barely noticed any of it before parking in the Hines family's driveway.

Nobody answered my knock, so I hurried around the side of the home to the back. Kira Hines sat on a chair on her back patio with an expressionless face. Her eyes passed over me, but it took her a moment to recognize me. Then she pointed toward the tree line behind the home. A rope hung from a beautiful old sugar maple. On that rope hung a body.

I crossed the lawn to ID the corpse. It was Dr. Hines, all right. His hands hung at his side, while a ladder lay on the ground. He wore a wrinkled white button-down shirt and gray slacks. Several days' worth of growth adorned his chin and cheeks, giving him a haggard appearance. He had hung himself with a white cotton rope. He didn't use a noose. Instead, it looked like he had tied the rope into a slipknot. Dr. Hines's son was the right age for the Cub Scouts, so I wondered whether the doctor had learned the knot while working on a merit badge with his kid.

I stepped back and then walked toward Mrs. Hines. She blinked heavy, moist eyes when she saw me. Multiple sirens shrieked in the distance, but not even the best paramedic or doctor could help Dr. Hines now.

"I'm sorry for your loss," I said. "If you'd like, we can go to the front yard so you don't have to see him."

She looked down and blinked away tears.

"He was a good man," she said. "He loved me."

"I'm sure he did."

She said nothing for a few minutes. Then she cleared her throat.

"There's a note in the kitchen," she said. "I found it and came out here."

"Did you touch anything else?"

She looked up, her brow furrowed.

"Why does that matter?"

"Until we learn otherwise, we'll treat this as a homicide," I said. "It's standard procedure for a suspicious death."

She brought a hand to her throat.

"You think I killed him?"

"Not at all," I said. "We treat every suspicious or violent death as a homicide until our coroner tells us it wasn't. That's our procedure. If we treat this as a murder from the beginning, we're not caught unawares down the line. Where's this note?"

She opened her mouth, her face ashen, but she said nothing. I gave her a minute. Two paramedics ran around the side of the house. I waved them toward the body but focused on Mrs. Hines.

"It's okay to feel upset," I said. "Is there someone I can call for you? A family member, or maybe a minister or priest?"

She shut her mouth and shook her head.

"No," she said. "I want to be alone."

"I understand," I said, looking toward the paramedics. They were running toward Dr. Hines, but then they stopped. One made the sign of the cross over his chest.

Neither of them touched the body. Officer Katie Martelle came running up the side of the house a second after the paramedics. I waved her over. She looked at the paramedics and then walked toward the porch.

"Mrs. Hines, I'd like you to go with Officer Martelle," I said. "She'll put you in her cruiser and talk to you about your day and where you've been and why you came home."

Mrs. Hines's mouth opened, and her lower lip trembled. She brought a shaky hand to her face as she began sobbing.

"Clothes," she said. "I was getting clothes for the kids."

I softened my voice.

"It's all right," I said, looking to Katie. She knelt in front of the grief-stricken woman. "Officer Martelle will take you to her cruiser and get you some water. I'll find that note your husband left."

Mrs. Hines agreed, so Katie put her arm around the woman's shoulders to guide her off the porch. Katie was the youngest officer we had in the department. She was also one of the gentlest and kindest young women I had ever met. I had worried that this job would chip away at her nature and change her into someone none of us recognized, but it hadn't so far. She was stronger than I had thought. Hopefully, that strength would hold out.

I followed Katie and Mrs. Hines to the front of the house. While they went to Katie's cruiser, I opened my Volvo's back door and grabbed a pair of nitrile gloves and a self-sealing polyethylene evidence bag from my evidence kit. If the note was wet, I'd have to store it in paper, but as long as it was dry, the clear bag would work fine. As I closed my door, the sheriff's black SUV pulled into the driveway. I updated him on what had happened and told him Officer Martelle was with Mrs. Hines. He told me to bag the note while he checked out the body in back.

The home's front door was open, so I walked into a two-story entryway with a polished marble floor and gleaming white woodwork. It was a beautiful home, and judging by the pile of dirty children's shoes on the ground beside the front door and the paper-covered table in the dining room to my left, it was well loved. I followed a hallway past a small powder room beneath the steps and to the kitchen. There, on a brown granite countertop, I found a short, handwritten note.

Kira-

I gave you everything. My life, my love…my very soul. I would have made you queen of the world if I could. If you wanted something, all you had to do was ask, and I would have moved heaven and earth to give it to you. You meant everything to me. I'm sorry I wasn't enough for you, but I hope he makes you happy.

-Nico

I slipped the note into my evidence bag and then sighed and carried it to the sheriff, who was standing near Katie Martelle's cruiser and listening as she interviewed Mrs.

Hines. The two of us walked to his SUV, where he read the note.

"Unless the coroner finds something surprising, I guess that's that," he said. "Mrs. Hines has identified the writing?"

"She said it was from her husband," I said. "I'd like to find the source of the rope he used and check the ladder for prints. It'd be nice if we could get the note verified, too. I'll also track down her boyfriend and talk to him about where he's been lately."

Kalil considered and then crossed his arms.

"Has Mrs. Hines been anything but straightforward since her husband went missing?"

I looked at Katie's cruiser.

"She held back some details, but I think she's honest," I said. "She even alluded to her affair when she reported her husband missing. At the time, I assumed Dr. Hines's disappearance had to do with his illicit pharmaceutical sales, but now it looks like he disappeared because he discovered the affair."

Kalil sighed.

"I feel bad for the guy's wife and kids, but I can't say I feel bad that he's gone."

A lot of people probably shared that sentiment. I didn't know how many would have voiced it aloud, though.

"We've all got some work to do," I said. "If I need you, I'll call."

"Okay," he said, drawing in a breath. "Tie up the loose ends. If I don't see you until tomorrow, have a good one."

I said likewise to him and then watched him drive off. This didn't sit well with me. It was too easy. Maybe the county had just gotten lucky and another of its biggest problem children had just expired by his own hand, but I doubted it. Something here was very wrong.

Chapter 36

For the next hour, I went from house to house, talking to neighbors. Unfortunately, the company that had built Pinehurst and the surrounding streets had designed the development to maximize privacy and recreation space. Each house sat on a five- to ten-acre lot, and each lot had a row of arborvitae, pine, or fir trees to give it privacy from other homes.

Nobody saw Dr. Hines hang himself, but several neighbors mentioned that Kira Hines entertained a handsome male guest often. Her lover drove a gray Toyota SUV, and he stayed for several hours at a time—but only after Kira's husband and kids had left for the day. I already knew about the affair, but I appreciated that they told me anyway. It made me think they would have told me had they seen someone strange lurking about today.

Kevius Reed collected fingerprints from the doorknobs and other flat surfaces inside the home, but I didn't expect him to find anything interesting there. Everything I saw pointed to a suicide. The note Dr. Hines had left didn't mention that he planned to kill himself, but it supported the notion.

I wondered about the kids, though. The house had pictures everywhere, and many of them showed Dr. Hines on his hands and knees, playing with his children. He wrestled with them, he drew pictures with them, and he held their hands. Pictures always gave a distorted image of reality, but the smiles looked genuine. Dr. Hines's kids had loved him, and he had seemed to love them. Despite that, he didn't even mention them in his note. That didn't sit well with me.

This case hinged on the body. If the coroner found irregularities, we'd investigate further, but if Mr. Rivers called Dr. Hines's death a suicide, we'd close the case. I wished I could trust Mr. Rivers's judgment, but he had neither the education nor the experience required to render a reliable opinion.

We left the crime scene at a little after six. Technically, Mrs. Hines and her family could move back into the house, but I doubted they'd be back soon. The moment Dr. Hines died, that place had become a tomb. Despite the happy memories they had of the place, I couldn't imagine his kids wanting to return.

I drove to my station and typed up my notes, but I doubted anything I did would make it to court. Everybody had lost today. It was just a tragedy.

At a little before seven, I shut my computer down for the night and pushed back from my desk but then was startled by a knock on my door before I could stand.

"You got a minute, Detective?"

I looked up to find George Delgado in my doorway. He had a thick file folder in hand.

"What do you need?" I asked.

"Marcus says you were interested in Vic Conroy's death."

I crossed my arms and pressed my lips into a thin line before answering.

"It doesn't matter. He's dead, and Marcus closed the case. Dale Wixson killed Vic Conroy, and Conroy's widow skipped town. Then Wixson killed himself."

Delgado shook his head.

"Wixson didn't kill himself."

I tilted my head to the side.

"Marcus said you two had doubts, but the sheriff and Darren Rogers shut you down. You didn't have the evidence."

"Because the coroner's an idiot," said Delgado. His voice was sharp. "Dr. Sheridan never would have written that report."

"Sheridan's not the coroner anymore. Rivers is, and he called Dale Wixson's death a suicide."

"And we both know that's horseshit," said Delgado, closing his eyes. "We've got a murderer in town, and he's taking out people Darren Rogers doesn't like."

I didn't know how to respond, so I smiled and looked down.

"I didn't realize you were practicing a comedy routine. Darren Rogers is an old man. He's not murdering anyone."

"I didn't say that he was," said Delgado. "A year ago, Darren Rogers fired the most competent medical examiner I've ever worked with and hired a mortician so ignorant he doesn't know how ignorant he is. Rogers then forced me to drive you away. You had the highest homicide clearance rate in our department's history. In one swoop, he cleared the ground."

The smile left my face.

"How'd he force you to fire me?"

"He told me that if I didn't fire you, the county would find itself in a fiscal emergency, and the only solution to that emergency would be to fire most of my staff. I supervised forty-eight employees. You were young, and you had resources. I knew you'd land on your feet. My other officers wouldn't have fared so well, so it was an easy choice."

My skin started growing hot, and I exhaled a slow breath through my nose to keep my temper from boiling over.

"Shut the door," I said. He did as I asked. I took another slow breath and then clenched my jaw tight before speaking. "Go on."

"I never got the chance to fire you, but I would have if you hadn't resigned. I thought that was the end of things, but then, lo and behold, Dean Kalil shows up and runs for sheriff. You know how much my campaign budget was?"

"At the moment, I don't give a shit about your campaign. Let's go back to you trying to ruin my life."

Delgado closed his eyes.

"I didn't try to ruin your life."

"You forced me out of the department at the request of Darren Rogers."

Delgado looked at me, but his expression didn't change.

"You can get pissed at me all you want, but if given the choice, I'd make the same one again. By forcing you out, I kept a lot of people working. Seems like your anger would be better directed at Darren Rogers."

He may have been right, but that didn't excuse what he did. Still, screaming at him wouldn't have gotten me anywhere, so I took a couple of deep breaths.

"Fine. Tell me about your campaign."

"My budget was three thousand dollars, which I thought was excessive," said Delgado. "It bought some signs, but I thought that'd be all I needed. Kalil rolled into town with a quarter-million dollars. That's almost twenty-five dollars for every person in this county. He bought billboards and even hired people to go from house-to-house talking him up. I knocked on as many doors as I could, but I couldn't keep up. Dean Kalil and his backers bought that election. They didn't win it."

A heavy feeling began growing in my stomach.

"And who are his backers?"

"I don't know," said Delgado. "But whoever they are, they wanted Kalil in charge of our department. You can see what he's done with it. We can't even log into our computers without Darren Rogers knowing about it."

I shifted my weight on my seat.

"Put this together for me," I said. "What are you saying?"

Delgado raised his eyebrows.

"You know what I'm saying."

"I do," I said, "but I want to hear it from you."

"I think Darren Rogers has a list of people who stood in the way of his vision for St. Augustine County, and he decided to get rid of them. To eliminate the chance of getting caught, he forced our coroner, best detective, and sheriff out. In their places, he installed people he can control."

I said nothing. He must have seen that I was incredulous because he held up his hands as if he were directing traffic.

"I didn't believe it either until Zach Brugler and Arthur Murdoch died."

I shook my head and closed my eyes.

"Just stop," I said. "Murdoch was an old man without a criminal record, and Brugler was a drunk who worked outside in the dirt."

Delgado opened the folder he was carrying and leafed through the pages inside until he came to the one he wanted. He handed me a printout of a newspaper article from the St.

Louis Post-Dispatch website. I skimmed it and then raised an eyebrow.

"So Mr. Brugler was involved in a car accident two years ago that resulted in a woman's death. That's a tragedy, but I'm not sure what it's supposed to show me."

"It happened in St. Augustine, and the victim was Emily Matthews," said Delgado. I raised my eyebrows and waited for him to continue. "Emily's maiden name was Rogers. She was Darren's only daughter."

I straightened.

"Oh."

"Yeah. Brugler was sober and doing the speed limit," he continued. "Emily ran a red light. Brugler tried to stop, but he T-boned her at forty-five miles an hour in a full-sized truck. She died before reaching the hospital. I worked the case myself. Brugler was broken up. He had just gotten out of the Navy and had bought a house. It was awful."

I brought a hand to my face.

"Jeez," I said before pausing. "What else have you got?"

"Murdoch was a real estate developer," said Delgado. "He owned apartment buildings, strip malls, and commercial spaces across the county. He specialized in low-income areas, but he wasn't a slumlord. His places are clean and well kept. He owned most of the waterfront south of downtown."

That was a blue-collar area, one of the few in the town of St. Augustine that hadn't begun gentrifying. The town needed it. We had housing for the wealthy, and we had more than enough restaurants with twenty-dollar hamburgers and fifty-dollar steaks. We needed places where waiters and cooks and grocery store workers could afford to live.

"I'm with you," I said.

"Darren Rogers has plans for St. Augustine. He wanted to turn the waterfront into a park and convention center. Rogers, on behalf of the county, offered Murdoch twice the appraised value of his waterfront property, but Murdoch refused to sell. Rogers then instructed the county attorneys to begin eminent domain proceedings against Murdoch to take the property. So far, Murdoch's lawyers have been able to fend them off. I'd be willing to bet Mr. Murdoch's kids will be much more open to a sale than their father, though."

I let my mind process that without forming a judgment. Then I blinked.

"So your theory is that Darren Rogers loves St. Augustine so much that he's willing to knock off everybody who stands in the way of him turning it into a major tourist attraction. That's…hard to believe."

Delgado shook his head.

"He's not doing it because he loves the town," he said. "Rogers is doing this because he loves money. For the past ten years, he and his family have bought up every farm, commercial building, and residential plot they could get their hands on in St. Augustine. If I had to guess, he's leveraged to his neck and is afraid the banks will ask for payments he can't make. If that convention center goes through, though, the value of his commercial downtown property will skyrocket. He'll make millions."

I drew in a breath as I fit the pieces together.

"Okay," I said, considering. "I could see why he would want to knock off Brugler and Murdoch. What about Vic Conroy, Nico Hines, and Dale Wixson? And what about Richard Clarke? Clarke's dead, too."

"Because they stood in Darren Rogers's way," said Conroy. "Would you want to hold a conference in a town that had a bordello on its border, a doctor openly selling opioids from a medical practice, and a minister who operated a virulently racist church?"

The theory made sense, but that didn't mean he was right. Still, Rogers had some explaining to do.

"We know Rogers didn't kill Conroy, though," I said. "Dale Wixson did. Isn't it possible that all this is a coincidence?"

Delgado shrugged.

"Sure," he said. "Maybe Rogers just happened to sideline everyone in the sheriff's department who's ever worked a homicide right before everyone who's ever pissed him off or thwarted his goals died in suspicious circumstances."

"Don't get testy," I said. "There's stuff here to think about, but I need more evidence before I believe Darren Rogers is knocking people off."

Delgado considered me and then reached into his pocket. He pulled out a thumb drive, which he then handed to me.

"And what's this?" I asked.

"A record of every account paid, every check written, and every dollar spent by St. Augustine County for the past five years. It includes Darren Rogers's slush fund. Darren Rogers is in his seventies. He's not killing people on his own. He hired it out, and I doubt he paid for it himself."

I lowered my chin and narrowed my eyes, incredulous.

"So you think he used the county's money to hire a hitman?"

"We've got so much dirty money flowing through this county, nobody even knows what's legitimate anymore. Follow the money. That's what this is all about."

I closed my eyes, leaned back, and shook my head.

"Fuck. My life is a mediocre crime novel."

"What do you mean?" asked Delgado.

"Nothing," I said, opening my eyes and standing. "Thank you for the chat. I'll look at the file. If there's anything there, we'll talk later."

"Nope," said Delgado, shaking his head. "Sorry, but today's the day. I've got enough vacation and sick days saved up to take off until I retire. I'm putting in my papers."

My eyes widened, but I said nothing. He crossed his arms.

"Something you want to say?" he asked.

I forced my eyes shut and then shook my head.

"I don't know what I could say. You just told me Darren Rogers is a murderer who slowly and methodically dismantled our department to cover up a far-ranging criminal enterprise, and then you told me you were leaving. I've got nothing, man."

Delgado considered me.

"Fine. St. Louis police officers have a bead on Tyvos Sizer and Nick Moore. They plan to pick them up tonight. With them in custody, my last case is closed. I've already called Sheriff Kalil and told him I plan to retire, so I'm going to slip my official papers under his door."

"Sure," I said, closing my eyes and shrugging. "You talked to Makayla and told her you've closed her case?"

Delgado shook his head.

"I planned to wait until we had Tyvos and Nick in custody."

I sighed.

"I'll do it, then," I said. "I'm sure her family will feel better once they get the police officers out of their driveway."

Delgado grunted.

"The sheriff already called them off."

I furrowed my brow.

"You think that was premature?"

George shrugged.

"I don't work here anymore, so it's not my call," he said. "When I did work here, though, Sheriff Kalil made it clear that my opinion didn't matter. You're free to babysit if you want. Our perps should be in custody in a few hours."

I clenched my jaw before speaking.

"I'll babysit until then."

"Your time to waste," said Delgado. "Good luck with that thumb drive. Blow this place to hell, but keep my name out of it. And don't plug that thumb drive into your work computer. If Rogers knows you've got that, you'll be a target."

He sounded paranoid, but that didn't mean he was wrong.

"All right. Thanks, George," I said before pausing. Then I tilted my head to the side. "Happy retirement."

"Thank you," said George before looking to the hallway and sighing. He looked at me again. "Word of advice? Keep your guard up around the new sheriff. He's dangerous."

"I'll keep that in mind."

He grunted before leaving. I watched the doorway, half expecting him to come back in and say he was just kidding about everything. He didn't, so I leaned forward and rested my elbows on my desk as I rubbed my eyes. Delgado had hurt my career, harassed me, and questioned my judgment nearly every day since I became a detective. My department would be better off without him in it, and yet I wished he had chosen another time to retire.

Then again, maybe it was for the best that he left now. St. Augustine was my home, and if Delgado was right, it faced a problem far bigger than any I had seen before. If he could run from that, maybe it was better that he did. As for me, I had run enough in my life, and I didn't have time to babysit a colleague.

I had work to do.

Chapter 37

Before going to Makayla's house, I locked my office door and drove home, where I made some sandwiches, fed Roy, and got my laptop. Then the dog and I returned to my station, where I signed out a cruiser for the night. It was probably against regulations to bring a dog with me, but I wanted the company. Roy sat on the backseat and watched while I ate a peanut butter and jelly sandwich for dinner. After I finished eating, he stretched and lay down. I had a leash for him in case he wanted to go for a walk later, but he seemed content for now.

It was a cool, cloudless night, so I cracked open my windows, pushed my seat back as far as it would go, and settled in. Someone nearby must have lit a fire because the sweet smell of wood smoke wafted into my car. Roy snored on the backseat, so I opened my laptop, inserted George's thumb drive, and got to work.

I wasn't an accountant, but George's spreadsheet was easy to understand. It had thousands of rows, each of which represented a payment with a unique reference number. Each row was divided by almost a dozen columns that contained a description of the payment, the date of the payment, and a lot of other information.

Delgado, as far as I knew, had no formal training in accounting, which meant any problems he had found must have been obvious to a police officer. That led me to reorder the spreadsheet so I could focus on the sheriff's department's purchases. Within moments, I closed my eyes, sighed, and swore under my breath.

My department didn't pay as well as departments in bigger cities, but the county didn't skimp on our personal protective equipment. Every sworn officer in St. Augustine County had a top-of-the-line bulletproof vest fit to his or her body, and every officer received a new vest every five years—if not sooner. Those vests kept us safe and likely lowered the department's insurance cost. They retailed for about five hundred bucks each, but, according to the spreadsheet, the St. Augustine County Treasury Department had paid almost two thousand dollars apiece.

The wonky expenses didn't stop there, either. The department required every sworn officer to practice at a firing range with the same rounds we carried on duty. Those rounds cost about forty cents each at a gun shop. The expert negotiators at the St. Augustine County Treasury Department paid well over twice that per round, and they had purchased thousands of rounds each month—far more than we used.

We had similar problems with disposable zip-tie handcuffs. We used them during Spring Fair when we had to make more arrests than usual, but they stayed in a storage room most of the year otherwise. According to the records, though, the department was purchasing two thousand a month at a dollar each. They should have cost a tenth of that price.

Gasoline was the real kicker, though. The price fluctuated every month, just as one would expect, and the price the county paid seemed in line with the market. Unfortunately, the usage was outrageous. Our department had about thirty vehicles, most of which were four-door passenger cars. The department, allegedly, purchased over a hundred gallons of gas each day for each vehicle, but our cruisers couldn't have burned through a hundred gallons of gas a day even if they had driven a hundred miles an hour nonstop. The spreadsheet said the department was spending almost three hundred thousand dollars a month on gas when it should have been spending sixty to seventy thousand.

There was something else interesting, too. Most of the county's expenses were paid to the vendor who supplied the good or service, but the goods with inflated prices or obviously fraudulent quantities went through a payment processor called St. Augustine Express Pay. Presumably, the person behind the Express Pay account then forwarded payment to the proper vendor and pocketed the rest. I knew the county had a slush fund, but it felt almost surreal to see how it had been created.

I studied the spreadsheet for a while but looked up when Roy started whining. The clock on my dashboard said it was almost ten, so I yawned and stretched and looked at the dog.

"You want to go for a walk?"

He sprang to his feet and started panting, so I got out, stretched, and opened the rear door. Roy jumped out and then dove into a play bow before walking to my side so I could scratch his back. I hooked my leash on his collar and looked around. The streets were empty. The Jefferson family ought to be okay with a police car in front of their house, and I needed a break to think.

For ten minutes, Roy and I crunched through fallen leaves and walked around the neighborhood. The houses were all fifty to a hundred years old, but the homeowners maintained them well. No clouds blocked the moon or stars, and the weather was cold but not bitterly so. For those ten minutes, I tried not to think about the spreadsheet, Lily Henderson, or Darren Rogers, but I found my thoughts drifting to them anyway. Unfortunately, those thoughts didn't get me anywhere.

When I returned to my car, I leaned back and sighed. For the moment, I didn't know what to do with the spreadsheet, so I focused on Makayla Simpson's case. With Delgado's retirement, the case would become mine solely, which meant I needed to get caught up. I had already looked up Sean Kirby, so I focused on Tyvos Sizer and Nick Moore. Both lived in St. Louis. Tyvos was twenty-two years old, while

THE MEN ON THE FARM

Nick was nineteen. Both men had long, serious criminal records despite their ages.

The St. Louis police suspected Tyvos was involved in at least two open homicides, while Nick had arrests for coercion, third-degree kidnapping, and second-degree robbery. Neither men had ever been convicted of a crime as an adult, but the St. Louis police had picked them both up for various drug offenses as juveniles. Each was also suspected to be involved in a gang. These were dangerous guys, and it didn't surprise me that they'd push a teenage girl down the stairs and leave her to die. It made me wonder how the hell they knew her, though.

Even if Makayla dealt marijuana, she wouldn't have been a threat to any business they may have had. She had an ounce and a half of weed on her. An ounce and a half was a pittance. Makayla and her attackers may have worked in the same business, but it was like comparing the Washington Post to a high school journalism student's blog.

I closed our criminal record database and opened a web browser. When I was sixteen, people my age used Facebook. Some young people still used it, but few of them wanted to share a social media site with their grandma and crazy racist uncle. Kids now were on Instagram, Snapchat, YouTube, and a few other places. If they were on Facebook still, they often used fake names. That put me at a serious disadvantage, but I still had a few resources.

I started by searching for Sean Kirby on Instagram. We had his cell phone number, but I didn't know his username on any of the major social media sites. My department, however, had a fake Instagram account in which we pretended to be a high school student from St. Mary, a town to our south. Our fake account accepted friend requests from everybody, including one from someone named SeanTheMan420. That was him.

I browsed the pictures and videos he had posted. The kid smoked a lot of weed and played a lot of basketball. I browsed his pictures but didn't see any of Makayla. I did, however, find pictures that Tyvos had commented on, so I clicked on his username and browsed his photos. His feed led me to Nick Moore's feed. Then I got lucky.

Nick had no pictures of Makayla, but he had several pictures of Mr. and Mrs. Jefferson, the house in front of me, and the other kids who had lived there. He tagged those photos *FosterFam*. That was how he knew Makayla. They were foster siblings. That changed things.

I pulled out my phone and dialed Delgado's number to ask who in the St. Louis Metro Police Department he was working with, but his phone rang four times before going to voicemail. I didn't leave a message. Instead, I texted him.

Call me when you get this. Need to talk about Tyvos and Nick.

I hoped he'd call me back, but he didn't, so I settled in to wait. Roy snored on the backseat, and my police radio occasionally crackled with static and voices, but I tuned all that out. Half an hour after I texted Delgado, I called his cell phone again, but once more, he didn't respond. This time, I left him a voicemail asking him to call me back. I drummed my fingers on the steering wheel. He was probably out celebrating his retirement.

I searched through my phone's directory until I found the direct line for the North County Precinct in St. Louis. The watch sergeant answered on the first ring. I introduced myself and asked whether they had picked up Tyvos and Nick.

"I was under the impression that we were working with Detective George Delgado on that case."

I sighed.

"I was under that same impression," I said, "but George unexpectedly retired this evening."

"Good for him," said the sergeant. He paused, and I heard papers shuffling. "Looks like we're still looking for your suspects."

"George implied that you knew where they were."

"We thought so, too, but they disappeared before we could arrest them. They'll turn up."

I started to thank him but then stopped when I heard a loud beeping noise. Roy lifted his head and perked his ears forward. The beeping increased in speed until it became a shrill, piercing note. It was coming from the house. A light popped on from the second story, and I reached for my door handle. I hung up with the St. Louis officer and called my station. Zuckerburg answered quickly.

"Jason, send me some officers," I said. "Somebody just broke into the Jefferson's house and set off the alarm."

Chapter 38

I unholstered my pistol and slammed my door shut so Roy wouldn't wander out after me. Then I jogged toward the home. My station received a lot of calls from alarm companies, and the vast majority turned out to be innocuous. Teenagers got caught sneaking out, dogs or cats escaped their rooms and tripped motion sensors, or homeowners forgot they had their alarms armed and then went outside to get something from their cars. Still, I pulled the receiver back on my firearm to chamber a round as I ran alongside the house toward the backyard.

Lights continued to pop on inside the home, and the alarm continued to shriek. A tall privacy fence surrounded the backyard, so I opened the gate and hurried along a concrete stepping-stone walkway to the back patio. The Jefferson family had a big patio table set and grill near the home. Their grass had grown dormant and yellow for winter. Nobody moved outside, but the back door hung open, leading into a dark kitchen.

I slowed as leaves crunched beneath my feet. My heart started beating faster as I reached the back door.

"Sheriff's Department," I called. "I'm coming in."

The moment I stepped inside, the lights popped on, illuminating a cheery kitchen with golden-colored cabinets, soft green walls, and rich wood countertops. Two young men stood inside with their hands in the air. A shirtless man carrying a shotgun stood in the hallway. I presumed he was Mr. Jefferson, the homeowner. He lowered the weapon when he saw me but kept his focus on the young men.

"Nick?" he asked, furrowing his brow and looking to the young men.

The young men started lowering their hands, but I shook my head.

"Nope. Hands in the air, boys," I said. "And put the shotgun down, Mr. Jefferson."

Mr. Jefferson put his shotgun on the ground and then held up his hands. The man I recognized as Tyvos Sizer from Instagram turned to me but kept his hands in the air.

"I ain't saying shit to you."

"Cool," I said, stepping back. Muscles all over my body felt tight, and my heart hammered against my chest. "We're going to the yard. There, I will take you into custody. I've got backup on the way. I know what you guys did to Makayla, so I know you're dangerous. If you two make any sudden moves or scare me, I'll shoot."

"What'd you do to Makayla, son?" asked Mr. Jefferson, his voice lowering.

"We're not talking until we get lawyers," said Tyvos. "Isn't that right, Nick?"

Nick nodded.

"Mr. Jefferson, you stay in the house. Sit at the dining room table until I come for you," I said. "I'll take these guys outside. No one needs to get hurt."

Mr. Jefferson stepped back. I led the two young men outside and made them lie facedown on the ground with their arms extended above their heads. Officers Scott Hall and Paul Tidwell arrived in separate cruisers about five minutes after my initial call. They took Tyvos and Nick into custody. Mr. and Mrs. Jefferson came into the backyard a moment later. Mr. Jefferson had found a shirt, while his wife wore pink flannel pajama bottoms and a white T-shirt.

"Did I hear you right?" asked Mr. Jefferson. "Nick hurt Makayla?"

"Yeah," I said. "A young man named Sean Kirby helped them. You know him?"

"I know the name," said Mrs. Jefferson. "I think Makayla's mentioned him."

"Were they friends?"

Mrs. Jefferson tilted her head to the side.

"Makayla doesn't have too many friends," she said. "She's had a rough life. She has a hard time trusting people."

"I can imagine," I said. "Let her know we got the people who hurt her, and tell her I'm sorry for how I treated her earlier. When I arrested her, I was just trying to get her to talk to me. It was unfair of me, and I shouldn't have done it."

"I'll tell her you said that," said Mrs. Jefferson. "If there's nothing else, I'd like to check on the kids."

"Before you go, let me ask you something," I said. "What brought this on? Why would Nick hurt Makayla?"

Mrs. Jefferson looked at her husband. He raised his eyebrows and shrugged before looking to me.

"They've barely met," he said. "Makayla moved in after Nick moved out."

I straightened and blinked.

"That makes no sense."

"It is what it is," said Mrs. Jefferson. "I don't know what to say."

I tried to smile.

"I guess it doesn't matter," I said. "We've got the bad guys. That's what's important." I paused. "Could I talk to Makayla?"

Mrs. Jefferson snorted and shook her head.

"No," she said. "After what you did, she's not interested in talking to you. She hardly talks to us."

"We'll work on her," said Mr. Jefferson, almost stepping in front of his wife. "She's a bright young woman, but she's gone through a lot in her life. It'll take time for her to feel safe enough to talk to you."

I stepped back.

"I understand," I said. "In the meantime, I'll leave you alone. If she's willing to talk, please call me."

They said they would, so I walked back to my car. Officers Hall and Tidwell stood outside their cruisers, so I walked toward them.

"You guys mind taking Mr. Moore and Mr. Sizer to the station?" I asked. "We'll book them on first-degree burglary for now, but we'll add to those charges tomorrow morning when the prosecutor gets in."

"Can do," said Hall. "You want us to put them in interrogation rooms?"

"No," I said, shaking my head. "I'm tired. They can stew in a cell overnight."

"Understood," said Hall. "We'll write this up and book 'em."

I thanked him and then got in my cruiser. We drove in a mini caravan back to our station. There, I returned my cruiser and picked up my car to go home. I fell asleep the moment I reached my bed.

The morning came quicker than I wanted. Roy woke me up at a little after six. I let him outside and didn't even try to go back to bed afterward. My mind was too busy. We had Makayla Simpson's attackers in custody, but the case made no sense. Sean Kirby, Tyvos Sizer, and Nick Moore attacked her on camera, so we had picked up the correct people. Why Makayla still refused to talk to us and why three young men who had no reason to attack Makayla tried to murder her remained a mystery, though. That pissed me off.

George Delgado's spreadsheet never strayed far from my mind, either. Corruption cases were always tough to work. The spreadsheet showed that St. Augustine County had a problem, but I didn't know how deep that problem ran, who knew about it, or where the money was going. Until I figured that out, I couldn't even know which government agency had original jurisdiction to investigate. Before I could do anything, I needed information.

I showered, dressed, and took care of Roy before driving into work. The morning briefing was short and pointless. As I walked back to my office afterwards, I took out my cell phone and called Agent Costa. He answered quickly.

"Bryan, it's Joe Court," I said. "I haven't heard from you for a while, so I'm just checking in."

"Morning, Joe," he said, his voice somber. "Before you ask, they're still out there, and we haven't found Lily Henderson's body."

I paused midstep in the second-floor hallway. Marcus Washington sidestepped me and whispered a greeting. I smiled, but I couldn't put much feeling behind it. My stomach tightened a little.

"So you think Lily's dead."

"We think it's a strong possibility. I spoke to her mother yesterday. She's preparing for the worst."

I nodded and walked the rest of the way to my office. Death was a part of life, one I had to confront often in my job, but it still hurt every time I heard that a child or young person had died. I swallowed the lump in my throat as I unlocked my office door.

"Strength only carries you so far," I said. "I hope she's got a support network."

"She does," said Costa. Neither of us spoke for a moment, so I sat at my desk and turned on my computer.

"Has Robin Brady contacted her brother yet?"

"No," said Costa. "I've got two agents following him at all times, and we've cloned his cell phone. If Robin contacts him or tries to pick him up, we'll know."

"She was willing to go broke to pay for his care," I said. "She'll come for him, I'm sure."

Costa paused.

"We'll see," he said, sighing. "For now, Robin and the other ladies are an agency priority, but the threat they pose will fade. I can keep agents on him for a week or two, but I'll have to call them off and reassign them to active cases soon. In the meantime, we're monitoring the homes and credit cards of all our suspects, and we've given their pictures to every police department within five hundred miles. They'll turn up."

I leaned back in my chair.

"We need a plan," I said. "Wendy Brady is dead. If that didn't force her sister and her partners to come in from the cold, they won't come in until they finish whatever they're doing. I think they're on a job."

"Or they know we're on to them. If so, they may never return."

I shook my head, remembering something Julia Green, my mom, once told me.

"Robin Brady is a mother. We couldn't keep her from her kids if we shot her in the gut and forced her to crawl across broken glass to reach them. She'll come back for her children. Nadine Kaiser has a husband with a cognitive disability from his time in the Army. She won't abandon him, either. Ursa Bauer will come along to support her friends."

Costa clicked his tongue but said nothing for a moment.

"All right," he said. "Suppose you're right. Suppose they are working a job. Where does that get us?"

I leaned forward.

"It limits their targets," I said. "They won't hit a truck unless they know there's a good payout, and I doubt they've left town."

Costa sighed and then paused.

"You're making a lot of assumptions," he said.

"Assumptions based on their past behavior," I said. "These ladies care about each other. They've demonstrated that. We know they're former military, and they've all spent time in combat zones, so they're accustomed to sacrifice, but they also recognize the importance of finishing their mission. If they weren't on a mission, they would have escaped with their families by now. We need to look at high-value targets in the St. Louis region. It's our best chance for getting them."

Costa paused, seeming to consider.

"It's worth thinking about," he said. "I'll start calling around to armored-car companies and see what they have to say. Will you be around if I need you?"

"Yeah," I said. "George Delgado retired yesterday, and he left me a lot of work."

Costa wished me luck and then hung up. I probably should have interrogated Tyvos and Nick, but I didn't care to think about them. Besides, they had broken into a home they knew to be occupied in the middle of the night. That made their burglary a pretty serious felony. They weren't going anywhere, and I had better shit to do.

Chapter 39

I put my phone in my pocket and walked to Marcus Washington's office. Family pictures decorated his desk, and manila file folders were stacked on his chairs. He smiled and waved me in once I knocked on the door.

"Hey, Joe," he said. "Have you heard the big news about Delgado's retirement?"

"He told me last night," I said. "Place isn't going to be the same without him."

Marcus smiled.

"That a good thing or a bad thing?"

I let a smile crack my lips.

"Whatever it means, we'll both have more work until we hire somebody new," I said. "In the meantime, how are you with Arthur Murdoch and Zach Brugler?"

"Case is closed," he said, leaning back in his chair. "The coroner autopsied both of them already. Murdoch died due to a stab wound to his chest that punctured his heart. That was a murder. Zach Brugler died due to blunt-force trauma to the back of his skull. Rivers ruled it an accident, and the sheriff told me to move on. I'm working a domestic dispute now."

I crossed my arms.

"It doesn't feel right to close the case."

Marcus tilted his head to the side.

"I'll keep the files, but unless we find something new, it's closed."

Before I could respond, my phone rang. I looked at the screen and saw Agent Costa's number.

"I've got to take this," I said, ducking out of the office. "Good luck on your new case."

"You, too," he said, already focusing on his computer screen. I walked into the hall and answered the phone. "Bryan, hey. I'm walking to my office. Give me a second."

"Sure."

Once I reached my office, I pulled my door closed and then shut my blinds. That should have given me ample privacy, but I lowered my voice anyway.

"Before you tell me about your search, let me ask you something," I said. "Do you have somebody in your office who works public corruption cases?"

Costa paused.

"I've got a lot of agents who work corruption cases. Officially, it's the Bureau's top priority. Why?"

"A colleague sent me a spreadsheet containing St. Augustine County's expenditures for the past five years, and we've got a serious problem."

I talked him through the spreadsheet, the deaths of Vic Conroy and the others, and George Delgado's theory about Darren Rogers. When I finished, Costa paused.

"What direct evidence do you have against Rogers?"

"Nothing. Everything's circumstantial."

Costa made a low noise in the back of his throat.

"Can you tie him to the expenses on the spreadsheet?"

"I've just started looking at it. If we can tie him to the third-party payment processor, though, we might get him on embezzlement."

Costa drew in a slow breath.

"Focus on the financial crimes. If your spreadsheet's accurate, somebody's embezzling money. There should be a paper trail. Follow it and then send your findings to the US Attorney's Office and the Missouri Attorney General's Office. They should be able to help you out."

"What about the suspicious deaths?"

Agent Costa grunted.

"I don't know. Rogers might have profited from them, but I can't see how he's involved. Take Vic Conroy. He's the big name on your list, and you've got video of Dale Wixson getting into a fight with him and then shooting him with the same pistol he later used to shoot himself. Rogers may have had a motive for all those men to die, but I can't see how he's involved."

"What if he hired it out?" I asked.

Costa paused.

"Like a hitman?"

I closed my eyes, almost feeling embarrassed to discuss the possibility.

"Yeah. Like a hitman. Like in a movie. Saying that aloud makes me sound naïve, doesn't it?"

Costa paused again. I hoped he wasn't laughing at me.

"It's possible, I guess, but professional murderers are rare, and most work for drug cartels or organized crime groups," said Costa. "I don't think Darren Rogers runs in those circles."

I grimaced and slid down in my chair as I sighed.

"You're right," I said. "And you didn't call to talk about small-town corruption. You find any probable targets for our armored-car robbers?"

"I did. An armored car is leaving the St. Louis branch of the Federal Reserve in four hours with forty million dollars cash in the back. It's on its way to the Federal Reserve branch in Little Rock, Arkansas."

That made me sit straighter.

"Who would know about that?"

"The president of the bank, the senior VP of the Little Rock branch, various bank workers, and a couple dozen sworn officers with the Federal Reserve police. My office has already been in touch with the Federal Reserve, so they've increased security. The armored car will be escorted by four unmarked vehicles, each of which will hold four armed officers. The armored car will have two armed officers in the cab and two armed officers in the vault, bringing the entire force to twenty."

I considered but then shook my head.

"It's a lot of money, but it's too big and too risky for our ladies," I said. "What else do you have?"

"Let me email you the list."

His email arrived in moments and contained the schedules of four different armored-car companies over the next three days. There were hundreds of different shipments, some of which piqued my interest. A jewelry store planned to receive two million dollars' worth of diamonds from the airport, an armored car planned to carry eight million dollars cash between two different bank branches before heading to the Federal Reserve, and a third armored car planned to carry a million dollars' worth of stamps from the post office downtown to various branch offices in St. Louis County. They all sounded like suitable targets, but they didn't jump out at me the way another one did.

"Tell me about number forty-three. It's scheduled for today."

Costa mumbled something under his breath and then cleared his throat as he read.

"It's a private transport from a residence in Ladue to an address on Fine Arts Drive in St. Louis. The only thing on Fine Arts Drive is the St. Louis Art Museum. Ladue's got a lot of wealthy people. I bet somebody's donating art. The insurance value is two million dollars."

I raised my eyebrows.

"Do we know specifically what they're donating?"

"No," he said. "Give me a few minutes. I'll call you back."

I thanked him and hung up. While Costa called the armored transport company, I read through the list again and noted shipments that seemed like the kind of thing a three-person crew might want to target. Costa called me back twenty minutes later.

"It's ancient Egyptian jewelry owned by a wealthy collector," he said. "The armored-car company has insured it for two million dollars, but the Art Museum has taken a supplemental insurance plan for an additional four million dollars."

"That's what they'll be hitting," I said.

Costa paused.

"The high-end art world is specialized. If these ladies steal this stuff and try to pawn it, we'll know right away. Not only that, we'll send notices to everyone who deals in this stuff. If they rob this car and try to profit from it, they might as well turn themselves in. I don't think they're that stupid."

"All that's true, but if you take a gold scarab pin from ancient Egypt and melt it down, what are you left with?"

Costa sighed.

"Gold."

"And whatever jewels were in that pin," I said. "This jewelry is valuable to the museum and art collectors because of the history behind the items and the workmanship. To our thieves, though, they're collections of raw materials that become untraceable when melted. The jewelry may lose seventy-five percent of its value, but twenty-five percent of six million dollars is still a lot of money."

Costa said nothing, but I could hear him breathe. Then he sighed.

"How would they have learned about this?"

I leaned forward.

"They're locals, and they're veterans," I said. "Armored-car companies recruit veterans and off-duty police officers as guards. I bet they've got a friend on the inside."

"You're making a lot of assumptions again."

"That doesn't mean I'm wrong."

"No, it doesn't," said Costa. "And you're right that we need to be proactive. If we wait for these ladies to show up to their homes or to pick up their relatives, more people will die." He paused. "I'll call the armored-car company and tell them to increase the security on their deliveries, and I'll call the St. Louis County police to assist. We'll set something up."

"I want to be in on this," I said.

Costa chuckled.

"I figured you'd say that. You know where my office is. Head to St. Louis. I'll let the gatehouse know you're on your way."

Chapter 40

After my phone call with Agent Costa, I got in my car and headed north. Sheriff Kalil had already given me permission to work with the FBI on the shootings at Henderson Angus, and this was part of that case, so I didn't tell him much except that the Bureau needed me.

Once I reached the FBI's compound, a guard hustled me to a conference room, where I met Agent Costa, his deputy, a tactical officer, and Heath Peart, the director of security at Rapid Transit, the armored-car company scheduled to pick up the jewelry from the home in Ladue. Though we had never met, Peart was a former St. Louis County detective and had known my adoptive mother. When he heard we suspected a group of armed robbers might target his company's shipment, he wanted to cancel everything. I couldn't blame him, but if he canceled, our perps would know we were on to them. They'd disappear, taking Lily Henderson with them.

So Costa made a deal. I'd ride in the back of the armored car with an armed guard, and an FBI agent would ride in the front with the driver. Twelve FBI agents with tactical experience would then follow in unmarked vehicles. We'd also have the local police departments on notice that we might need help.

If the ladies came, a dozen highly trained FBI agents would swarm the vehicle, and a dozen more uniformed officers from St. Louis County would hurry to meet us. While he appreciated the security arrangements, Peart finally relented when Agent Costa said the operation would fall under the Bureau's umbrella insurance policy. No one would hold him or his company responsible for a robbery attempt.

After that, Peart gave Rapid Transit uniforms to Special Agent Jake Wallace and me and drove us to his company's headquarters north of downtown St. Louis. He introduced us to the other guards assigned to the pickup in Ladue and told them we were from the Kansas City office. Guards moved around often enough, so they seemed to accept that. If Nadine, Robin, and Ursa had learned of the jewelry pickup, they had learned about it because someone at that company told them about it, so we didn't reveal our actual identities for fear of tipping off our bad guys.

About four hours after Agent Costa called me, I was sitting in the back of an armored car with a bulletproof vest strapped across my chest and back, a forty-caliber pistol in a holster on my hip, and a stiff cotton uniform on my torso. The woman sitting across from me was named Brittney. She had straight brown hair pulled away from her face into a ponytail, and she wore the same uniform I did. It hid the contours of the muscles on her arms and legs but did little to hide their size. She looked a little soft around the middle, but she was a weightlifter and likely had thirty or forty pounds on me. Like me, she wore a pistol and a bulletproof vest.

I smiled at her as the armored car bounced along the interstate. Special Agent Wallace sat in front with a driver named Buck. A thick steel wall separated us, so I'd be on my own in emergencies back here.

"Have you worked for Rapid Transit long?" I asked. Brittney tilted her head to the side and shrugged.

"A few years," she said. "You?"

"Not long," I said. "Until about a year ago, I was a cop."

Brittney raised her eyebrows.

"Oh, yeah? Where at?"

"North Carolina," I said, tilting my head to the side. "I was a reserve officer. The town I worked for called me in during emergencies. Other times, I was a little girl's nanny."

Brittney eyed me for a moment.

"You look like a nanny."

I smiled and pretended it was a compliment. Steel lockboxes lined the walls. O-rings built into the floor allowed guards to use ratcheting straps to secure heavy loads. We had yet to reach the home in Ladue, so the truck was empty. I looked out the thick rear windows at the traffic behind us.

"Why are you here?" asked Brittney.

I glanced at her and furrowed my brow.

"Excuse me?"

"Why are you here?" she asked again. "This is a two-person job. Why are you and Jake working it?"

I shrugged and forced myself to smile.

"Client asked for us," I said. "They're rich, so they get what they want."

"If you know the client's rich, you know more than I do. Who are you?"

I glanced at her and tried to think through my potential responses.

"I'm just trying to do my job," I said. "Are you going to let me, or are you going to keep asking stupid questions?"

"That depends," she said. "What's your job?"

I licked my lips and forced a smile to my face.

"I just work here, okay?" I said. "This morning, my boss told me to go to St. Louis with Jake. When I got here, somebody I never met before told me I was assisting with a residential job. That's all I know. That good enough for you?"

She considered me.

"You here to spy on us for the company?" she asked. I said nothing. "Buck and I bust our asses, and we do good work. You tell your boss that, honey. We don't need Barbie looking over our shoulders."

I considered her.

"Just do your job, and I'll do mine. Clear?"

She grunted and looked out the rear window. I put my hand over my firearm and watched her out of the corner of my eye.

Nadine Kaiser and her murderous friends had conducted each of their previous robberies when the guards were most vulnerable. If they were going to hit us, they'd do it while we stopped to pick up the jewelry or at the Art Museum, where we planned to drop it off.

Eventually, we exited the highway on Lindbergh Boulevard and then headed east on Clayton Road before eventually turning south on Warson Road. It was a beautiful street with rolling hills, mature trees, and expansive lawns and gardens that stretched toward homes the size of private schools. Buck drove about a mile before turning into a neighborhood and stopping in front of a red brick Federalist-style mansion.

The home's estate manager, Mr. Nelson, met us in the driveway and led us through narrow servants' hallways to the vault in the basement, where we found a cart laden with metal lockboxes. I didn't know how much those boxes weighed, but Brittney grunted as she pulled the handle. I tried to help, but she shook her head and waved me off.

"Keep your eyes open," she said. "You're working security. I'm the messenger."

I kept my hand over my firearm as we left the building. Every muscle in my body tensed as I gripped my still-holstered weapon and stepped into the sunlight. This was it. On previous robberies, our perps had first shot a guard with a sniper's rifle and then had run toward the vehicle. If the driver got out, he was killed with a sniper's rifle, too. An FBI helicopter with a forward-looking infrared camera had scouted the surrounding area for anyone hiding with a gun, but technology wasn't perfect. If they were out there, they'd move any moment.

"You see something, Barbie?" asked Brittney, her footsteps slowing. I shook my head.

"No," I said. "After hearing about that robbery at the Galleria, I'm paranoid."

Brittney looked around.

"If they were out there, we'd be dead already," she said. "Keep walking. The quicker we're in the truck, the safer we'll be."

She was right, but that didn't help my nerves. Once we reached the truck, we loaded each of the twelve steel lockboxes and secured them on the ground with a ratcheting clamp. As Brittney slammed the back door, I breathed a little easier. Brittney looked at me and furrowed her brow.

"Is this your first job, Barbie?"

I glanced at her.

"Would it matter?"

"It'd explain a few things," she said, her voice softer than it had been earlier. "That's nothing to feel ashamed about. Everybody's jittery for the first job."

I considered my answer and then exhaled a slow breath as Buck started the truck.

"Thank you," I said. "I've never done this before. Aren't you nervous?"

"Oh, yeah," she said. "The key is relaxing despite your nervousness. Whatever's going to happen is going to happen. Our feelings don't matter."

I cocked my head as we exited the driveway.

"I wish I could have that same attitude."

"It's like anything," she said. "You do it enough, you're not bothered by it. For now, take some breaths. Breathe in for a four count and hold it in your belly for a four count. Then exhale for an eight count. It'll calm you down."

It had been a long time since I practiced it, but my instructors in the police academy had taught similar breathing techniques for staying calm in stressful situations. I took long, deep breaths, and my heartbeat slowed.

"Good," said Brittney. "You're doing well."

"They didn't teach us that in my training," I said.

Brittney chuckled.

"That's because the people who work for Rapid Transit don't know what the fuck they're doing," she said. "I learned that in the Air Force. You stick with me, and you'll be okay."

She smiled and looked out the back window. With her attention away from me, I brought my hand to my waist and unhooked the strap that kept my pistol in its holster in case I had to draw it. The ladies we were hunting were all veterans, so their partners probably would be, too. Not that it mattered. Our team was already racing ahead to the Art

Museum. If the ladies came after us, they'd find a dozen FBI agents and dozens more St. Louis police officers waiting for them. This would be easy...

Or so I thought.

Chapter 41

The heavy armored vehicle rolled on its shocks as we rounded the interstate on-ramp. My skin tingled, and I nearly jumped out of my seat as the wheels hit a pothole. Brittney gave me a look that was half pity and half annoyance. Then she sighed and looked out the rear window again. Thankfully, the road became smoother once we hit the interstate. Buck settled into the far right lane at a steady speed.

About five minutes later, Brittney's cell phone beeped. She pulled it from a pocket, looked at the screen, and then slipped it back into her pocket. Afterward, she glanced at me and sat straighter and held her breath. Her back was rigid. She locked her eyes on mine, every muscle in her body tense. Something was happening. I drew in a breath.

"What's going—"

Before I could say another word, the heavy armored vehicle's tires screeched, and we decelerated. The momentum carried me off my seat and onto the ground. Dozens of cars around us honked their horns. Then something slammed into us from the side, knocking even Brittney from her seat.

My head hit the hardened steel floor, and my vision swam white.

As my eyes focused again, I realized we were no longer moving. Brittney was staring at me, her eyes open.

"You okay?" I asked.

She nodded and began pushing herself up. I did likewise. Then a noise roared like thunder through the cab, and the entire vehicle rocked. Then it happened again. And then a third time.

"What the fuck is that?" I asked, reaching for my pistol.

"Sorry, Barbie," said Brittney, unholstering her weapon. As she raised her pistol toward me, I shot my hand out to push the barrel away. Brittney's face contorted as she squeezed the trigger. Inside the enclosed space of the armored car, the sound was deafening. The round pinged off the wall to my left.

Then Brittney pulled her hand back and fired again. This time, I pushed the firearm upward. The round hit the ceiling. It ricocheted and dug into the lockbox to Brittney's right.

I didn't have time to reach for my weapon. Instead, I wrapped my left arm around Brittney's gun hand and vaulted as hard as I could toward her, using my legs like a spring. I didn't bother trying to punch her. Instead, I rammed the crown of my head against her jaw with all the force I could muster.

Her head snapped back. Before she could move, I pulled my right arm back and struck her with an open-handed blow to her face. She didn't drop her pistol, so I hit her again. She tried to pull her weapon arm back again, so I struck her again, and then again and again until her body went limp.

I grabbed her weapon and slid it into a pocket. Then I knelt beside her and checked her neck for a pulse. She was breathing, but I had broken her nose and maybe her orbital socket and probably her jaw. She looked rough, and my head and palms throbbed, but I was alive.

I opened the truck's rear door. Around me, the scene was chaotic. A line of cars stretched behind and around us like soldiers at attention. Westbound traffic moved at an even pace, but the eastbound traffic on our side of the divided highway had stopped. Behind us, a line of four FBI agents in tactical gear strode between the rows of now-parked cars. All of them held black tactical rifles.

I held up my hands to show them I wasn't a threat, but before I could ask what the hell was going on, gunfire erupted from the front of the armored car and tore into a four-door sedan to my right. The driver, a woman, ducked below the dashboard. The engine block would give her some cover, but a stray round could still hit her. Immediately, the FBI agents hustled back to seek cover and regroup. Stuck behind the armored car, I was safe, but the civilians around us might as well have been targets at a shooting range.

I pulled out an earpiece from my pocket and connected it to my cell phone, which we had set up as a radio. The line was silent.

"This is Joe Court. I'm behind the armored truck. What's going on?"

"Stay put, Joe," said Agent Costa. "They hit one of our teams with a spike strip and took out their SUV. Your truck almost rammed them. We've got accidents up and down the interstate now. Our remaining tactical teams are getting into place, but our perps are well armed. They've got a .50-caliber rifle in the back of an SUV. They've pinned Jake and a guard inside the cab of the armored truck, so he's not going anywhere. We're moving our other teams into position now."

The moment Costa said that, the line of FBI agents started hopping the concrete jersey barrier that separated the east- and westbound lanes of traffic.

"Can the armored truck still move?" I asked.

Agent Costa paused.

"Probably," said Costa. "Can you drive, Jake?"

He said he could, so I drew in a breath.

"Then ram our perps from behind. That concrete barrier will give our team cover, but these ladies have already opened fire on a civilian vehicle. We need to take them out now before they hurt anybody else."

Jake paused.

THE MEN ON THE FARM

"They've got a big rifle in the back of that car," said Jake. "If we ram them, they'll fire on us again. The glass won't hold."

"Then duck," I said. "You're in an armored car. If we don't do this, they'll open up on a minivan full of kids. If we hit them hard enough, the jolt should buy us a few moments for our tactical teams to move in."

Jake, again, paused. I heard some muffled voices, but I didn't know who was speaking.

"Buck says we can do it," he said. "It's your call, Bryan."

"Do it," said Costa. "Get our teams in position. Our perps are in a green Dodge SUV. Team one, you'll come in from the north from behind the jersey barrier. Team two, you're moving in from the east. We'll go on Jake's cue."

"Understood," said Jake. Immediately, the armored truck rumbled and then inched forward before its brake lights lit. "We're ready. On three."

He counted to three, and then the heavy vehicle accelerated. It was slow, but massive. Unfortunately, as it barreled forward, I lost my cover, so I ran south toward the side of the road. Several civilians started opening their doors, but I shouted at them to stay inside.

The heavy armored vehicle slammed into the green SUV at about twenty-five miles an hour and then shoved it forward like a snowplow before coming to a stop. Immediately, men in black tactical outfits swarmed over the concrete barrier to the north and from between cars to the east. They dragged two stunned blonde women from the SUV and held them at gunpoint.

"Two subjects secured," said a voice I didn't recognize through my earpiece. "No further casualties."

"Where's the third?" asked Costa. "There should be a third woman."

I focused on the armored truck and the green SUV, but out of the corner of my eye, I saw movement. A blonde woman in a baseball cap was scrambling up the embankment toward McKnight Road. My parents lived about two miles from that exit, so I knew the area well. There were residential neighborhoods to the south and then a commercial district beyond that. It wouldn't take much to lose her in that quagmire.

"She's going south," I shouted into my phone. "She's heading toward McKnight Road. I'm in pursuit."

Costa may have said something, but my earpiece fell out. I sprinted after her, first on the interstate's shoulder and then up the same grassy embankment she had run across. As I reached the top, a car honked at me, but I ignored it and ran south. McKnight was a crowded two-lane road through an upper-middle-class neighborhood. Mature trees, rolling hills, and family homes surrounded us. She veered to the right down Lindworth Drive. Then she ran to the left as the road forked. I sprinted after her.

The world disappeared as we ran. She was fast, but I was a little quicker. As I closed on her, she pivoted to the left and ran between two brick homes. A thick row of Lombardy poplar trees gave the homes privacy from one another and blocked her from my view. I slowed and unholstered my pistol, ready for her to pop out from cover.

She didn't, so I hurried through the tree line and found her vaulting over a short fence that surrounded a resident's in-ground swimming pool. I veered around the pool. She vaulted over the fence on the far side of the pool and rushed headlong through shrubs at the edge of the property. This time, I didn't slow down when I reached them.

I plunged through the trees and instantly wished I hadn't. Something hard and strong hit me in the stomach. It was her shoulder. I fell to the side, the wind knocked out of me. She landed on top. I tried rolling and pushing onto my stomach, but then a burning pain passed through my gut. I gasped and looked down. As well as Kevlar protected against gunshots, it didn't do shit against knives, and Nadine Kaiser had just stabbed me in the gut.

She stood. Blood dripped down her hand and the small knife she held. She tossed that to the ground and then reached for her pistol.

"You shouldn't have—"

Before Nadine could finish speaking, a door nearby opened.

"Hey! I see you!"

It was a man's voice, and it was coming closer. Nadine looked up and then dropped her right foot back as she unholstered her firearm. I grimaced and pulled my gun out. She and I fired simultaneously. My first round hit her in the shoulder. She spun toward me, and I squeezed the trigger twice more, hitting her in the chest. That pushed her back, but she was wearing a vest. I adjusted my aim and squeezed the trigger again. This time, the round hit her in the neck.

She fell to the ground, and I scrambled toward her to disarm her. My blood felt hot as it poured down my side and onto my legs. Nadine was dead, but already I could feel the periphery of my vision going white. I looked up to find the homeowner crouching behind a retaining wall in his yard, so I gritted my teeth and pulled out my cell phone. I didn't have my earpiece, but my phone was still set up to use the FBI's radio frequency. My breath was shallow.

"Bryan, it's Joe," I said before gritting my teeth. "Nadine Kaiser is dead. Did you find Lily?"

"Yeah," he said. "We found her in the front seat of the SUV we assaulted. She's alive, but her breathing is shallow. We've got an ambulance inbound. Where are you?"

"In the backyard of a brick ranch home on Lindworth Drive," I said. "I need help. Nadine stabbed me, and I'm bleeding a lot."

The white spots in my vision started growing darker. My head felt light, but my arms felt heavy.

"You know the address?"

"No," I said, looking to the homeowner. He was standing and looking at me, so I waved him over. "I'm going to hand my phone to the guy who lives here. Talk to him. I'm going to pass out now."

Chapter 42

So getting stabbed sucked. I stayed awake as long as I could but then passed out and awoke in a hospital bed a day later. An IV line snaked around my arm to a stand beside my bed, and I wore a white hospital gown with light blue polka dots. A pair of tight gray boots covered my feet and calves. Nothing hurt at all. In fact, I felt amazing.

I blinked and looked around the room. A whiteboard hung on the wall. According to it, my nurse was named Geraldo. I said the name aloud twice and laughed hysterically. My dad started laughing, too. That's when I realized my dad was sitting in the recliner beside my bed, reading a book.

"When'd you get there?" I asked, looking at him and smiling. I laughed. "Your name's Doug. That's funny."

I laughed again, and he looked at his watch.

"I got here about an hour ago," he said. "Audrey spent the night, but your mom was here yesterday. And don't worry about Geraldo. He's taken excellent care of you. Everybody has."

As soon as he said Geraldo, I giggled.

"Geraldo is a funny name."

Dad smiled.

"You only think that because you're on a morphine drip."

I smiled and allowed my head to fall into my pillow.

"I love morphine."

Dad said something else, but my eyes closed, and I fell asleep once more. When I woke up a second time, it was dark, and my gut hurt. I groaned and tried to sit up, but the muscles in my stomach felt...wrong. It was like they weren't there. My mom stood from the chair beside my bed and put a hand on my shoulder. I reached up and squeezed her fingers. My eyelids fluttered, and I swallowed.

"You want some water?" Mom asked. "Kate, your nurse, brought some by in case you woke up."

"Sure," I said. "Did she bring any illegal drugs by, too? Those were awesome. Bring back Geraldo."

Mom chuckled.

"They've got you on something, but I'm not sure what," she said. "And the drugs aren't illegal if they're prescribed by a physician. The morphine was a little strong, so they took you off it. Are you in pain?"

"A little, but it's okay," I said. "They sew me up?"

"Yeah," she said. "If you want the gory details, ask your doctor. You got lucky, though. The knife didn't penetrate any organs. I think they plan to release you tomorrow with some oral antibiotics. For now, they want you to rest."

I swallowed and shifted my weight, fearful of what my mother would say next.

"I was trying to save a little girl named Lily," I said.

"She's okay," said Mom. "She's with her mom and grandmother. Roy's with your father."

I wanted to ask her more questions, but I was tired and fell asleep again. When I woke up the next morning, Mom was still there, asleep in the chair beside my bed. Things moved quickly after that. A doctor came in and reiterated that I had been stabbed but that the stab wound hadn't reached my liver or other internal organs. I had bled a lot, but I had gotten to the hospital quickly. After that, a nurse helped me change into some loose-fitting sweatpants and a T-shirt, and then Mom drove me home.

I felt okay, but she and my dad insisted on staying with me for a few days while I recovered. The company was enjoyable.

Agent Costa came by the day I got home from the hospital to update me on our case. He had arrested Robin Brady and Ursa Bauer for multiple counts of murder, attempted murder, kidnapping, assault, grand theft, and half a dozen other crimes. Neither of them would ever walk free again.

Despite a massive search, Agent Costa's agents never found a single dollar the four ladies stole. They also never found Nadine Kaiser's husband, Robin's children, or Robin and Wendy's mother and brother. They disappeared, taking with them several million dollars in cash. As much as they likely appreciated the money, I'd bet those same people would have given it all back to hug their loved ones again. As usually happened in cases like this, everybody lost. At least Lily and Cassie had survived.

Since I was injured in the line of duty, my department placed me on paid leave, but that didn't mean I stopped working. Certain things still bothered me about the Makayla Simpson assault case, and George Delgado's spreadsheet never strayed far from my mind. I couldn't do a lot about the spreadsheet, but I asked Marcus Washington to send me everything our station had on Makayla Simpson's investigation so I could review it at home. He emailed me everything I needed; I read it and thought.

The case made no sense for two days. And then it did.

I called Marcus and ran my theory past him. He came to the house and looked through some phone and text records with me, and then we set up an appointment to meet the Jefferson family to relay our findings. When we got to the Jefferson's home, we met Officers Dave Skelton and Alisa Maycock. They'd stay outside until we needed them, but I appreciated having them close.

Marcus rang the doorbell. Mrs. Jefferson opened the door.

"Detective Court," she said, nodding but making no move to invite us inside.

"Morning, Mrs. Jefferson," I said, smiling before looking to my right. "This is Detective Marcus Washington. He works with me. And thank you for leaving work to see us."

Mrs. Jefferson blinked but said nothing. Her expression made her look bored. Or maybe annoyed.

"Can we come in?" I asked. "We can also talk on the porch if it's more comfortable."

She considered me and then sighed before crossing her arms.

"Why are you here?"

I kept the smile on my lips.

"As I told you on the phone, I wanted to give you a final update on our investigation into Makayla's assault. We've made some arrests."

She held my gaze and then shook her head and sighed.

"Fine," she said. "Come in. My husband and Makayla are inside."

The home's interior smelled clean and looked neat. Hardwood floors led from the front door and down a center hall to the kitchen, where baskets stacked on a wooden frame held shoes, gloves, and boots beside the rear door. A red backpack leaned against the wall. Mrs. Jefferson led us down a short hallway and then left into the dining room.

Makayla and her foster father sat on opposite sides of an old oak table. Mrs. Jefferson sat between them on the end. Marcus pulled a chair out for me so I could sit. My injury had healed some, but it still hurt to pull things, so I appreciated his help.

"Okay," I said. "Thanks for asking us in. I promise not to take too much of your time."

"That's all right," said Mr. Jefferson. "What can we do for you, Detective?"

"First, I wanted to let you know that Sean Kirby, Tyvos Sizer, and Nick Moore have all sought plea deals for the assault on Makayla. Because Sean is a minor, he'll be placed in a juvenile detention facility until his twenty-first birthday. Nick and Tyvos have both pled guilty to assault in the first degree. Nick will spend eleven years in prison. Tyvos, because he pushed Makayla, will spend seventeen years in prison. None of them will hurt Makayla or this family again."

"Thank you," said Mr. Jefferson.

I smiled and focused on Makayla.

"I've got a couple of quick questions," I said. "Do you know why these guys attacked you?"

"Why don't you ask them?" asked Mrs. Jefferson.

"We did," I said. "Their attorneys said they had no interest in talking except for a reduced sentence. Our prosecutor didn't want to deal."

"Why are you here, then?" she asked. "You've arrested the people who hurt Makayla. Aren't you done?"

"I didn't become a cop to make arrests," I said, shaking my head. "I became a cop to help people. Tyvos Sizer, Nick Moore, and Sean Kirby weren't after her. They had no reason to hurt her. That tripped me up until I realized they weren't trying to hurt her. She was just a message."

I looked at Mrs. Jefferson and then to Mr. Jefferson.

"You guys care to guess who she was a message to?"

Neither answered, so I reached into my pocket for my cell phone and dialed a number from memory. A phone rang, but I couldn't tell which of the Jeffersons it belonged to. Then Mrs. Jefferson closed her eyes and sighed.

"It's mine."

"Can you stand up, Mrs. Jefferson?" asked Marcus. "I need to pat you down for weapons and take your phone."

Mrs. Jefferson didn't respond, so Marcus repeated the command. As she stood, Mr. Jefferson put a hand on his wife's shoulder.

"My wife did nothing wrong."

"Leave it alone, Vance," she said. "I'll get a lawyer and figure this out."

He looked at me.

"What are you charging my wife with?"

"Hindering prosecution and tampering with evidence, but we'll probably add to those charges," I said, looking to Mrs. Jefferson. "You want to take it from here, or do you want me to keep talking?"

She looked at the table but said nothing, so I focused on her husband.

"Nick Moore lived in your house for two years as your foster son," I said. "Prior to living here, he dealt drugs and had ties to a gang in north St. Louis."

Jefferson nodded.

"He was lost, but he was a good kid. We gave him a home, the first genuine one he ever had."

"Every kid deserves a home," I said. "A now-retired colleague of mine found Nick and Tyvos by examining the phone records of Sean Kirby. They planned the assault over text message."

Mr. Jefferson crossed his arms.

"What's this have to do with my wife and her phone?"

I glanced at her.

"George, my colleague, looked at two weeks of text messages. I looked at two years' worth of messages. Nick Moore had Sunday dinner with your family once a month. Why?"

Mr. Jefferson rolled his eyes.

"Because we were his family. I taught him how to drive and how to wear a tie and how to dress for an interview."

"You're a good foster parent. I wish the system had more men like you," I said, smiling at him. My smile left when I looked at Mrs. Jefferson, though. "What'd you find in Nick's room two years ago?"

Mrs. Jefferson's lower lip trembled. Her mouth opened, but no sound came out.

"Sam?" asked Mr. Jefferson. She looked at her husband.

"I'm sorry."

"What did you do?" he asked.

She looked at me.

"I found a gun," she said. "I don't know where he got it or why he had it, but I found it in his backpack."

"But you kept it."

"He asked me to," she said. "As long as I kept it hidden, he paid me a thousand dollars a month. We used that money to pay for the other kids. That's why Nick came back for dinner. He didn't care about seeing us. He came to pay me. I never even asked why he had a gun. I should have."

"He or one of his friends probably used it in a murder," I said. "Where is it now?"

"I threw it in the Mississippi. It's gone."

I grimaced and then looked away.

"Let's not focus on that. Two months ago, he sent you a text message that said he refused to keep paying."

She nodded.

"I threatened to go to the police if he didn't give me the money he owed me, but he didn't respond. Then he hurt Makayla."

I looked at her.

"Why didn't you tell us who hurt you?"

Before Makayla could answer, Mrs. Jefferson spoke again.

"I told her not to," she said. "Nick and his friends scared me. I thought he'd go after the younger kids."

"How could you do this without even telling me?" asked Mr. Jefferson. "Makayla could have died."

She opened her mouth but said nothing. Her shoulders trembled.

"The money made things easier," she said, finally. "I didn't have to worry about whether I had a coupon to buy ice cream or whether the bread I liked was on sale at the grocery store. I just bought it. Before Nick started paying us, we were barely holding on, but his money let us live. We even went on vacation last year. The Lake of the Ozarks. We took the kids."

Mr. Jefferson shook his head. Makayla put her head on the table and cried.

"The lake wasn't worth it," said Mr. Jefferson, putting a hand on his foster daughter's back.

"Samantha Jefferson," said Marcus, "you're under arrest."

Marcus recited her Miranda rights and led her to the car. I left the house and got in the front passenger seat of Marcus's cruiser. Mrs. Jefferson sobbed on the backseat. She had brought this on herself, but my stomach hurt, and my throat felt tight. The Jeffersons weren't perfect, but they had provided a home for a lot of kids. I thought I had done the right thing, but it sure didn't feel right.

"This sucks," I said, glancing at Marcus.

"Yep."

We drove to our station with Mrs. Jefferson crying on the backseat. Marcus took over from there, while I went to my office to write a report. About twenty minutes after I sat down, Sheriff Kalil knocked on my door.

"Marcus told me you arrested Samantha Jefferson. That was a tough call."

I shook my head.

"It wasn't. Because of her, an innocent kid almost died. I don't care if she didn't intend that to happen. She hid a firearm for a gangbanger. We don't even know what he used the weapon for, but Nick wouldn't have paid her what he did if it didn't scare him."

He considered me and then crossed his arms.

"Maybe it was an easy case, then."

I turned back to my computer. The sheriff sighed.

"I need you to stand up, Joe."

I wasn't in the mood for twenty questions, but I clenched my jaw and pushed back from my desk. Instead of standing, I swiveled my chair to face the door. That was when I noticed the two men in suits standing behind the sheriff. One of them, a bald, heavyset man in his late forties, pulled his jacket back to show me the gold badge on his belt.

"I'm Detective Jim Hargitay," he said. "My partner is Detective Roger Vega. We're from the Cape Girardeau Police Department, and we're here to talk to you about George Delgado."

I straightened.

"What happened to George?"

"We found his body in the Mississippi River," said Hargitay. "He was shot in the chest six times with a .40-caliber pistol."

I brought a hand to my mouth. Skin all over my body tingled.

"As we understand it," said Detective Vega, "you and Mr. Delgado had a contentious relationship."

For a moment, my mind refused to process his comment. Then I took two breaths.

"George and I worked together. We didn't always get along, but he was a good cop. He tried to do what was right."

Detective Vega nodded. He had a thin rat-like face and a pompadour haircut that added two or three inches to his height.

"Do you have a .40-caliber pistol?"

I furrowed my brow and shook my head.

"You can't think I killed him."

The two detectives looked at one another. Detective Hargitay drew in a breath and crossed his arms.

"We were just at your home. We found a shotgun, a nine-millimeter pistol, and a Smith & Wesson revolver. Do you have a .40-caliber pistol?"

I raised my eyebrows.

"You searched my house?"

"This is a serious matter, Joe," said Kalil. "You need to answer their questions."

I leaned back. My throat felt tight, and a weight pressed against my chest.

"My mom and dad were at the house, but they don't have authority to let you search. How'd you get in, and where are my parents?"

"Your mother and father are fine," said Kalil. "We had a warrant."

"We?" I asked, lowering my chin and opening my eyes wide.

"These are serious charges," said Kalil. "You need to talk to us."

I put my hands on the arms of my chair and pushed myself to a standing position.

"No, I don't need to talk to you," I said. "Unless I'm under arrest, I'm going home."

The two detectives parted, but Sheriff Kalil didn't move.

"You have a firearm in a holster on your waist," he said, crossing his arms.

"Yeah. It's a .40-caliber Glock 23. I assume you want it."

Kalil nodded, so I looked at the detectives from Cape Girardeau.

"Who will test this?"

"The state crime lab," said Vega. I pulled my weapon from the holster, removed the magazine, and handed it to the detective. He thanked me and said he'd give me a receipt. Sheriff Kalil stood aside to let me pass. I walked into the hallway.

"Thank you for the weapon, but I can't help you if you don't talk to me," said Kalil.

I looked at him up and down. My head felt light. If I hadn't said the same thing to murder suspects dozens of times over the years, I would have believed him. More than anything, that showed me how badly I had misjudged him.

"Delgado was right about you," I said. "You are dangerous."

Kalil tilted his head to the side.

"I'm not under investigation."

"I didn't kill George," I said, looking to Kalil. Then I looked at the two detectives. "I'll have my attorney contact you about an interview, but it's a waste of your time and mine. When'd George die? I'll tell you where I was."

"We'll be in touch," said Hargitay, reaching into his jacket. He pulled out a business card from the inside pocket and handed it to me. "Thank you for your cooperation."

I walked out of the station. Trisha watched me go but said nothing. I wondered whether she thought I had killed him. It didn't matter. I knew what I had done and what I hadn't done. George had kicked a hornet's nest before he left, and now I had to clean up. First, though, I had to protect myself.

As I walked to my car, I called Brenda Collins, an attorney in St. Louis who oversaw the trust fund my biological mother had left for me.

"Brenda, hey, it's Mary Joe Court," I said. "I need a hundred thousand dollars. Can you sell that much stock?"

She paused.

"I can," she said. "Sneeze if you're in trouble and need help."

I smiled despite the situation.

"I'm in trouble, but not that kind," I said. "Sell the stock. And do you know a good defense attorney? I'm pretty sure the police are going to arrest me for murder soon."

***

I hope you liked the book! It's really getting good now! To see what happens next, click below to check out The Man in the River, the next, gripping novel in the Joe Court series:

Amazon US

Amazon UK

Amazon Canada

Or, turn the page for a free Joe Court novella…

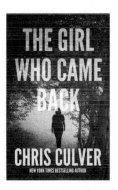

You know what the best part of being an author is? Goofing off while my spouse is at work and my kids are at school. You know what the second part is? Interacting with my readers. About once a month, I write a newsletter about my books, writing process, research, and funny events from my life. I also include information about sales and discounts. I try to make it fun.

As if hearing from me on a regular basis wasn't enough, if you join, you get a FREE Joe Court novella. The story is a lot of fun, and it's available exclusively to readers on my mailing list. You won't get it anywhere else.

If you're interested, sign up here:

http://www.chrisculver.com/magnet.html

As much as I enjoy writing, I like hearing from readers even more. If you want to keep up with my world, there are a couple of ways you can do that.

First and easiest, I've got a mailing list. If you join, you'll receive an email whenever I have a new novel out or when I run sales. You can join that by going to this address:

http://www.indiecrime.com/mailinglist.html

If my mailing list doesn't appeal to you, you can also connect with me on Facebook here:

http://www.facebook.com/ChrisCulverbooks

And you can always email me at chris@indiecrime.com. I love receiving email!

Chris Culver is the *New York Times* bestselling author of the Ash Rashid series and other novels. After graduate school, Chris taught courses in ethics and comparative religion at a small liberal arts university in southern Arkansas. While there and when he really should have been grading exams, he wrote *The Abbey*, which spent sixteen weeks on the *New York Times* bestsellers list and introduced the world to Detective Ash Rashid.

Chris has been a storyteller since he was a kid, but he decided to write crime fiction after picking up a dog-eared, coffee-stained paperback copy of Mickey Spillane's *I, the Jury* in a library book sale. Many years later, his wife, despite considerable effort, still can't stop him from bringing more orphan books home. He lives with his family near St. Louis.

Made in the USA
Columbia, SC
06 August 2025